04/03

P9-AZX-646

The Bronze Bow

THE

Bronze Bow

Elizabeth George Speare

Houghton Mifflin Company Boston

The Riverside Press Cambridge

1961

To my husband

The Bronze Bow

I · THE BRONZE BOW

A BOY STOOD on the path of the mountain overlooking the sea. He was a tall boy, with little trace of youth in his lean, hard body. At eighteen Daniel bar Jamin was unmistakably a Galilean, with the bold features of his countrymen, the sun-browned skin, and the brilliant dark eyes that could light with fierce patriotism and blacken with swift anger. A proud race, the Galileans, violent and restless, unreconciled that Palestine was a conquered nation, refusing to acknowledge as their lord the Emperor Tiberius in far-off Rome.

Looking down into the valley, the boy could see the silver-gray terraces of olive trees splashed with burgeoning thickets of oleander. He remembered that in the brown, mud-roofed town every clump of earth, every cranny in a stone wall, would have burst into springtime flower. Remembering, he scowled up against the hot noonday sun.

He was waiting for two figures to reappear among the boulders that tumbled on either side of the path just above him. He was puzzled and uneasy, at odds with himself. Who were these two who had been so foolhardy as to climb the mountain? He was resentful that they had reminded him of the village, fearful that they might look back and discover him, yet unwilling to let them out of his sight. Why was he so bent on following them, when

1

all he had wanted for five years was to forget that other world in the valley?

He glimpsed the boy again, some distance up, then the girl. Some memory nagged at him. Twins they were, that was evident. They moved alike, with a sort of free, swinging ease. They had the same high cheekbones and dark ruddy complexions. Their voices were sharp in the clean air. Daniel could see the girl clearly. She had stopped to snatch a cluster of pink flax blossoms and she stood now, poised on a rock, her face lifted, her yellow head covering slipped back off her dark hair.

"Look, Joel!" she cried, her voice coming down to him distinctly. "How blue the lake is! You can see the tetrarch's palace in Tiberias."

Daniel's black brows drew together fiercely. Now he recognized the boy. He was Joel bar Hezron, the red-cheeked boy who used to come to the synagogue school, the scribe's son, the one the rabbi held up for an example, the one they used to tease because his sister was always waiting outside to walk home with him. She had an odd name—Malthace. Five years ago that was, and Daniel could still feel the hurt of seeing her waiting there outside the school, while his own sister—

"We're almost there!" the boy's voice rang out. The girl sprang down from the rock. The two flicked out of sight, sending a quick hail of pebbles bounding down the path. Daniel moved forward with the caution of an animal stalking its prey.

He reached the top just as the girl, flushed and out of breath, flung herself down on the patch of grass where Joel waited. She snatched the head covering clear off, letting the wind pull at her hair. Daniel could see them pointing out to each other the landmarks below.

From where he crouched he could not see the valley, but he knew the sight of it well enough. How many times had he sat where those two sat now, looking down on the village of Ketzah that had been his home? Not so often these last years, but at first, before he had got used to life in the cave. Sometimes he had climbed up and sat here till dark, straining his eyes to catch the specks of light, picturing Leah and his grandmother at their evening meal, wondering if he would ever see them again. He never had, and he had stopped remembering and wondering—until today.

Now that Joel and his sister were no longer shouting, the wind hid their voices. He stared at them, disappointed and baffled. He had to hear them. More than that, he was fighting back a longing to speak to them. His own people—after five years! He looked down at his bare calloused feet, at the goatskin tunic bound with a thong around his waist. What would they think of him, those two in their clean robes and leather sandals? Suppose he should risk his freedom for nothing? But he could not help himself. Like an animal lured out of hiding, he edged slowly from behind the rock.

Instantly the boy was on his feet, the girl swiftly up beside him. He might have known they would be off at the sight of him. To his astonishment, they stood still. He saw Joel's hands clench; the boy was no coward. Daniel stood on the trail, his heart pounding. If they ran from him now he could not bear it. He fumbled for the remembered greeting.

"Peace be with you," he said.

Joel did not relax his guard. "Peace," he said shortly; then, "What do you want?"

"No harm, Joel bar Hezron," said Daniel.

"How do you know me?"

"I heard your sister call you. I am Daniel bar Jamin."

Joel stared, remembrance suddenly livening his face. "The apprentice who ran away from the blacksmith?"

Daniel scowled.

"No one blamed you," said Joel quickly. "Everyone knows how Amalek treats his boys."

"I care nothing for Amalek," Daniel said. "Can you tell me about my grandmother and my sister?"

Joel frowned and shook his head. "I'm afraid I can't. Do you know them, Thace?"

The girl had been frightened, and her breath was still uneven, but she spoke with a frankness like Joel's.

"There is an old woman who comes to the well in the morning," she said. "She lives in a house behind the Street of the Cheesemakers."

"Yes," Daniel said hungrily.

The girl hesitated. "They say she has a little girl who never goes out of the house."

Still? He had thought perhaps in all this time—"That is my sister Leah," he said. He wished he had not asked. It had been better not knowing.

"No one has ever seen her," the girl went on. "But I know that she's there. I'm sorry. I wish I could tell you more."

Daniel hesitated, embarrassed, but unwilling to give up.

"There was a boy named Simon," he said. "Six or seven years older. He was bound to Amalek too."

"You must mean Simon the Zealot," said Joel.

"You know him?"

"I've heard of him. He has his own shop now. They say he gets more business than Amalek."

"He used to help me," said Daniel.

4

"He has a reputation for being a good man—and a good patriot."

"Would you give him a message for me? Would you tell him I'm up here? I'd like him to know."

Joel looked surprised. "You mean you live up here?"

"Yes."

"Alone? Is it safe? I mean—they say the mountain is full of robbers."

Daniel said nothing.

"Aren't you lonely?"

"I don't live alone," said Daniel.

"Oh." Joel was baffled. "Don't you ever come back to the village?"

"I'd just get dragged back to Amalek's shop."

"I suppose so. Yes, I'll tell Simon, of course. How long since you ran away?"

"Five years, about. Simon will remember me, though."

The girl spoke, in a straightforward voice that matched the look in her eyes. "Five years! Do you mean your grandmother hasn't known where you were in all this time?"

Daniel looked at the ground, his lips tightening.

"Tomorrow, when she comes to the well, can I tell her I've seen you?"

Daniel looked back at her with resentment. He had long since managed to quiet his conscience, and he did not like having it stirred up again. "If you like," he said. He felt angry at himself now, and disappointed. Why had he given himself away after all these years? What had he expected? There was nothing more to stay for.

"You'd better go back," he said, turning away. "You shouldn't have come up here?"

"Why not?" asked Joel, looking not at all alarmed.

5

"I'm warning you. After this, stay in the village." He walked away from them.

"Wait," called Joel. He looked at his sister with a swift question, and she nodded. "We—we brought our lunch. Will you eat it with us?"

The blood rushed up into Daniel's face. He had not asked for their charity.

"It's not much," Joel said. "But we'd like to talk to you some more."

Was it possible this boy had made the offer in friendship? Slowly, like a wary animal, Daniel took a few steps back and let himself down on the grass. From the pocket of the wide striped girdle that bound her waist, the girl pulled a neatly wrapped bundle. Joel produced a small flask which he handed to his sister, then sat down and solemnly held out his hands. With astonishment Daniel watched the girl pour a little stream of water over her brother's hands. Hand-washing before a meal—he hadn't given a thought to it for five years. He wouldn't have imagined that even a scribe's son would carry water all the way up the mountain just to observe the law. Then the girl turned toward him. He saw the question in her eyes and the slight shrinking, and a stubborn pride stiffened him. He was a Jew, wasn't he? He held out his hands, and watched the drops trickle over his blackened knuckles, embarrassed, thinking how the men in the cave would hoot if they could see him.

The girl unwrapped the bundle and made three small piles, equal piles, he noticed, not skimping herself the way his mother used to do. Then Joel spoke a blessing and they handed Daniel his share, a few olives, a flat little loaf of wheat bread, and a small honey cake whose taste his tongue suddenly remembered from childhood. For the first time Daniel felt his tight muscles begin to relax. His eyes met Joel's, and the two boys studied each other without hostility.

"Why did you come up here?" Joel asked, wiping the last crumbs of cake off his chin.

In some way the food had made it easier to speak. "I knew there were caves up here," Daniel answered. "All I wanted was a place to hide where Amalek couldn't catch me. But I couldn't find any caves, and I wandered around for three days, and then—a man found me."

He thought of how Rosh had found him lying flat on his face, starving, half frozen, his back still raw from the last flogging. How could he tell this boy what that night had been like? He remembered the terrible moment when he had seen the man bending over him, and how Rosh had reached out a hand, not to strike him but to help him to his feet, and then, when he had flopped over, how Rosh had picked him up and carried him like a baby all the way to the cave.

"A robber?" Joel questioned.

"A good man," said Daniel fiercely. "He took me to live with him."

"What's it like up here? What do you do all the time?"

"Hunt. Wolves and jackals, even panthers. Sometimes we hunt as far north as Merom. I work at my trade too. I made a forge to work on."

Joel looked impressed. Even the girl was listening with dark eyes as lively as her brother's. Daniel looked at the other boy with curiosity. He had been trying to find a distinguishing mark about Joel. "What is your trade?" he asked.

"I'm still at school," said Joel. "I'm going to go on to be a rabbi, probably. But I studied sandal-making too. I could earn my living at it, but I'm sorry for the man who has to wear my sandals."

Daniel nodded. Of course Joel would be a rabbi. He had always been the smartest boy in the school. But even a rabbi must learn a trade, like any other man.

"Why did you come today?" he asked. "No one comes up here from the village."

The girl laughed. "We'll be skinned alive if anyone finds out we've come," she said.

"We always planned to," Joel explained. "Ever since we were children. We weren't allowed to because it's supposed to be dangerous. Today's a holiday, and we just decided to come without telling anyone. It was our last chance. We're leaving the village and going to live in Capernaum."

His sister frowned at him. "I don't see why you always have to sound so dismal about it," she protested. "I think Capernaum is going to be wonderful."

Joel's face looked suddenly closed. His fingers snapped the tops off the red blossoms, one after another. It was plain to Daniel that this was an old argument between them.

"What more do you want?" she demanded, forgetting Daniel in her insistence. "A big house to live in, shops, and people, and a school with the best teachers in Galilee!"

Joel went on snipping the blossoms savagely. "Father doesn't want to go," he said. "He's only going to please Mother."

"Well," she answered, "Mother left it all to please him once. It hasn't been easy for her, living in Ketzah. Why shouldn't she go back, now that Grandfather's left his house to her? It doesn't really matter to Father where he is, so long as he has his books."

8

Daniel listened, shut out again from the clean, safe world that they shared. But all at once his attention was diverted. Far down the mountain, on the narrow ribbon of road, he spotted a moving line that threw off reddish flashes of metal in the sunlight. Legionaries. At the sight, black hatred churned up in him. Out of habit he spat violently. The shocked attention of the two jerked back to him, and they followed his savage gaze, leaning to peer at the moving line.

"Romans!" snorted Joel. Daniel liked the way he said the word. He spat again for good measure.

"You hate them too," said Joel, his voice low.

Daniel closed his teeth on a familiar oath. "I curse the air they breathe," he muttered.

"I envy you," said Joel. "Up here you're free."

"No one is free," said Daniel. "So long as the land is cursed by the Romans."

"No. But at least you don't have to look at them. There's a fortress at Capernaum. I'll have to watch them all the time, strutting around the streets."

"Oh, Joel!" the girl protested. "Do they have to bother us?"

"Bother us? Bother—!" The boy's voice broke. "I should think even a girl could see—"

"Of course I see!" She was stung almost to tears by her brother's contempt. "But what use is it to be always making yourself miserable? The Romans won't be here forever. We know that deliverance will come."

"You're talking like Father!"

"But he's right! The Jews have been worse off before. There have always been conquerors—and there was always deliverance, Joel."

Joel was not listening. He had caught Daniel's eye,

9

and the two boys were studying each other, each asking a silent question.

Malthace sprang to her feet, recognizing well enough that this time it was she who was shut out. "I'm not going to have my holiday spoiled by those soldiers," she said, with the trace of a childish pout. "We've climbed all the way up here and you've scarcely looked at the things we came to see."

Joel turned back to her good-naturedly. "We've seen something we didn't expect," he said. "Daniel."

She tossed her head. "What about the places we used to talk about? The plain where Joshua marched out against the heathen kings?"

Joel shaded his eyes, taking his bearings. Just below them the village clung to the rocky slope, the dark block of the synagogue showing clearly among the clustering flat-roofed houses. Around it circled the gray-green olive orchards and the fresh, clear green fields of grain, banded by purple iris and shining yellow daffodils. To the south lay the lake, intensely blue. To the north, beyond the line of hills, through the shimmering, misty green of the valley, the silver thread of the Jordan wound up to the shining little jewel that was the Lake of Merom. Suddenly bold, Daniel got to his feet.

"There," he pointed out. "On that plain. Horses and chariots drawn up against him, and a great host of men like the sands of the shore. And Joshua fell on them and drove them as far as the Great Sea."

He saw surprise on their faces. They thought he was an ignorant savage. The girl did, anyway. This was something he knew. Five years ago, that first morning, when he was warm and fed and slept out, Rosh had brought him up here, and stood with an arm across his shoulders, and pointed to the plain in the distance, and told him how a few brave men had dared to go out against a great army, and how they had won a great victory for Israel. Up here, in the clean sunlight, Daniel bar Jamin, orphan, runaway slave, had found something to live for.

"All the mighty ones," he said, remembering Rosh's very words. "Joshua, Gideon, David, all of them fought on the soil of Galilee. No one could stand against them. It will be so again."

"Yes," breathed Joel. "It will be so again. God will send us another David." His eyes glistened, as though he too could see the shadow of a vast army moving on the distant plain.

"You mean the Messiah!" Malthace cried. "Oh Joel, do you remember? We always thought that up here we'd see him."

"I was sure," said Joel. "I knew that if we could only climb up here, that would be the day he would come. I believed it so hard, it seemed to me I could *make* it happen."

"So did I. And we would be the ones to rush down the mountain and tell them. And all the people in the village would drop their work and follow him. Do all children have such wild imaginations?"

Joel was instantly sober. "The Messiah is not imagination. It's the truth. It is promised."

"But straining our eyes at every cloud in the distance, and thinking we would be the first ones—"

"I still want to be!" cried Joel, so passionately that the other two were startled. "Call it childish if you like. That's why I don't want to go to Capernaum."

"But it may be years!"

"No. It must be soon. Not the way we imagined it,

Thacia. I used to think he would come with a great host of angels. Now I know it must be men, real men, trained and armed and ready—" He checked himself.

"There are such men," said Daniel, keeping his eyes on the distant hills. Without looking, he felt the other boy's muscles tighten.

"I know," Joel answered. Excitement leaped from one boy to the other. The question had been answered.

Malthace looked at her brother, puzzled by something she could not understand. "We should start back now," she said. "We must be home for supper."

"I'll walk a way with you," Daniel offered. He was thinking that he would like to see them safely onto the main road.

They started down the steep slope of the mountain. Once they left the summit behind, the breeze died down, the golden sun hung close above them, and not a leaf moved beside the path. They did not talk now. Daniel could see that Joel was still seething with hidden thoughts. He suspected that for the girl this holiday had not turned out as she had hoped. As for himself, he was already beginning to wish that they had never come. He had been satisfied up here, not thinking too much, shutting out the things he didn't want to remember—working for Rosh, and waiting, nursing his hatred, for the hour that would come. He had never had a friend of his own, and he had never thought about wanting one. Why hadn't he let well enough alone?

Malthace was impatient now. Probably her conscience was beginning to trouble her. But Joel lingered, trying deliberately to fall behind. When his sister was distracted by a clump of myrrh blossoms just ahead, he spoke half under his breath.

"There was something else I hoped for when I came up here," he said. "I've heard that Rosh the outlaw lives on the mountain. I hoped I might be lucky enough to see him."

"Why?"

"He's a hero to every boy at school. But no one has ever seen him. Have you?"

Daniel hesitated. "Yes," he said.

Joel stopped in the pathway, forgetting his caution. "What I'd give—! Are the things they say about him true?"

"What do they say?"

"That he fought beside the great leader Judas when they rebelled against the Romans at Sepphoris, and that when the others were crucified, he escaped and hid in the hills. Some men say he's nothing but a bandit who robs even his fellow Jews. But others say he takes the money from the rich and gives it to the poor. Do you know him? What is he really like?"

No caution in the world could hide the fierce pride that rushed over Daniel. "He's the bravest man in the world! Let them say what they like. Some day every man in Israel will know his name!"

"Then it's true!" cried Joel. "He's raising an army to fight against Rome! That's what you meant up there, isn't it? And you—you are one of them. I knew it!"

"Rosh is the man I told you about, the one who found me. I've been with him ever since."

"I envy you! I've dreamed of joining Rosh."

"Then come. No one could find you up here."

Malthace had stopped and turned back, waiting. Joel looked down at her and made a small helpless gesture. "It's not so simple as all that," he said. "My father—"

"Oh Joel, why are you so slow? What are you talking about?" The girl stood in the pathway, her arms full of crimson blossoms, her dark hair, still uncovered, falling about her shoulders, her cheeks flushed with the sun.

If he were Joel would he run away? Daniel wondered suddenly. Suppose his father and mother waited, with the lamps lighted and a good supper laid out? Suppose he had a sister who could run to the top of the mountain with him and be scarcely winded?

Then abruptly he stopped wondering. Just below Malthace he caught sight of another figure. In the middle of the trail, blocking their way, stood one of Rosh's sentries, Ebol, waiting for them to come down.

2　　　　THE BRONZE BOW

Wait here," Daniel said to Joel. He strode down the path past Malthace. "Go up and wait with your brother," he ordered, scarcely giving her a glance.

"Where have you been all day?" Ebol greeted him. "Rosh needs you."

"Rosh? Where?"

The man jerked his head toward the rocky hillside. "Seven of us. There's a job to do."

Even to Daniel's practiced eye there was not a sign of life on the barren slope. "Right now?"

"Now. There's a pack train coming from Damascus with a string of slaves. They've almost reached the pass. Easy. No guard to speak of. All we're to take is one slave."

"No money?"

"Not a thing but the slave. A black fellow, big as an ox. Rosh spotted him yesterday when they stopped at Merom. Too good to waste on the galleys, Rosh says. Who are those two up there?"

"A boy I used to know in the village and his sister."

"What are they doing on the mountain?"

"They climbed up here—for a holiday."

The man snorted. "Get rid of them. There's no time to waste."

Daniel climbed back to where the two stood waiting.

"I can't go on with you," he said, ignoring the curiosity in both their faces. "You'll be safe from here on—if you hurry."

Joel didn't move. "Is that one of Rosh's men?" he demanded.

Daniel did not answer.

"I know it is," said Joel. "And there's something going on." His eager look scanned the hillside. "Rosh is somewhere near here. I'm sure of it, and I want to see him. Please, Daniel. I may never have another chance."

With the certainty that Rosh's eyes were on them even at this moment, Daniel dared not delay. "No!" he almost shouted. "Forget Rosh and get down the road as fast as you can."

He was astonished at the anger that flashed in Joel's eyes. "Who are you to order me around?"

"Do what I tell you!" Daniel insisted. "There's going to be trouble. Any minute now!"

Excitement flared into Joel's face. "Romans?"

"No, you fool. Not Romans."

The boy's jaw had a stubborn set. "You don't own this mountain. And neither does Rosh. I'll go where I please!"

Two pairs of eyes stared hotly at each other.

"What about your sister?" Daniel asked, and watched the defiance blank out of the boy's face. Too bad, he thought briefly. He's the kind we need.

There was a sound of running feet. A boy about twelve, thin as a scarecrow, came racing up the road, face crimson, eyes bugging. "C-coming!" he stammered. "They've passed the dead oak tree." He scrambled up the steep bank of rock and vanished like a lizard into one of the jagged crevices.

Distinctly now Daniel heard the first sounds of an approaching caravan, the groaning protest of the camels, the bump of heavy loads against the rocky sides of the pass, an occasional muttered order. "Too late!" he warned. "Get up that bank, both of you, and out of sight."

Joel whirled on his sister in sudden fear. "Thace—you heard him! Get up there—quick—as far as you can!"

The girl lingered maddeningly. "Joel—what—?"

"*Hurry*, Thace! I'll explain later!" Then, with a snort of despair, Joel grasped her hand, jerked her toward the bank and gave her a push. "Up there!" he repeated. "Lie flat and keep your head down. And don't make a sound, no matter what happens."

Daniel watched with approval. Once he had caught on, the boy had acted fast. The girl too. She had gone up those rocks like a mountain goat. Then he saw that Joel had turned and was coming back.

"I'm staying with you," the boy said.

There was no time to argue. Daniel grasped him by the arm and dragged him up the opposite bank. As they crouched behind a boulder Ebol loomed beside them.

"He's all right," Daniel spoke quickly. "I vouch for him."

"One sound from him—" The man made one swift gesture.

"He won't," said Daniel.

"See to it, then. Now mark this. Wait for the signal. The one in the yellow and purple is yours. No sport about it, Rosh says. No killing." He was gone, as though he had melted into the rocky bank.

In the still air Joel's breathing was loud. The boy's eyes, fixed on Daniel's face, were feverish. Daniel felt

17

his own heart begin to pound. This was Rosh for you, he wanted to say. You could never be sure what would happen next. Days on end with no excitement, and then, all of a sudden, Rosh would see something he needed or wanted, and like a hawk he would pounce. Daniel began to feel the crawling in his stomach, half fear and half pleasure. Only recently had he been allowed a part. He wasn't used to it yet, especially the waiting.

Joel nudged him. "What do we do?" he whispered.

"I do it," Daniel answered. "You stay here."

Joel's eyes sparkled. His young face was taut, his hands clenched so that the knuckles knobbed out. Daniel saw that he had no intention of staying there, and an elation he had never felt before leaped up in him. Suddenly he grinned back at Joel, and in that instant they heard a sound just below them. Close together they edged their foreheads around the rock.

The first of the train came in view, a burly guard armed with a heavy staff, and behind that a second guard with a sword at his side, both walking silently, glancing uneasily at the rocky banks. They knew they were approaching a bad spot on the trade route, lonely, narrow, and treacherous. Above them the boys waited, holding their breaths, as the rest of the caravan wound slowly into sight. It was not much to brag about. Four mangy camels, lurching grudgingly up the steep path, their burdens swaying. A string of underfed mules. One litter with dingy curtains. Four ordinary tradesmen. With disgust Daniel marked the one in the purple and yellow headdress. The man was fat and out of breath, and looked scared to death already. How long would it be before Rosh would give him a full-sized job to do?

Behind the tradesmen plodded the slaves, first the men

18

and then a drab cluster of women, herded close together, urged on by the flicking whips of two more guards in the rear. No question of which one Rosh wanted. Over the whole party towered one murderous-looking slave, with lash-ridged shoulders and an ugly scar. What would Rosh want with such a brute? Daniel wondered. Still, it ought to be easy. Only eight men to account for. He caught Joel's eye and grinned again, and then both of them jumped to the shrill whistle.

Instantly the hillside erupted. Out of the corner of his eye, even as he moved, Daniel saw Rosh, always one jump ahead, hurl himself at the first guard. Accurate as hawks, other figures dropped to their chosen targets.

It was too easy. The man in the striped headdress was fumbling for his dagger when Daniel caught his arm, twisted it back, and, seizing the weapon from the fat unresisting fingers, poked it against the roll of fat that covered the man's ribs. He stared down into the pudgy face, at the moist eyes blinking with terror, the cheeks gray with sweat, the fat lips trembling, and he felt cheated. There was no sport in a match like this. But he had his orders, and he held the knife steady. Around him there was a brief efficient struggle, a few blows, some wailing shouts, the scream of a camel, all muffled in a spurt of choking dust. Then silence, and the familiar hoarse bark of Rosh giving orders. The skirmish was over. He drew back his dagger, let go of the man's arm, and stood back.

Slowly the caravan pulled itself together and moved on. Grateful to escape with the loss of one slave, the tradesmen knew better than to argue. When they had straggled out of sight, Daniel took quick stock. One of Rosh's men lay on the path, his legs thrashing, another mopped blood from his arm. No one else appeared to be even winded.

Joel stood rubbing his shoulder.

"Is that all there is to it?" he demanded.

Daniel strode across the path and pulled the cloak down from Joel's shoulder, revealing a bruise already darkening and swelling. "Who gave you that?" he demanded.

Joel reddened. "I meant to get the other arm of your man," he said. "But his plagued mule—"

Daniel choked back a roar of laughter.

"At any rate, we got the slave," Joel added, looking ridiculously pleased with himself.

The cause of the fracas stood motionless in the middle of the path, a giant of a man, naked except for a filthy loincloth, his black skin mottled with purplish bruises and patches of mud. Daniel, with an ironsmith's eye, noted that the bands binding wrists and ankles were of double weight. The slave stood like a beast of stone, unaware that they had gone to this trouble to free him, indifferent that he had exchanged one master for another. Once again Daniel doubted Rosh's choice. There was power there, all right. Those huge arms could crack the ribs of a man as easily as a child could snap a twig. But the broad face with the livid scar showed no sign of intelligence, only an animal wariness that would mark the time to strike.

Then Daniel saw Rosh coming toward them. Rosh had a squat, thick body, with a short muscular neck, and a grizzled head which seemed to thrust forward directly from the powerful shoulders. Now, under the bristling eyebrows, his small black eyes glittered at Joel, not with surprise, because Rosh never allowed himself to be surprised, but with a hostility that made Daniel step forward and speak first.

"We've got a new recruit, Rosh," he said.

Heavy legs braced, Rosh measured the newcomer.

20

"Speak up, boy," he barked. "Who are you?"

Rosh was used to seeing men cringe. Joel did not cringe, and though he was speechless, the pure hero-worship that shone from his eyes must have melted even Rosh's suspicion.

"Joel bar Hezron, sir," he managed finally.

"Your father know you're here?"

"N-no, sir."

"In trouble in the town, are you?"

"Oh, no."

"Then what do you want with me?"

Joel stood his ground. "I wanted to see you," he said, "because they say that someday you will drive the Romans out of Israel. When you do, I want to be with you."

Rosh's teeth flashed from the midst of his matted black beard. As his gnarled hand came down on the injured shoulder Daniel saw the tears start into Joel's eyes, but the boy did not flinch.

"Well said!" Rosh thundered. "Any man who hates the Romans is welcome here."

"I didn't come to stay," Joel explained unhappily. "I'd like to, but I can't, not now. I just came up here for a holiday, and my sister is with me. And in a few days we're moving to Capernaum."

Rosh's approval twisted to anger. "Not after what you've just seen," he said, his voice ugly. "Now you stay here."

Daniel knew that Rosh was bluffing. Rosh had had a price on his head for too long to care now what news reached the village. But Joel could not know that, and Daniel felt a surge of pride at the steadiness in the boy's eyes.

"I'm taking my sister home," Joel answered. "But if

you mean I'd talk, you're wrong. If keeping silent is all I can do for now, then you can count on that."

Rosh studied the boy. "You're certain you want to work for me?"

"I'm certain."

"You think you know how to keep your eyes open and your mouth shut?"

"Yes."

"Then go along to Capernaum. There's time enough. When your turn comes, you'll hear from me."

Rosh turned away, the matter settled. Suddenly, without warning, Daniel was shaken by a flood of jealousy. Not a word, not a look at him. Who had captured the merchant and held him while they took the slave? What had Joel done, besides getting in the way of a mule's hind leg? He wished again that he had never laid eyes on the boy.

"What do you think of him?" Rosh was shouting to his men, waving a hand at the black slave. "Worth a little trouble, eh?"

"By the look of him," one man muttered, "we're all like to wake up dead some morning."

"That's no joke," said another. "He could crack two of our heads together like a pair of walnuts."

Rosh only grinned. He walked up to the slave and clapped a hand on the trunklike forearm. His own powerful body was dwarfed beside that of his prisoner. "Don't look so glum, man," he roared. "Don't you know when you're in luck?"

The slave stared down at him, uncomprehending.

"Do you understand me?" Rosh questioned, impatiently. "Do you have a name?"

Not a flicker livened the stony features. There was

22

some laughter. "Samson," someone suggested. "Goliath."

"Deaf, maybe," one man guessed.

"Dumb too, I wager. Lots of those black ones are mutes."

Rosh shrugged. "We'll see. We took him for his muscles, not his tongue. He'll prove his worth soon enough."

"If he ever learns which side he's fighting on," someone muttered.

Rosh's good humor vanished. The joke had gone too far. "I'll do the choosing!" he roared. "I don't ask for a vote by a pack of lily-livered jackals. Bring him along."

He stamped scornfully up the trail without a backward look. The men eyed each other, each waiting for someone else to make a move. Then, without knowing what prompted him, Daniel stepped into the path. "I'll take him," he said, reaching for the short length of chain that dangled from the iron wristbands. Five of the men tripped over each other to follow their leader. Even the man who had lain writhing on the trail got hastily to his feet. Two reluctantly stood by, willing to reinforce Daniel from a distance.

Daniel looked back at Joel. With the slave's chain in his hand he felt he had regained his former advantage. There was nothing to say now. The affair was over. Joel's eyes met his in a brief salute, and between the two boys something flashed, a wordless exchange that was both a farewell and a beginning.

Though the slave plodded forward without urging, Daniel was forced to check his own pace when he realized how narrow a stride the iron shackles allowed. At the first turn in the trail he looked back. Joel still stood in the path looking after them. Then he saw Malthace, coming down the rocky bank in one sure fluid course, her dark hair falling about her shoulders. He remembered with sudden clearness what he had not even been aware of seeing up there on the mountain, the way that hair had sprung, clean and alive and shining, like a bird's wing, back from the smooth forehead. He watched till the girl joined her brother, and then he set his face toward the mountain with his prisoner. He left the trail and struck off toward the right to follow a steep-pitched course among the boulders. Once again, prompted by the sure grace of the girl, the thought of his own sister stirred in him like an old wound.

Daniel already regretted the impulse that had prompted him to lead the slave. He knew well enough why he had done it. It had been nothing but a boast, an urge to make up for the fact that Joel had found favor with Rosh. He had plenty of chance now to curse his own childishness as he inched his way up the rocky course beside the chained ox. The two men who had stayed behind chafed at the slow pace, their crude jests about the prisoner soon changing to oaths at his lumbering progress. Once the sun dropped below the horizon, the dark came on swiftly, making their way even more difficult. It was like a release from a nightmare to smell at last the fragrance of roasting meat, to hear the sound of voices, and to emerge at the familiar clearing. A roaring fire near the mouth of the cave lit up the circle of men sprawled on the hard dirt. The meal was almost over, and Daniel's two companions lost no time in flinging themselves down for their share. No one paid the slightest attention to the slave for whom they had a few hours earlier risked their necks. Daniel stood uncertainly, the chain in his hand.

Rosh waved a greasy mutton bone in his direction.

"See that Samson gets his big belly full," he shouted. "After tonight he works for it like the rest of us." A roar of laughter applauded him, but no one moved to carry out his command. Daniel perceived that in his absence the matter had been settled. Samson they had christened the slave, and Samson he would remain, no matter what his proper name might be. And Daniel had only himself to thank that he had been promoted to Samson's keeper.

He went to the chill depths of the cave where the goat-skin water bags were kept, and after he had taken a long deliberate draught for himself he carried a gourd of water to the slave. The gourd contained only enough for two tremendous gulps, and he went back to fill it twice more. Then he brought a huge slab of mutton. The black man snatched it from his hands, and sank his teeth into it with a ferocity that turned the boy's stomach. He tore off two chunks of barley bread and laid them down within the slave's reach. Then he went to the other side of the fire and sat down apart from the others. He had lost interest in his own supper.

Rosh did not let him rest for long. "What are you waiting for?" the leader prodded him. "Get your file to those chains."

"Tonight?" Daniel was startled.

Around the fire the sprawling figures reared up in protest.

"Leave the shackles on him!"

"He won't know the difference."

"He'll know, right enough, and so will we when we get our heads smashed in!"

"Shut your mouths!" roared Rosh. "What kind of patriots are you? We'll have no slaves on this mountain. He's one of us—get that through your heads. I'll double

25

the watch so you pigeonhearted can sleep. But the man sleeps free."

With a sigh Daniel got to his feet. This job would have fallen to him anyway, since he was trained to the trade of blacksmith. It was not the first time he had removed manacles. Two of the men who now sat near the fire had made their escape from the Roman mines. He went now to get the chisel and mallet and a heavy file.

The slave crouched in a sort of stupor after his meal. When Daniel signed to him to stretch out his arms, he blinked stupidly. Gradually he seemed to comprehend what was required of him. He shifted his heavy frame and allowed Daniel to stretch the manacled wrists across a flat surface of rock. Then Daniel bent himself to the task that he knew would take half the night.

Rosh stumbled to the pile of skins in the cave. Most of the men stretched out where they lay, pulling their cloaks over their heads and falling at once into slumber. The man who had first watch, planning to wake reinforcements before the slave was freed, settled down to observe Daniel's labor. From time to time he renewed the fire so that Daniel could see to work, but beyond that he had no intention of helping.

Daniel's shoulders began to ache. The steady rasp of the file, which seemed to make little headway on the double thickness of metal, wore his nerves thin instead. After an interminable time a narrow channel sank almost through the first band. The slave did not move. The guard, bored, prowled about the fire, poking in the ashes for scraps from the meal. To keep himself awake, Daniel began to talk, expecting and getting no response.

"I know this is hard on you," he said. "But it's no joke for me either. Rosh was right about the chains, but if he'd had to do the job himself I wager it could have waited till morning. Still, what Rosh says goes, and you might as well learn that tonight."

The black eyes, in the half-darkness, looked like bits of polished basalt.

"You don't know what's happened, do you?" Daniel asked. "You've got Rosh to thank that you're not on the way to the galleys. You don't know what the galleys are either, I suppose. But you do know the taste of a whip, that's plain. Well, that is over. It's not easy here in the cave, but there are no chains, and no whips. You're safe now."

The slave gave no sign that he either heard or understood, but Daniel went on, thinking out loud, shutting out the grating of the file with the sound of his own voice.

"Rosh is the finest leader you could ask for. He pretends to be careless, but actually he leaves nothing to chance, not the slightest trifle. He has eyes in the back of his head. That's why he's been successful, and his band is growing, while other bands break apart or get captured. And he is afraid of nothing on earth, nothing. He laughs at the Romans.

"There are more coming to join us every day. Someday there'll be enough. Rosh asks of them all just one thing. They must hate the Romans, and be willing to go on fighting till the last cursed one of them is driven from the land and Israel is free. We live only for that. And so will you. Rosh knows he's not taking much of a chance with you. Any man who has worn these things on his wrists will die before he'll have them on again. Do you know what I'm saying, Samson? I can see you don't. But soon I'll show you something you can understand."

The fire had died down to a flicker and the night was far

gone when the last of the four iron bands had worn thin. Daniel whistled to the guard, who jumped nervously to wake two comrades. The three stood watching, swords in hand.

Daniel picked up the chisel and mallet. The bands fell with a clatter that woke half the camp. Then he stood back. The slave still knelt, looking down at his hands, not moving. Finally Daniel bent toward him, touched his shoulder. The heavy man shifted, heaved up, and reared over Daniel. For an instant Daniel knew a shaft of real fear, as the massive arms slowly reached, stretched to their appalling length, and the chest expanded in a deep breath. Then suddenly, in one incredible swift motion, the man went down on his knees, and before Daniel could move he had seized the boy's foot in his huge hands and bent to lay his forehead against it.

Daniel jerked his foot away. "Get up!" he snapped. "It is Rosh who freed you." When the slave did not move he turned and walked away. "That's done," he said, trying to hide from the guards his quivering embarrassment. "I could sleep for a week."

He located his sheepskin cloak, wrapped it around him, and lay down just outside the circle of firelight. Samson came crawling toward him and hunched at his feet. Exasperated, he got up again, rummaged in the cave for another tattered cloak, came back and flung it over the naked shoulders, and lay down again. Then he pulled his own cloak over his head and slept. He was too tired even to wonder why he was not afraid.

UNDER THE MIDDAY SUN the rock would blister one's fingers. The air over the smelting oven quivered. When Daniel bent over it to poke at the doughy mass of red-hot ore, the fumes scorched his nostrils. He glanced at Samson, who for a full half-day had been kneading the bellows without ceasing. Perhaps Samson, wherever he had lived, had learned early to endure the heat of the sun. Daniel had had enough for this day. The small lump of iron could be left now till it had cooled enough to be broken into pieces.

He picked up a goatskin bag, tipped it up, and let the warm water run down his throat and splash over his chin and chest. Then he handed the bag to Samson. After almost four weeks in the camp, Samson still never helped himself to anything. Daniel had to have it forever on his mind that the man might be hungry or thirsty. Now, watching the water sloshing out carelessly, he reminded himself that the man had earned it. They had twice as much water in the camp now that Samson helped to haul it from the spring.

Had the big man any idea that he was free? He seldom made a move without an order from Daniel. Rosh had given him up in disgust. Rosh was used to seeing men jump when he gave an order, but no matter how he shouted and cursed at Samson the giant stood immovable. Baffled, not sure whether Samson was utterly stupid or only defiant, Rosh had shrugged the man off on Daniel. All day long the giant was at the boy's heels, and at night he slept so close that Daniel could barely stretch his legs without kicking him. It was like being chained to a huge rock, having to drag it with him wherever he went.

Daniel had to admit that his work was easier. There was never a lack of firewood, and with Samson to help with the bellows instead of the skinny twelve-year-old Joktan he could keep a steady heat in the furnace. The other men were grateful for Samson's muscles too. They came to Daniel as though they were asking to borrow a hammer or an ax. A boulder that five of them were heaving and tugging Samson could roll into place like a child's pebble. The whole eastern end of the camp had been fortified in the last two weeks. Even Rosh had to admit that Samson earned his keep. But the men still hated and feared him and made him the butt of all their jokes. That was one more reason for Daniel to resent his burden; he felt more than ever shut out from the rest, for the jibes that were aimed at Samson usually included him as well.

Was Samson actually deaf? Sometimes he suspected the man understood a great deal more than they realized, and once he had made the mistake of saying so. The only result had been that the men had plagued Samson cruelly, devising all sorts of tests to trick him. They had finally tired of trying to surprise a reaction out of Samson, but they had not convinced Daniel.

Was Samson dumb? Were the sounds he occasionally made just gibberish, or were they fragments of a language it was useless to speak? Where had he come from? What thoughts went on behind that impassive face? What

30

memories were locked inside where they could never be shared? At times Daniel hated him, with a dull resentment. At other times, like now, as Samson set down the water skin, wiped a huge hand across his mouth, and looked at Daniel with a slow childish grin spreading across his face, Daniel felt a grudging liking.

He helped himself and Samson from the stock of raw vegetables in the cave, cabbage and cucumbers and onions pilfered from the farms in the valley, and they lay down in the dark shade of the cave to doze away the midday hours.

He was roused by Rosh's voice shouting his name. He came out of the cave, still half asleep, blinking in the sunlight. Ebol, the sentry, had come into camp leading a man who was tied and blindfolded, as Rosh ordered all strangers and prisoners must be.

"Come out here, Daniel," Rosh barked. "This fellow claims he was looking for you. Ever see him before?"

Daniel came nearer, staring at the young, dark-bearded stranger. Unhampered by blindfold or thongs, the man stood in the center of the suspicious ring of outlaws with the easy confidence of one who had nothing to hide.

"Is this Daniel?" he spoke in a deep voice. "Peace be with you, my friend. It's been a long time."

Daniel came closer. "Simon?" he asked uncertainly. He could scarcely associate his memory of a tattered apprentice with this tall vigorous man. "Joel gave you my message?"

"I was glad to get it. You'd be surprised how often I've wondered what happened to you."

"So you know him?" Rosh was puzzled, but he signaled for the man to be released. "The boy's been well taken care of," he said affably. "You can't deny that."

The blindfold removed, Simon looked Daniel over, with a twinkle of amusement that the boy was taller than he. "He's grown, that's certain," he allowed. "I wouldn't have expected so much muscle."

"That's from the forge," said Daniel, flattered. "Did Joel tell you I've kept at my trade? I'll show you."

"Later," said Simon. "First I'd like some water, if you have some. You people give a man a warm welcome up here."

Chagrined, Daniel hastened to find the coolest water in the back of the cave. Rosh left them, and the other men made a show of some business well within earshot. Daniel was clumsy with pleasure and importance. Never before had anything like this happened to him.

"How did you know where to find me?" he asked.

"I had an idea that once I got up the mountain I'd have plenty of assistance."

"You might have got hurt instead."

"I don't think so," said Simon. He seemed very sure of himself.

Proudly Daniel showed Simon his forge. He knew he had reason to be proud of it, but it was gratifying to see Simon's surprise. He had discovered, in his first year on the mountain, patches where the soil was rusty with iron. Gradually he had learned to smelt it, constructing an oven against a rocky wall, lining it with clay, and devising a primitive sort of bellows from a pair of goatskins.

"This is very good," said Simon, poking at the lump of ore that lay cooling in the ashes. "No wonder you have muscles."

"Samson helps me," said Daniel, pointing toward the big man who crouched near the mouth of the cave.

Simon started. "Beard of Moses! Where did you get that giant?"

"He—escaped from a caravan," said Daniel. "We don't know where he came from."

"Hmm." With a long look at Samson, Simon turned back to the blade Daniel had put in his hand, running an expert finger along its edge. "Not bad. Not bad at all. Amalek taught you well. Do you make anything besides daggers and swords?"

Daniel hesitated. "Hooks sometimes. We don't have horses, and we're not farmers."

"I see." Simon sat down on a flat stone, his back to the curious eyes. "Are you happy here, Daniel?"

"Rosh is good to me," Daniel answered. "Nothing like old Amalek."

"You always wanted to fight the Romans, didn't you?"

"So did you," said Daniel. "Joel told me you are called Simon the Zealot. You ought to know Rosh. If you knew him, you'd join him too." A sudden hope sprang up in him. "Is that why you came today?"

Simon shook his head. "I've known about Rosh for a long time," he said. "I'm a Zealot, yes. Rosh and I work for the same end, but we don't exactly see eye to eye."

"If you really knew him—"

"Perhaps. Today I came only to find you. Amalek died a fortnight ago, Daniel. You could come back to the village if you like."

Old Amalek dead! Should he feel something—pleasure? remorse? pity? It was too far away. He had not thought about going back for a long long time.

"What about my bond?" he asked. "I had four more years to go."

"There's no one to hold you to it. He hadn't a relative to his name, nor a friend either, poor man. I doubt anyone would even remember."

Daniel tried to imagine going back. He couldn't tell whether he would like it or not.

Simon let him think for a moment. "Don't you want to see your grandmother again, and your sister?"

Daniel did not answer. He was ashamed to say that he did not want to see them, but it was true.

"They have worried about you, just as I have," said Simon. "If you go back with me you need stay only a day or two. Just to let them see you are well. It would please them."

"Rosh might need me." Daniel felt upset and resentful, as he had that day on the mountain top with Joel. What was there in the village for him but the old troubles that had ceased to bother him up here?

In the end, however, he let Simon persuade him, Simon and his own curiosity. Rosh grumbled, but there was an irresistible confidence about Simon that Rosh admired. The difficulty came from the one Daniel had not reckoned with at all. As he and Simon walked to the edge of the clearing, a vast shape rose from the mouth of the cave and moved after them. Looking back, Daniel found Samson at his heels.

"Go back, Samson," he ordered. "I go alone this time." He called Joktan, and the red-haired boy jumped to answer. "See that he gets his meals," he told the boy.

Joktan shut his lips tight, looking stubborn and scared.

"He won't touch you," Daniel urged. "Just for one day, Jok. I'll do your work for you when I get back."

Joktan agreed sullenly.

"Anyone who tries any tricks will have me to reckon with," Daniel shot back over his shoulder.

But when he and Simon started forward again the big man moved behind them.

"No!" shouted Daniel, angry now. He waved his arms. The man stared at him without expression—or was there an expression that Daniel did not want to see? "You cannot follow me," the boy said. "Wait. I'll be back." Then he turned and stamped down the trail behind Simon. At the first turn he looked back. Samson stood at the top of the trail looking down. He did not move, and Daniel raised a hand briefly to him and went on.

As they walked, Daniel tried again to persuade Simon. "If you're a Zealot, if you work for the same end as Rosh, why won't you join him?"

"When the day comes." said Simon. "When the one comes who will lead us, then we will all join together. In the meantime, as I said before, Rosh and I don't see eye to eye. For one thing, I prefer to earn my own bread and meat."

The insult to Rosh was like a blow to Daniel. "Doesn't a warrior earn his keep?" he demanded hotly. "Rosh would give his life for Israel. Why should the farmers begrudge him a few scraps? They owe him far more than he takes."

"Perhaps so," said Simon mildly. "I did not mean to anger you, my friend. There will be need for warriors. But just now there is always a need for a good blacksmith."

Daniel subsided into scowling silence. They left the rocky trail and came out on the road through the green pastureland that sloped down to the village. Presently they reached a small ford that crossed a mountain stream which gathered in a pebbly hollow richly overgrown with fern and clusters of rosy oleander and purple iris. Simon stopped and studied the spot.

"This will do, I think, he said. He began to remove his head covering. Daniel watched, puzzled.

"We will have to bathe here," said Simon. "When we reach the village it will be too late."

"Too late?"

"It will be sundown, and the Sabbath will have begun."

Daniel reddened. How could he have kept track of the Sabbath? Had Simon guessed that in the cave one day was the same as another? Simon, not looking at him, was carefully folding his cloak and spreading it on a bush. To Daniel's eyes Simon had no need to bathe. Daniel looked down at his own arms, streaked with soot and sweat. If Simon had said another word, or even looked up, he would have abandoned the whole visit. But after a moment he stamped into the fern, stripped off his own filthy tunic, and splashed into the pool. The feel of the water, after weeks of measuring it by drops from a goatskin bag, was sharp pleasure. Daniel scooped up handfuls of sand and pebbles and scraped his hands and feet. Then he got down on his knees and plunged his whole head into the stream. He came up dripping, to find Simon already dressed, sitting on the bank and smiling at him. This time he managed a sheepish grin in return.

They reached the village just as the thin clear note of the ram's horn sounded the first call to the Sabbath, signaling the workers to leave the fields. Nothing had really changed in five years, except that it all looked much smaller than Daniel had remembered, the streets narrower and dirtier, the dooryards shabbier and more cluttered.

There were a few new houses with fresh mud walls and thatch still green on the roofs. He tried to recall who lived in this house or that one. They passed the shop of Amalek, so crumbling and out of repair that no new occupant had attempted to restore it to use. They passed the deserted square, and the well where four weary donkeys were being hastily watered. They entered a dark narrow street, at the end of which stood the small remembered house, its clay walls dark and crumbling, its roof sagging. Here Simon halted.

"I will leave you," he said. "You will do better to go in by yourself."

Daniel looked at the house uneasily. "How do I know they—"

"They are expecting you. I told them you were coming."

Daniel glared at him. What right had Simon to be so sure he would come? Simon smiled a brief encouragement and strode away. Daniel stood, resentful, overcome with panic, and as he hesitated the door opened and a very old woman stood on the threshold.

How bent she was, and thin!

"Daniel?" Could that quavering voice belong to his grandmother? "Is that you, Daniel?"

"Yes, Grandmother," he stammered. "Peace be with you." As he spoke he heard the second call of the horn across the village.

"My boy! It is time you came home!" Her eyes, pale and clouded, peered up into his face. Her hands clutched at him.

At the door he hesitated, and the strong habit of his childhood reaching out to him, scarcely aware of what he did, he touched his finger to the mezuzah, the little niche in the door frame that contained the sacred verses of the Shema. Then he stepped over the threshold.

The room seemed to be empty. One smoking oil lamp hung from the rafters. On the mat beneath it the supper dishes were set and the Sabbath lamp stood ready. He peered about him with dread.

"Come Leah," his grandmother said. "You should not be working after the second call. Come and greet your brother."

Then he saw the girl, seated behind the loom in the corner, the long golden hair flowing over her shoulders. He stood tongue-tied. He had remembered a little girl. She was almost a woman, and he realized that she was beautiful.

"Leah," his grandmother fussed again. "It is Daniel, come home after all these years."

He ran his tongue over his lips. "Peace, Leah," he said.

The girl raised her head from her work, so that he caught a glimpse of the clear blue of her eyes. The fear in them struck like a sickness behind his ribs.

"Don't mind her," the old woman said. "She will know you before long. Shame, Leah. Get some water for your brother. Where are your manners?"

The girl did not move. Daniel waited, sick at heart. "Leah," he stammered. "Don't you know me?" He pleaded with her. "Don't you remember how you always brought me water when I came home to visit?"

She raised her head again. Slowly into the blue eyes he watched recognition come. "You really are Daniel?" Her voice was faint and tremulous. "You have been away so long."

"Please bring me the water, Leah."

Obediently she moved from the loom to the earthen jar by the door and poured out water into a hollow bowl, every motion gentle and graceful. But the bowl she held out to him was shaking so that the water spilled over. He took it awkwardly and bent to wash his feet. What had he expected or hoped? It was just as it had been when he left five years ago. No, it was worse. His sister Leah was fifteen years old, and fear still looked out of her eyes.

The last call of the horn came clearly, announcing the start of the Sabbath. His grandmother lighted a wick from the lamp and held it to the Sabbath lamp. "Speak the blessing, Daniel," she said. "It is fitting the man should say it."

He hesitated, then the words came falteringly to his lips. "Praised be Thou, O Lord our God, King of the Universe, Who hast sanctified us by Thy commandments and commanded us to kindle the Sabbath light."

They sat on the hard dirt floor around the frayed mat, and once again his grandmother looked to him. Long ago, for the first months in the cave, he had repeated a blessing silently over his food. This he remembered well. "Blessed art Thou, O Lord our God, Who bringeth forth bread from the earth—"

There was certainly little to bless God for, a watery stew made of lentils, some coarse barley bread. In a moment he noticed that the others were not eating at all, only watching him, their eyes following each morsel from the bowl to his mouth.

"Do you not eat with me?" he asked.

"We have eaten already," said his grandmother.

But Leah was more honest. "Grandmother said we must save it for you," she explained, in her sweet childish voice. "She said you would be very hungry."

His appetite left him. "You must eat with me," he insisted, pushing the bowl toward his sister.

With a frightened look toward the grandmother, the girl broke off a crust of bread and dipped it into the bowl. He saw the blue veins through the delicate flesh of her hand; the wrist was fragile as a bird's claw.

Where did they get their food, anyway? He tried to think how to ask. "It is good bread," he said. "Do you grow the grain?"

"It is pauper's share," his grandmother answered shortly.

He wished he had not asked. He hated the picture of his grandmother following after the reapers in the field, scrabbling for the sheaves they dropped, which had by law to be left for paupers to gather.

After the meal was cleared away they sat in silence. His grandmother did not ask any questions. Did she really care that he had come? She seemed too weary to care about anything; her chin had settled into the folds of her mantle and she drifted in and out of an uneasy sleep. He supposed she must still work in the fields of ketzah, the plant from which the village took its name. Stooping over all day, she sowed and weeded, and when the blue flowers had dropped, she beat off the seed covering with a staff and gathered the tiny seeds, so hot to the tongue, which were marketed as a seasoning for food.

He looked about him. The clay platform which had once divided the room into two levels had crumbled so that it was no more than a shelf, scarcely wide enough for sleeping. A hollow scooped out of the earthen floor held the cold ashes of an old fire. The only furniture was a battered wooden chest and the loom at which Leah had sat.

As darkness fell there was a soft thudding sound against the door. His grandmother roused herself and let in a small black goat. The little creature went straight to Leah, who reached out both arms toward it. The goat nuzzled against her, and settled down to sleep with its square chin in the girl's lap. She sat fondling it, twining the black hairs of its beard around her fingers, talking to it in a soft murmur like the sound of doves on the roof. Daniel watched them, his uneasiness lulled for a moment. She looks like our mother, he thought. Then he caught the words the soft voice was saying.

"You mustn't be afraid of him. He is our brother Daniel come home. When he milks you, you must be good and stand still. See how big and strong he is. He will take care of us and keep us safe."

Suddenly he was afraid again. He looked away, trying to shut out the sight of her with her golden hair shining in the lamplight, trying to shut out the sound of that murmuring voice. Everything he cared about and worked for was threatened by that small helpless figure.

His arms and legs were cramped. The airless little house seemed to hold all the heat of the day. The sputtering oil in the lamp filled the room with a rancid odor. His head was heavy, and he thought with longing of the evening breeze that would be moving among the branches above the cave. With relief he watched his grandmother lift down mats from a niche in the wall.

"I have made ready your old place on the roof," she said.

He took the worn roll of matting, bade her goodnight, let himself out the door, and climbed a tottering ladder up the outside wall to the flat rooftop. It was little cooler up here. Heat lay over the town like a smothering blanket. He sat for a time hugging his knees and looking about him.

Why did I come here? he thought. Already he yearned

41

to be away from this place. Hunger gnawed at him. Up on the mountain the men would be still sitting about the fire, their stomachs satisfied with stolen mutton and grape wine, joking and telling boastful stories. Later they would wrap their cloaks about them and sleep with their lungs full of clean mountain air, and the stars would come down, brilliant, close enough to touch. He wondered if Joktan had made sure that Samson had enough to eat. He wondered how long the man had waited at the top of the trail. Suddenly he flung himself on his face and buried his head in his arms and could have wept for homesickness.

THE SABBATH MORNING was very still. Not a grindstone rumbled, not a voice was upraised. No puff of smoke rose from the clay ovens. No women passed on their way to the well. Descending the ladder to the house, Daniel found a handful of olives and a cold crust of bread waiting for his breakfast. The little goat wandered in the small garden patch behind the house.

Very early in the day, when Daniel was already wondering how he could endure another hour, Simon came to the door. His knock sent Leah cowering into a corner. Daniel hastily went out into the road, shutting the door behind him.

"I'm on my way to the synagogue," Simon said. "I'd like you to go with me."

Daniel scowled. "I haven't been to a synagogue for five years," he countered. "One more Sabbath won't matter."

"On the contrary," Simon answered with a smile. "Today is none too soon."

Daniel's lips tightened. He bent and picked up a pebble and shied it at a little green lizard that had crawled from under the house. Simon's eyebrows lifted. Probably it was against the law to throw a stone on the Sabbath.

"There's a man I'd like you to see," Simon told him.

"They say he will visit our synagogue this morning."

Daniel glanced up. Beneath the words there was a hint he could not miss. "What sort of man?"

"I'm not sure," said Simon. "He comes from Nazareth."

"Good reason to stay away," grumbled Daniel. Then, feeling the pressure of Simon's silence, "A Zealot?"

"It may well be. Come and see what you make of him."

"In these clothes?"

"I have brought you a cloak and shoes."

Daniel stared at his friend. If Simon, stickler for the law, had carried a bundle on the Sabbath just so that Daniel could see this man, he must consider the matter important. Daniel took the cloak and went inside the house. His grandmother was nodding again in the corner. She looked up and muttered his father's name, her eyes confused with sleep. Leah crept forward shyly and bent to fasten the leather sandal.

"Will you go with me?" he asked on impulse, and could have bitten his tongue at the terror that leaped into her blue eyes.

"Never mind, I didn't mean it," he said miserably, jerking away from her.

Simon looked him over with approval as he stepped out into the roadway. "How does it seem to be home?" he inquired.

"You call this home?" Daniel burst out. "My grand-mother does nothing but sleep, and my sister is possessed by demons."

"She is no better?"

"Before I was apprenticed—when she was five years old, she hid herself in that house. In all this time she has never stepped outside the door."

"So I've heard. The demons must have a strong hold.

44

Yet she does good weaving, I understand. Your grandmother sells it in Chorazin."

Daniel had not paid much attention to the loom in the corner, but now Simon's words somewhat lightened his shame.

"Who is this man we go to see?" he asked, not wanting to think about Leah.

"Jesus, son of Joseph, a carpenter by trade. He has left his work and goes about preaching from town to town."

"Preaching? I thought you said he was a Zealot."

"He preaches the coming of the kingdom."

"You have heard him?"

"No, but I have seen him. I journeyed to Nazareth with a friend who went to arrange for a wife. While we were there this carpenter came back to preach in his own synagogue."

"A town like Nazareth must have boasted—"

"They did not boast. They tried to kill him."

Daniel glanced quickly at his friend, his curiosity roused not so much by the words as by the tone of Simon's voice. But Simon had no time to say more. They were approaching the small stone and plaster building in the center of the village, and men and women brushed close to them on either side of the road.

Daniel had to stoop to go through the low doorway. He sidled close to the wall, tensing his muscles, conscious of his shaggy height and his wide shoulders, trying to draw in and make himself smaller. But he soon realized that today there was no curiosity to spare for him.

He was sure that the synagogue had never been so full in his childhood. Close together on the low benches huddled the men of the town, their knees drawn up almost to their chins. They sat in order of their trades, the skilled artisans nearest the pulpit, the silversmiths, the tailors, and sandalmakers. Farther back sat the bakers, the cheese-makers and dyers, and along the walls where Daniel and Simon had taken their places, stood the lower tradesmen and the farmers. Still others crowded the doorway, and many, he saw, would have to stand outside in the road. By the rustle and murmur behind the grilled screen that separated the women's section, many of the men had brought their wives with them.

"Hear, O Israel: the Lord our God is one Lord, and you shall love the Lord your God with all your heart, and with all your soul, and with all your might—"

The great words of the Shema rolled through the syna-gogue. For a moment Daniel was caught up by them as he had been in his childhood. But as the long passage of the Law was read aloud in Hebrew and then carefully translated into Aramaic, the language which the people spoke and understood, his attention began to wander. Though the throng of men sat respectfully, he could feel their restlessness also, and the anticipation that mounted, moment by moment. They knew that by custom a visit-ing rabbi would be invited to come forward and read from the Torah. When the long-awaited moment came, every man turned to watch the stranger who made his way to the platform.

The man's figure was not in any way arresting. He was slight, with the knotted arms and shoulders of one who has done hard labor from childhood. He was not regal or commanding. He was dressed simply in a plain white tallith that reached to his feet. His white head covering, drawn closely over his forehead and hanging to his shoul-ders, hid his profile. Yet when he turned and stood before the congregation, Daniel was startled. All at once nothing in the room was distinct to him but this man's face. A thin face, strongly cut. A vital, radiant face, lighted from within by a burning intensity of spirit.

Yes! Daniel thought, his own spirit leaping up. This man is a fighter! He is one of us!

Jesus received the scroll and stood unrolling it with reverence, as though he were seeking for some passage already determined in his own mind. Then he raised his eyes and spoke from memory.

"The Spirit of the Lord is upon me, because He has anointed me to preach good news to the poor. He has sent me to proclaim release to the captives, and recovering of sight to the blind, to set at liberty those who are oppressed, to proclaim the acceptable year of the Lord."

A shock ran through Daniel at the first words. A gentle voice, barely raised, it carried to every corner of the room, warm, vibrant, with a promise of unlimited power. It was as though only a fraction of that voice were being used, as though if the full force of it were unstopped it would roll like thunder.

Jesus closed the book and gave it back to the attendant. The waiting congregation seemed to surge forward and to hold its breath. Again that voice made the blood leap in Daniel's veins.

"I say to you, the time is fulfilled, and the kingdom of God is at hand. Repent, and believe."

Now! Daniel leaned forward. Tell us that the moment has come! Tell us what we are to do! Longing swelled unbearably in his throat.

But Jesus went on speaking quietly. A rippling murmur passed across the crowd. Others too waited for the word that was not spoken. What had the man meant? He had

47

said liberty for the oppressed. Why didn't he call them to arms against the oppressor? Repent, he said now. Repent. As though that could rid them of the Romans. Disappointed and puzzled, Daniel leaned back. The fire that had leaped up in him died down. The man's voice had been like a trumpet call. Yet where did the call lead?

Had Simon understood? Daniel stayed close beside his friend as the crowds streamed from the synagogue at the close of the service. "Is he a Zealot or isn't he?" he demanded, as soon as they had outdistanced the others.

"What do you think?" countered Simon.

"I couldn't tell. Why did they try to kill him in Nazareth?"

"They said he blasphemed. Some of them said he had set himself up as God's anointed, a common carpenter's son. They were beside themselves."

"How did he get away?"

Simon slowed his steps. "I'm not quite sure," he said, "though I was there and saw it. I didn't know what it was all about, but you know how it is with a crowd—I ran with them, and I'm ashamed to tell it, I had a stone in my hand too. They dragged him up the hill to a cliff and they meant to push him over. But just at the edge of the cliff they fell back, and he stood there alone looking at them. I don't know how it was with them, but all at once I was ashamed, terribly ashamed, of the stone in my hand. Then he walked back down the hill, and not one of them touched him."

"Didn't he fight to defend himself?"

"No. He was not angry. He was just—not afraid. I have never seen anyone so completely not afraid."

Strange. Daniel would have liked the story better if

48

the man had fought back. He was vaguely disappointed, let down as he had been in the synagogue. He scuffed along the dusty road beside Simon.

"I can't make the man out," he said finally. "What did he mean that the day is at hand?"

Simon walked on for a moment, his eyes on the ground. "I don't know what he meant," he said slowly. "But I intend to find out."

At a crossroads Simon left him. "I will look in on you tomorrow," he said. "Keep the cloak. It is an old one, but you may have some use from it."

Daniel walked on through the noonday heat, lingering to peer furtively at the people who passed. Though he shrank from their curious glances, he was in no hurry to return to his grandmother's house.

Without warning, the sound of a trumpet split the Sabbath calm. Instantly the peace around him dissolved into terror. There was a frantic scramble to be out of the road. Ahead of Daniel two women and a child darted senselessly to one side and then the other. The younger ran back to jerk her child after her, the older woman shrieking at them both. Barely was the way cleared when a detachment of Roman cavalry trotted by, the horses' hoofs sending up a choking cloud of dust. In their rear four soldiers suddenly reined in, horses rearing, and stood guard. Some distance behind them marched a detachment of foot soldiers.

Paralyzed with hatred, Daniel watched them. This was not the same as looking down from the mountain. Here he could see them plainly. They were not even Romans but Samaritan auxiliaries, traitors, paid to fight in Caesar's army. He watched their brutish faces pass, one after another, looking neither right nor left. To smash those faces—even one of them! He bent and picked up a rock. "Infidels!" he shouted.

A hand slapped down over his mouth. Another hand gripped his upraised arm and forced it back. He felt himself jerked flat against a wall, held fast, while two men stepped in front of him, between him and the marching soldiers. With the sharp pressure of their hands on him, Daniel's senses came back. He stood still, not trying to fight them off. He saw that they had acted so quickly that not a soldier had noticed. The detachment went on down the road, their laced boots slapping an unbroken rhythm.

"Gone!" said a voice. "And no trouble, praise God."

"No thanks to this one," another voice rasped.

Abruptly the hands released his jaw and wrist. "Are you possessed?" one man hissed.

"One of those hotheads!" the other scoffed.

Another came closer, peering into his face. "Who are you, boy? Not one of ours, that's sure."

Daniel looked back at them sullenly. "I am Daniel bar Jamin."

"Son of Jamin? Wasn't it your father who—"

"Yes."

"Then you ought to know better. Do you want to bring the same curse down on all of us?"

"I despise them!" cried Daniel. "I have taken an oath!"

"Keep your oath to yourself," a man warned. "You Zealots cause nothing but trouble. You'll have every village in Galilee burned to the ground like Sepphoris."

Daniel knew he had behaved like a fool, but he would never admit it. He jerked away from them and walked scornfully down the road to the narrow alley that led to his grandmother's house.

At sundown the thin clear piping of the horn announced the end of the Sabbath. Promptly his grandmother snuffed out the Sabbath lamp, which had been burning ever since his arrival, and wrapped it carefully to put away for another week. The shadows settled closer around the one remaining flame in its saucer of smoking oil. With relief Daniel perceived that it was time to take himself to the rooftop for another night.

He was not sleepy. The long afternoon of inactivity had left his body restless. He was hungry, despite the sacrifice of the two women who had barely touched the food. He sat on the rooftop and felt the village steaming and seething around him in the dark, like a great pot of stew. He hated the stifling, foul-smelling streets, the miserable houses crowded close together. He hated this moldering house filled with the sighs of his grandmother and the murmuring voice of Leah. Here in the village who cared about the dream of freedom? Even Simon was content to wait and talk, never to act.

The man who had spoken, though, Jesus of Nazareth? There had been a moment, when he first stood up to speak, when it had seemed—but it had come to nothing. More words, nothing but words.

He knew one man who still dared to act. One of these days Rosh would show them all. One day Rosh's army would be strong enough, and then these timid men in the village would come scrambling to throw in their lot with him. And when that day came, he, Daniel bar Jamin. would show them too. When the Romans were defeated and the last of them had gone, he would come back. He would build a good house for his grandmother and Leah, and there would be plenty to eat, and a good life for them at last. And there would be no more giving way on the road and looking over their shoulders before they dared to whisper, but everyone would walk free.

In the darkness Daniel climbed down the ladder. He caught the faint note of a bell as the little goat shifted in its sleep. For an instant he wavered. Would Leah be sorry when she woke and found him gone? Then he pushed back his doubts. Someday, very soon, he would come back and make it up to her.

He walked through the narrow streets and struck off toward the hills. He walked swiftly, his feet sure on the rocky trail. Toward midnight he came to the foot of the steep ascent that led to the cave. His heart began to beat strongly and joyfully. As he started up the last climb a dark shape moved out from the boulders above, loomed for an instant against the sky, and then came soundlessly down toward him. In the dim light he could see the white gleaming arc that split the shadowy face.

"Ho, Samson!" he called out. "I've come back."

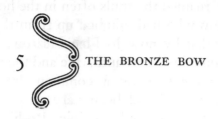

5   THE BRONZE BOW

THE MONTH of Nisan drew to a close. It was the time of
the first harvest. On the slopes at the foot of the mountain the villagers, men and women and children, moved
slowly through the fields of barley, the long hairy heads of
grain falling in rhythmic waves before their sickles. From
the mountain lookout Rosh's men watched them, specu-
lating from which unguarded field they might snatch their
own due share. Daniel, who had never before been dis-
contented with a mountain springtime, felt restless. He
chafed at the days of heavy labor required to make one
inferior sword. He yearned for the day when they could
cease to make swords and could at last put them to use.
He was impatient with Rosh's waiting.

Every day Rosh's spies brought news of caravans passing on the roads below. When the men least expected
it, Rosh would give sudden orders, and there would be a
spurt of furious activity. Then Daniel would hurl himself
into the short battle with all the fury he longed to expend
on the Romans. Afterwards he always felt let down.
What had been gained? Was the day actually any nearer?
That night on the rooftop of his grandmother's house he
had seen so clearly that all he longed and hoped for was
here in Rosh's band. Now it seemed to him that most of
the men did not really care, that they were just as bad

as the villagers who thought no further than the next meal.

He roamed the trails often in the hope of meeting again the boy who had climbed up from the village, though he knew that by now Joel bar Hezron must be living in the big house in Capernaum. He and the village boy had been drawn together by a common dream, and for a few moments Joel had been very close to giving up everything he possessed to join Rosh's band. Perhaps if he had another chance—? Joel was the sort Rosh needed, impatient, full of spirit, not afraid to take a risk. Slowly a daring plan began to form in Daniel's mind, and when he had mulled it over for several days he summoned his courage and took it to Rosh. Rosh heard him out, his button-black eyes twinkling with derision.

"Ever been to the city of Capernaum?" he inquired.

"No," said Daniel. "Still, I'd like to try. I'm sure I could find him."

Rosh considered. "Go ahead," he said finally. "You can look after yourself. But don't set your heart on that boy. He's got too much to lose. I checked on him. Grandfather was rich as old Hezekiah himself. But go along. He might be useful to us in Capernaum."

Daniel set off long before dawn, carrying the cloak Simon had given him. Leaving Samson was easier this time. The big man understood that he would come back. The dark trails held no terror; his feet knew every jutting rock and turn. With the first light he left the mountain behind and strode along the level road through the plain. In the east a yellow glow began to gather, sending out long spears of pink and pale amethyst. From the olive groves came the song of a lark, rising to a thin clear sweetness against the pearly sky. On every side sounded the urgent chirping of linnets and finches. Abruptly the sun burst forth. Daniel could see a golden field of mustard stretching as far as his eye could reach, the yellow blossoms so high that a man could walk through them unseen.

Presently he overtook a caravan. Prodded on by weary drivers, the camels swayed slowly. Above the smell of camel Daniel's nose caught an unfamiliar fragrance, sweet and spicy, which seeped from the toppling bags they carried. As the day grew brighter the road was busy with farmers trundling small wagons or bearing on their shoulders baskets of vegetables for the city market. Already the excitement of the city quickened his pulse.

He came out on the last long slope of the road. Below him lay the sea, like a great blue jewel in the sun, and at its edge the town of Capernaum, a mass of dark stone houses, thick-clustered. A transparent veil of mist and smoke hung over the rooftops. He fancied he could hear the hum of thousands of voices. He hurried on, forgetting the miles behind, feeling fresh and exhilarated.

It was far too early to look for Joel, but he was in no haste. There was much to see. He wandered through the streets, taking in great gulps the busyness, the color and sound and smell of them. In the marketplace the farmers were heaping squashes and cucumbers and melons, and merchants jabbered in outlandish tongues as they set up booths of cloth or baskets or pottery. He saw four elders of the Pharisees, the phylacteries bound to their proud foreheads, walking with great care that their tasseled robes did not brush the passers-by, lest the merest touch might make them unclean. Once he saw a black slave scurrying about his master's business. Did he, if Daniel could understand, speak the same language as Samson?

He came to the harbor and gazed at the multitude of boats, fishing dories and pleasure craft and flat-bottomed barges. Back and forth from the anchored barges moved an unending line of half-naked men, bearing on their backs the sacks of grain and baskets of fruit which the farmers had brought to the city. So this was where the food went that was borne away day after day from his own village? All this to feed the evil city of Tiberias, which Herod had built to the south and named for the emperor of Rome. Daniel was reminded suddenly of his own empty stomach, and he remembered that although Rosh had been free enough with his advice, he had not provided a single copper with which to buy food.

Further along the shore, where the fishing boats were drawn up, the fishermen were dragging in their night's catch, the great nets heaving and gleaming in the sun. Women had come down to meet them, and were spreading the fish on flat stones and sprinkling them with salt. Others stretched out the empty nets to dry. Above the smell of fish, Daniel detected a tantalizing odor, and saw that several of the families had lighted small fires and were preparing their breakfast.

"Hungry, boy?"

Daniel started, abashed to be caught staring. A smiling young woman in a bright red and blue headdress was holding out a small fish on a palm leaf. He backed away. "I have no money," he muttered.

"Who said anything about money? You can see there's plenty. Take it."

The fish was delicious, the skin smoky and crisp.

The woman eyed him admiringly. "Where would a handsome stranger like you have come from?" she demanded.

Embarrassed, he stammered the name of Ketzah.

"Are you waiting for the teacher?" she inquired.

"No."

"You should then. It's worth being late for work."

"What teacher?" he asked.

"The carpenter. Ah, there he is now." She called over her shoulder to another woman. "Come! He's about to begin."

Daniel turned curiously. A short way from them on the shore a cluster of fishermen had gathered, and from all sides others were leaving their nets. A few workers broke from the lines that labored on the barges. Through the shifting bodies Daniel caught a glimpse of the man in their midst. It was the man who had spoken in the synagogue. He stood on the beach among the fishing boats, in his plain white robe, smiling and greeting the men by name. Out here in the sun he did not look solemn as in the synagogue. He looked vigorous and confident and happy. Something he was saying drew a burst of laughter from the men. Daniel pushed his way nearer till he could get a good look.

How strong he is, he thought. Yet bodily the man was no match for the sturdy fishermen who surrounded him. The impression of strength came from an extraordinary vitality that seemed to pulse in the very air around him. Once more, as on that day in the synagogue, Daniel felt a spark leap up in his own body. Looking about him he could see the same spark reflected in the eyes of the men and women who jostled him.

Someone shouted a question that Daniel could not catch, and Jesus held up a hand to ask their silence.

"What is the kingdom of heaven?" he answered. "It is like a merchant in search of fine pearls, who, on finding one pearl of great value, went and sold all that he had and bought it. Or the kingdom of heaven is like a net which was thrown into the sea and gathered fish of every kind—"

A clink of metal distracted Daniel. Turning, he saw that two soldiers had joined the crowd. They sauntered close, and stood looking with curiosity at the speaker and his audience. Automatically, Daniel spat. Two fishermen glared at him. Plainly they resented his disturbance more than they did the presence of the soldiers. One of the Romans shot him a quick contemptuous glance. Jesus took no notice whatsoever. He could not have missed their tall helmets, yet his calm voice did not falter. Anger spiraled up in Daniel. He didn't want to hear any more. The nearness, the arrogance of those two choked him. He turned his back on them and walked away.

Yet he could not escape the sight of Roman soldiers. They stood on the docks, counting off bales of wheat and vegetables. They strolled through the marketplace. Everywhere, the Jews went about their business, paying no attention. The boy who had lived for five years in the solitude of the mountain, nursing his hatred and keeping it ever fresh, could not credit his own eyes. How could these city people endure to be reminded on every hand of their own helplessness? More shameful still, he saw merchants joking with the soldiers. He could not understand. Where was their pride? Had they forgotten altogether? If Rosh were here he would open their eyes. Why did that Jesus do nothing?

At the thought of Rosh he was reminded of the reason he had come to the city. It took him some time to find the house of Rabbi Hezron. Finally someone directed him up the steep hill that rose above the harbor. As he climbed the cobbled street his stomach began to clamor. He had counted on Joel to observe the unwritten law that provided that any stranger who came to one's door must receive food and shelter. But as the crowded stone dwellings gave way to the long forbidding walls of large estates, and he caught glimpses of gardens and terraces rising, one upon another, green and golden, he felt his first doubt. Rosh had warned him that Hezron had inherited great wealth. But Daniel had no acquaintance with wealth. He had not been prepared for the hugeness of it. Would such houses as these remember the law of hospitality? Or would they turn him away like a beggar?

He came to the heavy door in the wall to which he had been directed, and rang the bell that hung there. After some time the wooden door creaked open and a wizened man peered out at him. Hezron? In the nick of time he noticed that the man's ears had been pierced. He had almost made a fool of himself and bowed to a slave!

"I have come to speak with Joel bar Hezron," he announced much too loudly.

With reluctance the servant allowed him to step into a narrow tiled corridor. "You will wait here," he said. "What name shall I give to the young master?"

"Tell him it is Daniel bar Jamin, a friend from Ketzah."

The hallway where he waited was cool and dim, the oaken doors that led from it all closed. Through the open archway opposite him, Daniel stared with astonishment into a sunlit courtyard, at flowering trees and green borders and white marble. His ears caught the gentle splash of water and the trilling of birds. He had not dreamed that even Herod's palace could boast such wonders. What a fool he had been to think that Joel would even remember him!

There was a soft footstep, a rustle of silk, and a shadow fell between him and the sunlit opening. It was not Joel who stood there, but his sister Malthace. A robe of thin soft material fell in exquisite folds to delicate embroidered sandals. Her dark hair was bound back from her face with a thin fillet of gold. She started at sight of a stranger, and there leaped into her eyes recognition, and then something else, an unmistakable shrinking. His careful greeting fell back at his own feet. She made no greeting at all, only stared at him with dismay.

Then there was a thumping of feet. The boy who came charging across the courtyard had not changed at all. He was the same country boy who had jumped into the fight on the mountain road. He grasped Daniel by the elbows, his dark eyes glowing.

"Daniel! Welcome! I've been wishing—" He broke off with a quick glance over his shoulder. "You'll stay to eat with us? Of course you will!"

Pride battled with Daniel's clamoring stomach. "No," he said. "I came only to speak with you."

"You're certainly not going right away, after all this time."

"My clothes are dusty from the road."

"Oh—that! Just leave your cloak here in the hallway. For Father's sake, you know."

Daniel flushed, remembering that a common man who visited a Pharisee must leave his cloak at the door lest he make the household unclean. Slowly he undid Simon's coat, allowing Joel a glimpse of the torn and scanty garment underneath.

"Never mind," Joel said hastily. "Better wear it after all. It doesn't matter really."

Propelling his guest along the corridor, Joel was all at once aware of his sister, who still stood just inside the archway. "Thacia," he said, an uncertain note in his

60

voice. "Do you remember Daniel—the one who—" He floundered to a stop.

Her fine dark eyebrows lifted. "I remember," she said, in a cool light voice. Then she turned on her embroidered sandal and walked away from them.

Joel looked after her with annoyance, then he shrugged. "Don't mind Thacia," he said. "She's putting on city airs lately. Come, we'll go up to my room where we can talk. If you knew what it's like to see someone from home!"

Daniel had to follow so rapidly through the courtyard that he had only a blurred impression of green beauty. They passed beneath a row of slender columns into another corridor, up a flight of shallow steps and into a small square room. Apparently Joel slept in this room, and did not even have to share it with anyone. There was a single low couch, with a striped linen covering, two carved wooden benches, a painted chest, and a desk with quills and an inkpot and a scroll propped open as though Joel had just been working on it.

Joel poured water from a fine pottery jar and laid out a smooth linen towel. Self-consciously Daniel washed his hands and feet and retied his turban. It was plain that Joel did not care whether he was respectable or not, that the boy was overjoyed to see him. Daniel's wiry self-confidence reasserted itself. He would not let himself be shaken again by a silly girl.

"Did Rosh send you?" Joel demanded. "Have you held up any more caravans? How about the slave, the big black one? I didn't envy you when you led him off that day."

"I should have kept my mouth shut," Daniel answered.

"What happened?"

"The minute I took his chains off he took charge of me instead. He's made me the laughingstock of the camp. He works like a mule to keep my fire going. But he won't let me out of his sight."

Joel was amused at the picture. "Can he talk? Does he understand what you say?"

"The others don't think so. I'm not sure. Sometimes it seems as though he's trying to tell me something."

"You're not afraid of him?"

"Not for myself. But I have to watch him all the time. That strength of his—it's like a rock on the edge of the cliff. A feather could start it down. One night I got into an argument with Joktan, and Jok started at me with his fists. I looked up just in time. There was Samson reaching for Jok with those great arms of his. It was all I could do to stop him."

Joel whistled. "I should think—" he began, when a chiming gong interrupted him, and he rose to his feet. "Father insists that we're on time for meals," he said. "We'd better talk later."

Near the fountain in the courtyard Hezron stood waiting, a tall, narrow-faced man with graying hair. He bowed with a cool courtesy at Joel's introduction.

"Peace be with you," he said. "You are welcome." He gazed with distaste at Daniel's unlawful garment.

A camel would be as welcome, Daniel thought. The man will have to purify his whole house when I leave!

Side by side two women moved gracefully across the tile pavement, Malthace and an older woman who must once have looked much like her daughter. A tiny bird of vivid blue darted from a dwarf pear tree and lighted for a breath's space on the girl's shoulder, then flashed away.

The corner of Thacia's mouth curled slightly as she looked at Daniel, hinting, "I could tell them much if I cared." The mother smiled warmly and held out her hand to him.

They led Daniel through an archway into a spacious room. His muscles stiffened at the array of couches. Was he expected to eat his meal lying down like a Roman? But after an awkward wait he lowered his body gingerly and, imitating Joel, propped himself up on one elbow, aware of Thacia's amusement. For all her airs, he could wager she had never seen a couch herself up to a month ago. No one in the village boasted such heathen nonsense.

Joel's mother, with a gracious word, led her daughter behind a silken screen, where they would both be hidden from view while the men of the family ate. More nonsense. Daniel was sure that in the village they must have sat on mats and eaten their meal together like any other family.

Through the prolonged hand-washing Daniel fidgeted, affronted by the silver pitchers, the fine tiny napkins, the hovering slaves. Then at the sight of the food a fierceness sprang up in him. He had drained every drop from the cup of date wine before he noticed that the others were holding theirs untouched. Too late he set down what remained of his small loaf of bread. He had torn into it like Samson himself, and he saw Hezron's lips flatten together. Curse their finicky rules. Had they ever felt the gnawing of an empty stomach?

"Your home?" Hezron inquired, after the scant portions of fish and fruit had been consumed in silence. "Is it far from Capernaum?"

Daniel dragged his attention from his empty bowl. "In Ketzah, sir."

"Indeed?" Hezron looked surprised. "Your father too? I do not seem to recall—"

"My father was Jamin, chief overseer of the vineyards."

"So," said Hezron, frowning. "I remember. A very tragic affair. He was a good man, your father, but a rash one."

His cool tone pricked Daniel's thin skin and stirred the anger that always smoldered close under the surface. He glowered at his plate, holding his tongue.

"You are the support of your mother?"

"My mother is not living either."

Hezron hesitated. "You have been doubly unfortunate," he said in a kinder tone, mistaking Daniel's anger for grief. "Do you follow your father's trade?"

"No. I was bound to Amalek, the ironsmith." Sold! he felt like shouting. Sold into slavery for a term of six years, to a man who was not fit to own even a mule. Had the rabbis protested then, or a single soul in the village lifted a finger to help him?

"Well," said Hezron reasonably, "it is necessary for every boy to learn a trade. Joel, as you probably know, was trained as a sandalmaker, as I was myself. Though I must say I applied myself with more diligence. I do not seem to remember seeing you in Amalek's shop."

"I didn't work there long."

"You can tell he's a blacksmith," Joel broke in, in an effort to swerve his father's questions. "With those muscles you'd be a sensation in the gymnasium, Daniel. Have you ever been there?"

"The Roman gymnasium?" Daniel glared at his friend. "I would never set foot in it!"

64

"I should hope not," said Hezron, with a scowl at his own son. "That was an ill-considered jest."

"Of course it was a jest, Father," Joel amended hastily.

"It is not a matter for jesting," his father said. "It is an outrage that some of our Jewish youths have been tempted to take part in these disgraceful games. And some of their elders even go to watch their shame."

"Well, there are other things in the city worth seeing," Joel persisted cheerfully. "This afternoon I'll take you about, Daniel."

Daniel stared down at his empty cup. The morsels of food had not begun to whet his hunger. The rabbi had deliberately put him at a disadvantage with every question. His resentment turned now even against Joel.

"I have seen enough," he said rudely. "All I can see is the Roman fortress and the eagles in the streets. Everywhere I turn I hear the ring of Roman boots on the pavement."

Joel, a worried line puckering his forehead, still attempted to steer his friend to safety. "I felt that way at first," he said. "But you do get used to it. For the most part they mind their own business. Some of them even try to be friendly."

"Friendly!" Daniel reared up on his couch. "This morning on the road I passed an old man mending the axle of his wagon. He was deaf and he couldn't hear the chariot coming. It caught his rear wheel—he said there was room and to spare. He swore the soldier meant to do it. His cabbages were ruined, and the old man was shaking all over. Can you get used to that?" He glared across the table.

Joel looked down, dismayed. Hezron spoke sternly.

"Unfortunate things happen, we know," he said. "But your friend has doubtless found a market for his vegetables. We must remember that here in Capernaum we have reason to be grateful to the Romans for our beautiful synagogue."

But Daniel had gone too far to retreat. The dark tides had swelled to the brink, flooding out politeness, caution, even the memory of the errand that had brought him to this house.

"A Roman synagogue!" he growled. "Raised with Roman taxes. What is it better than the stadium?"

Joel gasped. Hezron, his eyes flashing, rose from his couch. "Watch your words, boy," he warned. "The synagogue is a house of God, no less because Roman funds helped to build it."

The boy also sprang to his feet. His dark eyes blazed back at the man. "I would never set foot in it!" he cried. "There is blood upon it!"

The passion in his words trembled through the quiet room.

"Young man!" Hezron's voice was like a whip. "You will learn to keep such thoughts to yourself. If you have no concern for your own life, you will respect the safety of those who offer you hospitality."

The stinging reminder restored Daniel to reason. A flush swept up over his face. "Forgive me, sir," he stammered. "I—I was not ungrateful for your kindness. But I can't understand. Have the city people forgotten? They don't seem to care. Everywhere I look I see them—their stupid faces, their armor clanking. How can you feel grateful to them? Grateful that they built us a synagogue to keep us contented—that they let us breathe the air they have polluted? I shouldn't have come here. I

66

don't belong in the city or in a house like this. I can't endure to go on as though nothing were wrong when my people are prisoners on their own land—"

He stammered to a stop, aghast at himself, and saw to his surprise that the man was no longer looking at him with scorn but with something like pity. Hezron stepped around the table and laid a hand firmly on Daniel's shoulder.

"My boy," he said quietly, "we have not forgotten. We feel as you do. In his heart every Jew grieves at our captivity. We have need of patriotism like yours. But we have need also of patience. We must not say we cannot endure what God in His judgment has visited upon us."

"But how long—must we endure it for ever?"

"God has not spoken His final word. Until He does, it is our part to endure."

"But—"

"I know. You have been listening to the Zealots. They stir up foolhardy young men like you to fill their ranks."

Daniel backed away, freeing his shoulder. "The Zealots are the finest men in Galilee. They are brave and honorable—"

Hezron stopped him. "Many brave men have come out of Galilee," he said. "But not many men of judgment. The Zealots have thrown themselves against the conquerors time and time again, and what have they to show for it? Rows of crosses, and burning villages, and heavier taxes. They see a few Romans marching, a cohort, and the Roman power seems slight and open to attack. They do not think that behind these few there are others, another cohort, a legion, countless legions, on and on as far as the mind can reach, all armed, all perfected in the art of killing. To a power that holds the whole world in its grip what is a swarm of reckless Zealots? Buzzing mosquitoes to be silenced and forgotten."

"They—"

"Mark my words, boy. Israel has one great strength, mightier than all the power of Rome. It is the Law, given to Moses and our fathers. When the last Roman emperor has vanished from the earth, the Law will still endure. It is to the Law that our loyalty must be devoted. I wish Joel to understand this, and I must forbid him to see any old friends who will turn his mind to violence. I ask you to go now, at once. Go in peace, Daniel, with a prayer that you may see the truth before that rash tongue of yours betrays you. But do not return." He motioned to a servant who stood near the door. "Go with our guest and see that he is started on the right road."

Joel made an impulsive gesture, swiftly checked, and stood quietly. Thoroughly silenced, too confused even to attempt a courteous leave-taking, Daniel flung back his head and followed the servant from the room.

As the outer door shut behind him, all his rage was turned against himself. How could he have bungled his errand so stupidly? He had failed Rosh. Rosh would never trust him again, and why should he? He could not even keep his own head. And he had lost Joel.

Yet beyond the humiliation of reporting his defeat to Rosh, he knew a sharper disappointment. He had lost not only a new recruit. He had lost something he had been close to having for the first time in his life—a friend of his own.

6 · THE BRONZE BOW

DANIEL TURNED his face toward the mountain. He intended to leave this city and never set foot in it again. Instead, smarting from Hezron's dismissal, dreading to face Rosh, smoldering with resentment against himself and the world, he blundered straight into trouble. At a crossroads he came to a well, and seeing a broken bowl nearby, he went down on his knees to scoop up water. Before he could even cool his tongue, a shadow fell across his bent shoulders. He saw close beside him the dark wet flanks of a horse, and looked straight up into the face of a Roman.

"Water for the horse, boy," the soldier ordered, not unpleasantly. "We have come a long way."

Daniel stiffened. But he noticed, against his will, the heaving sides of the overridden animal, the streaks of foam on the glossy neck. The beast too was helpless in the hands of the Roman. He could not deny it water. He lifted the bowl and held it steady while the animal quenched its thirst.

"Enough!" the Roman barked. "You will give him a swollen belly. Now some for me."

Daniel hesitated. Then, sullenly, he lifted the bowl toward the man.

A vicious kick, missing its aim, sent a shower of drops through the air. "Impudent scum!" the man roared. "Fresh water!"

Daniel's hatred brimmed over. Without a thought he hurled the contents of the bowl straight into the man's face. For the space of a breath he stood paralyzed. Then his wits came back and he ran. There was a shout behind him. A stunning blow against his ribs sent him staggering, and a spear clattered in the road just ahead of him. He regained his feet and ran on, ducked behind a stone wall, ran bent over under its shelter for a way, and then made a dash for a clump of trees. There was more shouting now, and the thud of feet. He dared not look back. He reached the trees and then a row of houses, saw an alley-way open before him, and fled along it. The feet pounded after him.

At the end of the alley he dodged one way and then another. He was running uphill now, and his breath was coming short. He stumbled, righted himself. He crawled over a low wall and crouched behind it to catch his breath, pressing hard against the pain in his ribs. His hands came away sticky and red. He saw that he was in a garden, and that opposite him a ladder led up to the terrace above. He barely managed the ladder, but it gave him a moment's advantage. He could still hear the running feet, but he dared now to climb more slowly and conserve his breath. He gained the next terrace and then the next.

He stopped finally, gasping, and leaned against a terrace wall. He had outrun them. In the quiet orchard there was no sound of pursuit. But he had used up almost all his strength. Pain gripped his whole chest now and ran down his arm into his fingers. Very soon, he would have to lie down and wait for them to find him.

Where could he go? Down there in that huddle of houses was there someone who might give him shelter? But Rosh had warned them against trusting even their fellow Jews. Roman methods were too sure. Would any man hide a stranger, knowing what it might mean to his family? No, he must keep on the hill. The Romans would not be so likely to look up here.

An icy fog kept drifting over his eyes. In panic he realized that he was not even thinking clearly. He clung now to one chance, and he knew that that chance had been in his mind all along, and had directed his feet even when he was running too fast to think. If he could get to Joel, Joel would take him in. He didn't know why he was sure of this. But on that first day on the mountain he had trusted Joel.

He never remembered how he got to the door in the long wall, or how he had sense enough to pull the folds of his robe to cover the dark stain that spread down his side. Afterwards he recalled that the doorman admitted him and went to summon Joel. But as he stood for the second time in the outer hallway, he was not thinking at all, only concentrating on staying on his feet. Presently he heard a step on the courtyard paving, and a figure approached him, wavering and indistinct against the light. Then his eyes focused, and he saw that once again it was not Joel, but Malthace. She came toward him swiftly.

"Daniel," she said. "You must go away quickly. Joel is not here. He and Father have gone to the synagogue, but they may be back any moment."

Daniel's wits moved slowly. He could not quite take in what she was saying, but he perceived that his one chance had failed. Still he could not seem to move.

"Don't you understand?" she said sharply. "If Father

finds you here he will have no patience. Why did you come back, anyway?"

He forced himself to one more attempt. "I must see Joel," he said, his voice harsh. "It is important."

"Nothing is so important as Joel's studies," she flared. "If you cared anything about Joel, you would leave him alone. He can be a famous rabbi someday. He's not going to risk his whole future for a band of outlaws."

Daniel looked at her stupidly. Her voice seemed to be coming from farther and farther away.

"Can't you see?" she cried. "Joel is torn in two directions. But he knows what is right. Please, Daniel, I beg you—go away and leave him alone."

Briefly the mist cleared. He realized that once again he had blundered. The girl was right. He could only bring danger and trouble for Joel. He turned away, saw the door wavering and dissolving in the wall, took two steps toward it, and plunged headlong into blackness.

Consciousness returned slowly. At first he was aware of something soft under his head. For the moment that was enough, and he lay motionless, while pain flowed in again across his chest and side. Finally, as the sharpening pain prodded him awake, he was able to open his eyes. It must be night; he could see nothing in the blackness. Then he realized that someone was bending over him, and gropingly he made out a woman's head with dark masses of hair, her face a white blur in the dimness. Then he remembered and struggled to move. Instantly the sick blackness roared over him. After a time it all started over again, the pain, the groping, the face of the girl still looking down at him.

"Where am I?" he asked carefully, not moving.

"Hush!" Malthace whispered. "Don't speak out loud. You're in a storage room."

The words reached him from a great distance. He lay trying to grasp their meaning.

"Daniel," she whispered again, "can you hear me?"

"Yes."

"I'm going to go and get something for your wound. Just lie still and don't make any noise. I'll come as soon as I can. Do you understand?"

"Yes."

There was a rustling and a streak of light, then blackness again. He understood only that she had gone and that he did not need to move.

After a time the streak of light fell across him again. The girl was bending over him once more.

"Are you awake?" she whispered. "Here. Drink this. I'll hold it for you."

The cool rim of a cup touched his lips. A gentle hand lifted his head. The wine was strong, with an unfamiliar bitter taste. It spread warmly down his throat into his chest, pushing back the pain.

She set down the cup. "Now I have to pull away this cloth. I'll try not to hurt you."

He clenched his teeth while she slowly eased the blood-stiffened tunic from his ribs. The wine made his head swim. He suspected there must have been medicine in it. He was aware that she was sponging his side, and he smelled the pungent odor of dill and the sweetish fragrance of oil, and felt a soft dry cloth against his side.

"How did I get here?" he murmured.

"I dragged you in. Why didn't you tell me you were hurt? Joel would never have forgiven me if I—if anything—"

She fell silent, bound the cloth snugly against him, and held the wine again to his lips.

73

"I can't stay any longer," she said then. "Joel will be here soon and he'll know what to do. Don't move. Just wait till we come."

He did not know how long he waited, drifting in a sluggish river. Finally the crack of light appeared, widened, and when it closed there was still light. Joel had brought a candle, the flame lighting up his worried face.

"Daniel—are you all right? Thank God you came here!"

"I—didn't know—where—" Daniel began.

"Don't talk. I heard what happened. They're searching all over town. When Thace told me I knew it must have been you. You were crazy, Daniel!"

"Don't make him talk, Joel." Malthace was close behind. "See, Daniel, I've brought some gruel for you. Can you eat a little?"

Joel held the candle while the girl dipped up spoonfuls of gruel. It tasted warm and good, but the effort was too great. After three attempts he had to close his eyes and rest. Presently he forced himself to speak again.

"I have put your house in danger."

"No. They'll never think of searching Father's house. Let me look at that wound, Daniel." Joel knelt down and cautiously pulled away the bandage. He let out a slow whistle. "You're lucky. Another inch or so! There's a nasty hole. No use arguing, you'll have to stay quiet."

Daniel did not attempt to argue. He knew he could not even get to his feet.

"I don't think this place is safe," Joel went on. "One of the slaves might come to get grain any moment. There's a passage between the two walls. Thace and I discovered it when we were children visiting here. If we lift you onto a mat and drag you, can you stand it?"

"Yes," he said. He could stand anything in his helpless gratitude.

The passage was scarcely two cubits wide. Joel, stooping over and tugging, with Thacia steadying behind, made slow progress, bumping along the rough earth floor for some distance before Joel was satisfied. Then he smoothed the mat carefully while Thacia went back to get grain sacks for a pillow and covering.

"I hate to leave you in this place," Joel said, shining the candle beam along the boxlike walls. "It's not too airy, but you won't suffocate, and I'm sure no one will find you."

Daniel tried to stammer his thanks.

"I wish I could do more," Joel answered. "I'm sorry things went wrong at dinner today. Father isn't like that, really. It's just that—he's suspected for a long time how I feel, and he's afraid I'll join the Zealots."

"I talked like a fool," Daniel said.

"Well—yes, you did." Joel smiled for the first time. "But I wish I had the courage to stand up to him like that."

"If he finds out—?"

"He'd never give you away. I'm sure of that. But he would start asking questions. About Amalek and—the mountain and all. No knowing where it would end. Just stay here and don't worry about it. Thace and I will come whenever we can."

Thacia murmured something to her brother.

"Yes, we have to go," Joel answered. "Will you be all right alone here, Daniel?"

"Yes," said Daniel. "I—"

"Sleep all you can. I'll be back."

He lay still while the candlelight and the footsteps receded. Just before the blackness closed down he thought he heard a whispered voice, "Goodnight, Daniel." He was not sure, and as the fever began to rise in him he imagined that it had been his mother's voice, speaking the words he had not heard for years.

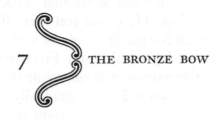

*"And the Kings and the mighty and exalted and those
    who rule the earth
Shall fall before Him on their faces . . ."*

J OEL'S VOICE, hardly more than a whisper, trembled with
earnestness as he read. He sat on the dirt floor of the
passage, stooping to hold the scroll so that it caught the
light from the one sputtering wick they dared to burn.
His two listeners sat motionless against the wall, scarcely
breathing, held by the music of the words and the spell of
the ancient prophecy.

*"And their faces shall be filled with shame,
And the darkness shall grow deeper on their faces,
And He will deliver them to the angels for punishment,
To execute vengeance on them because they have
    oppressed His children and His elect;
The elect shall rejoice over them,
Because the wrath of the Lord of Spirits resteth
    upon them,
And His sword is drunk with their blood."*

Daniel leaned back, his face hidden in the shadows. The words were like the wine that Thacia brought to him every evening. He could feel them like fire in his veins. And tonight for the first time he was conscious of his own strength stirring within him. Five days and nights he had spent in this narrow passage, while the fever burned itself out and the pain in his side gradually eased. Soon now he must leave this place, and he must store up these words to take back with him to the cave.

Joel came to the end of the scroll. For a moment there was not a sound. Then Joel began to roll the papyrus carefully, and the girl beside him let out her breath in a long sigh.

"Joel," she said thoughtfully, "has Father read the Book of Enoch?"

"Of course he has."

"Then why does he say that the Jews must not fight for their freedom?"

"Father believes we must leave the future to God. That when God is ready He will establish His kingdom on earth."

"Don't you believe that too, Joel?"

Joel's eyebrows drew together. "In a way I do," he said. "But the men of old didn't wait for God to win their battles for them. They rose up and fought, and God strengthened them. Maybe God is waiting for us now. It seems to me we've tried Father's way long enough. What do you say, Daniel?"

Daniel had been content just to listen. He envied Joel the ability to find so readily the right words. He scowled now with the effort to make them understand his thoughts.

"We've waited too long," he said. "This Phinehas—the one you read about last night—he pulled out his sword and killed the enemies of God, and God rewarded him for it."

"When will God send us another Phinehas?" Joel sighed.

"Suppose he did?" Daniel burst out, ignoring the stab of pain in his side. "One man is not enough. What could he do without an army? Without men, thousands of men, and weapons to fight with. Why aren't we making ready?"

"Isn't that what Rosh is doing up on the mountain?"

"Yes, but Rosh can't do it alone. There are only a few of us."

"Daniel—" Joel leaned forward, his eyes wide with sudden awe. His breath caught so that the words would scarcely come. "Did you ever think that Rosh—that he might be the leader we are waiting for?"

It was out at last, the thought that neither of them had dared admit to the other.

"I *know* he is," said Daniel.

They sat silent, trembling at the immensity of the secret they shared.

"He's like a lion!" Daniel said, his confidence mounting. "He has no fear at all. Up there in the cave, whatever he says, the men obey him without question. If there were more of us—if we could only get enough—Rosh would drive every cursed Roman back into the sea!"

Before Joel could speak, Malthace interrupted. "But this Rosh is an outlaw!" she protested. "Surely God would not choose a man like that to bring in His kingdom!"

Daniel bristled. He could not make this girl out. Was she for him or against him? She had hidden him and dressed his wound and brought him food. But before that she had pleaded with him to leave Joel alone. She had done all this for her brother, but wouldn't she still fight to keep Joel in his safe world?

"What difference does it make what Rosh is?" he demanded. "If he can rid us of the Romans the kingdom can take care of itself."

"But it is the same thing," said Joel. "Victory and the kingdom."

"Call it what you like," Daniel said impatiently. "All I know is I hate the Romans. I want their blood. That is what I live for. It's all I've lived for since—"

"Since what, Daniel?" Joel urged.

"Since they killed my father and mother."

There was a silence, and then Malthace said, very gently, "Tell us, Daniel."

Daniel wavered. He was torn, as he had been torn that first day on the mountain, between the desire to stay in hiding and the need to speak to them. No one in the cave knew all of his story. He never spoke of it. He dreaded to bring it up out of the secret places of his memory, but even more he longed to share the burden that he had carried alone for so many years.

"It's not a good story for a girl to hear," he said.

"Is it about your mother?" asked Malthace.

"About them both."

"If it's about my own people, about another woman like myself, then I can hear it."

Daniel stared at the blur of her face against the wall. Her eyes shone deep and steady. Was she for him or against him?

He began to grope his way back, far back to the beginning. "It was when I was eight years old," he told them. "I was in the synagogue school then. My father was overseer of the vineyards. It was a good job. I don't remember ever being hungry or afraid. He used to tell us stories after the evening meal. He knew them all by heart. My sister was only five. She had yellow hair and blue eyes like our mother. That's because my mother's mother was a Greek slave who married her Jewish master. But my mother never knew any foreign ways. She believed in the God of the Jews. She taught us verses from the scripture, and made us say them after her. I think we were like all the other families. Perhaps it is still like that, in the houses in the village."

Joel nodded. "It was so in our house," he said.

"My father had a brother, younger than he was, and they were very close. When I was very young my uncle lived in our house with us, but then he married and went to live in a house of his own not far away. I can remember the wedding. They let me walk in the procession, and I was so excited that I dropped my torch and burned a hole in my new coat."

Daniel stopped and waited for a moment. This part, the good part, had been buried very deep. The others did not speak, letting him find his difficult way back at his own halting pace.

"My uncle was so proud of his wife. When their first baby was born, a boy, you would have thought no one ever had had a son before. He did a very foolish thing. It was almost time for the taxes, and he took part of the money he had saved and bought his wife a present, a shawl with gold thread in it for her to wear to the naming. He planned to find extra work and make up the money. But that year the Romans were building a new section of road, and the collector came early. My uncle should have come to my father, but he was ashamed, because of course none of us ever had money to spare. So he tried to argue that it was not time. He was a very excitable man, and the collector was angry and reported him. The soldeirs came and put him in the guardhouse. As soon as my father heard, he went to all his friends and collected enough money for the tax. But my uncle had lost his head and tried to fight his way out, and the soldiers would not let him off. They said he would go to the quarries to work off his debt.

"We all knew they would never let him go, or that he would fight them and get killed. His wife was almost out of her mind. She came and put her arms around my father's knees and screamed at him. So my father made a plan. He was a peaceful man, but he armed himself. He and four others hid in a cornfield and waited till the Romans started for the city with my uncle, and then they attacked. Of course they were all captured. One of the soldiers was cut with a sickle and he died that night. They wanted to make an example for the village. They crucified all six of them, even my uncle, who had not done anything because his hands were tied behind him."

There was a sound like a moan from Thacia. Joel did not move. After a moment Daniel went on.

"My mother stood out by the crosses all day and all night for two days. It was cold and foggy at night, and when she finally came home she did nothing but cough and cry. She only lived a few weeks."

"Were you there too?" asked Thacia under her breath.

"Yes, I was there. After my father died I made a vow. Maybe they would say a boy eight years old couldn't make a vow, a real one that was binding. But I did. I vowed I would pay them back with my whole life. That I would hate them and fight them and kill them. That's all I live for."

When he stopped speaking he realized that he was trembling all over, and the wretched cold sickness was climbing up into his throat. He wished they would go away now and leave him alone. But Thacia questioned him again.

"Who took care of you after that?"

"My grandmother. She made me go to school for five years. But then she was ill, and there wasn't enough to eat, and she sold me to Amalek."

"What about your sister?"

Daniel hesitated. Yes, they had to know this, too. "I told you she was only five. That night she got away from a neighbor and ran out. They didn't know how long she had been there by the crosses before they found her and took her back. She used to scream in her sleep. Then she refused to go out of the house. If we tried to make her, she would howl till she was blue and fall into a sort of fit and we would think she was dead, and then she would be ill for days. So we gave up. She has always been sickly. She doesn't eat enough. I think she has forgotten everything, but the demons will not leave her. She has never gone out of the house."

He stopped, helpless in his longing to make them understand Leah. "She is very gentle and good," he added, looking humbly at Malthace.

To his surprise, her eyes glistened with tears. He had to look away.

Since the beginning of Daniel's story, Joel had not spoken a word. He sat now staring straight ahead of him. Somehow in a few moments he had grown older. The man he would become was revealed in his young face. All at once he came up to his knees, and knelt in the narrow space, his shoulders taut. Daniel saw that his lips were trembling.

"Daniel!" he choked. "I will take the oath too! Before heaven, I will avenge your father! I swear it! I will fight them as long as I live!"

Swept up by the boy's passion, Daniel was checked by a sudden stab of guilt. He had not intended this. Was it fair to win Joel in this way?

"No!" he exclaimed. "No, Joel! It is not your quarrel."

"But it is!" cried Joel. "Mine and every other Jew's. Your father is only one—out of thousands who have died at their hands. We must do anything—*anything* to make the country free again."

It was what he had wanted, what he had come to Capernaum to accomplish. But he was not sure. To drag Joel out of his safe scholar's life into the dark danger of his own world?

Thacia understood. After one gasp of dismay, she sat huddled against the wall, staring at her brother with terror in her eyes. But behind the terror there was pride.

Joel turned to her. "You see it has to be this way, don't you, Thace? I can't go on burying my head in a book while things like this are happening. You must see it. We've always seen things the same way."

Thacia looked back at him, struggling against her fear, and there flashed across to Daniel something of what it must mean to be a twin. Then she drew a long breath.

"Yes," she said steadily. "I do see. If I were a boy I would make a vow too."

Suddenly Joel's fire leaped up in her face. "Why can't I?" she cried. "Why can't a girl serve Israel too? What

84

about Deborah and Queen Esther? Let me swear it too, Joel! I promise to help you."

Jealousy beat suddenly up in Daniel. "No!" he exploded. "This is a man's vow! It's not for a pretty child!"

Her face went white. At the hurt in it Daniel cursed himself. What had made him say a thing like that to her?

But this time Joel came instantly to his sister's support. "Then we will make a new vow," he said. "The three of us together. We'll swear to fight for Israel—for—for—" He hesitated.

"For God's Victory," said Thacia swiftly. "Remember the watchword of the Maccabees?"

"Yes! That's it! Come swear it together. Now—on the Book of Enoch here. What could be better? Put your hands on mine, both of you. Swear to stand together. The three of us. For God's Victory."

Thacia laid her hand firmly over her brother's. "For God's Victory," she repeated. They looked at Daniel, waiting. The three of us, Joel had said, taking him, who had always stood outside, into the close circle of their lives. With an effort he leaned over and laid his hand over the girl's. He felt the small fine bones under his palm.

"For God's Victory!" he choked. He drew back quickly into the shadow, afraid for them to see his face. But they were far too lost in their own excitement to notice his.

"Now we must plan what to do," said Joel solemnly. "Tomorrow night I'll bring—"

"Oh—" Thacia remembered. "Tomorrow night will be the Sabbath."

Joel considered. "We can come anyway," he decided. "The Law doesn't forbid visiting the sick."

"We can't unbind the wound or put on a fresh dressing."

"No matter," put in Daniel. "The wound is almost healed."

"I'll bring the food before sunset," Thacia promised. "Enough to last through the Sabbath."

"We must plan," Joel went on, still lost in the wonder of his new resolve. "When you go back to the mountain I'm going with you."

"No," objected Daniel. "That's not what Rosh wants of you. He wants a man here in Capernaum. Right now it's better for you to stay in school."

He could see that in spite of his vow Joel was relieved. "I'm willing to give up school," Joel insisted. "I mean it. I'll do anything."

"Stay in school, then. We're not ready to fight yet. We've got to wait and work for it. Rosh has something in mind for you. I don't know what it is, but he'll send you word."

"You're sure?"

"Yes. You can count on it."

"I've been thinking of a plan," Joel said. "If you should bring a message from Rosh, or if you should ever need to get away from the Romans again, there's an opening in the outside wall, at the angle where this passage joins the storage room. It's used to bring the sacks of grain in from the street, and it's just big enough for a man to crawl through—I tried it. I'll make sure it's kept unlatched, and you can push it open. That way no one will ever suspect you're here."

"How will you know it?" Daniel asked.

"I thought of that. If you could mark some sign on the wall—"

"A bow!" Thacia exclaimed. "You know—from the Song of David you read last night!"

"The bronze bow," Daniel exclaimed, pleased that Thacia too had remembered. "Will you read that part again, Joel?"

"I didn't bring the scroll," Joel said, "but I know it by heart." He leaned back against the wall.

> "—*God is my strong refuge,*
> *and has made my way safe.*
> *He made my feet like hinds' feet,*
> *and set me secure on the heights.*
> *He trains my hands for war,*
> *so that my arms can bend a bow of bronze.*"

"It couldn't really be bronze," said Daniel, puzzled. "The strongest man could not bend a bow of bronze."

"Perhaps just the tips were metal," Joel suggested.

"No," Thacia spoke. "I think it was really bronze. I think David meant a bow that a man couldn't bend—that when God strengthens us we can do something that seems impossible."

"Perhaps," said Joel. "You do have an imagination, Thace!" He went on with the Song of David.

"Thou hast given me the shield of thy salvation . . ."

"Oh dear," Thacia broke in, dismayed. "I just remembered. Father asked me to play for his guests tonight."

"Then we must go," said Joel quickly, gathering up the scroll of Enoch. "Father likes to have Thace play the harp for him," he explained, seeing Daniel's bewilderment.

87

Daniel looked at Thacia. "I have never heard a harp," he said.

"Then I'll bring it and play for you tomorrow," she promised. "No—not on the Sabbath. But I won't forget."

"Do you want us to leave the light, Daniel?"

"No," said Daniel. "I'm used to the dark."

They crept along the passage, the light flickering and vanishing altogether. Then, very faintly, came the whispered words, "Goodnight, Daniel." This time he was certain he had heard them.

He lay in the darkness, and it seemed that a warmth and light still glowed all around him. Together, Joel had said. Three of us together. And Thacia was not against him.

He trains my hands for war,
  so that my arms can bend a bow of bronze ...

He could see the shining bow, the bow that no man could bend with his own strength alone.

Suddenly he sat up. It came to him that Joel had given him the answer to his most urgent question. It was time for him to leave this place. For two days, without their knowing, he had tested his strength, pacing back and forth in the narrow passage. Joel would try to keep him. Better simply to go. They would be horrified that he had chosen the Sabbath, when a man could walk no more than two thousand cubits from his home. But the Law was for the wealthy, for the scholars, not for the poor. By now he had broken so many points of the Law that he was beyond all redemption. What matter if he broke one more?

Toward morning, when he was sure that all the household would be asleep, he crawled along the passage. His fingers discovered a latch, and the little service door swung inward. He eased himself through the narrow slot, into the street, pulled himself to his feet, and made his way through the city toward the mountain.

I would like to have heard that harp, he thought once. But he put that behind him. Instead he repeated the Song of David.

> *He has made my feet like hinds' feet*
> *And set me secure on the heights.*

All the same, he would like to know how a harp sounded.

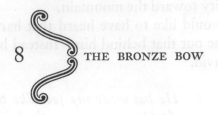

DANIEL HAD OVERESTIMATED his strength. Long before he reached the mountain he knew that he had left the shelter of Joel's passageway too soon. Toiling up hill under a merciless sun, he had to stop so often that it was late afternoon before he came to the steep zigzag rise up the cliff. He was not sure he could make it.

Suddenly it seemed to his wavering sight that one of the dark boulders high on the cliff detached itself from the rest and rolled toward him. Samson came leaping down the trail to kneel at his feet. Then, when Daniel tried to speak and no sound would come, the big man rose swiftly, lifted the boy in his great arms, and carried him gently up the trail to the cave.

Samson did not allow Daniel to get on his feet again for three days. Like a vast shadow he sheltered him. He brought water mixed with wine in which he steeped roots of the mountain lilies. He snatched the choicest bits of roasting game from beneath the very nose of Rosh to feed his patient.

Daniel noticed that the men were getting accustomed to Samson and treated him with better humor, though none of them ever disputed him. As for himself, Daniel had acquired new status. By the unfailing grapevine, word of his exploit in the town had reached the cave days before. They had all given him up, believing him dead or captured. Some of the men admired his nerve; others were relieved to have him in charge of Samson again. For a day or so they made a hero of him, and then they forgot the matter and ignored him, and life in the cave went on exactly as before.

For Daniel nothing could ever be the same. He had never admitted to himself that he was lonely here on the mountain. He had worshiped and feared Rosh. He had fought and eaten and slept side by side with the hard-eyed men who made up Rosh's band. But the few days in Joel's passageway had shown him a new world. He had found someone to talk to, someone who had shared his own thoughts, and who had instantly taken Daniel's burden as his own. The memory of the pact they had made glowed like a warm coal in the heart of the forge.

Lying in the sunlight, his back against the baked gray rock, Daniel repeated to himself the chronicles that Joel had read aloud, the glorious deeds of Joshua, of Phinehas, Saul, and David. Most of all he thought of Judas Maccabeus, who had given them a watchword. The other mighty ones had lived and fought in distant ages. But Judas had lived in a time like his own, not two hundred years ago, when Israel was helpless, as it was now, under the foot of the heathen. Judas, with his heroic father and brothers, had dared to rise up and defy the oppressor, and for a time Israel had breathed the free air again. Here in these very mountains Judas, young and daring and cunning as a panther, had hidden from his enemies and taken them by surprise. Many brave men had joyfully laid down their lives for Judas. But never enough—never quite enough. This time—! There were young men everywhere who longed for such a chance again. Together, he and Joel would find them.

The third member of the pact? He was not sure about Thacia. In all his life he had known only two girls, and he did not understand them. Compared to his own sister, Thacia was like a brilliant scarlet lily, glowing and proud. He could count on her loyalty to Joel; in all else she was unpredictable. The very thought of her was disturbing. He tried to shut her out of his mind, as he tried to shut out the thought of Leah. Both girls, so utterly unlike, seemed in some way to threaten his plans.

The prospect of seeing Joel again occupied all his thoughts, and the opportunity came unexpectedly soon. A week after he was back at the forge, doing the light work that Samson allowed him, Rosh brought him a dagger to mend. It was a special dagger that Rosh had carried for years as a talisman, and some mischance had sent it hurtling down a chasm. Five men had been sent to retrieve it. Four had come back empty-handed, but hours later the fifth, exhausted and bleeding, had brought the thing back. Rosh received it with scant gratitude. It was bent askew, twisted out of the shaft, and useless.

"Fix it," he demanded of Daniel.

Daniel took the blade in his hand. He thought that it might be mended, but he knew that he could not do the job.

"I don't have the right tools," he explained. "It needs a new collar and rivet. My forge doesn't give heat enough."

"Then get a rivet."

Daniel looked back at the man. He would think a new

dagger would be easier to come by, but he knew that Rosh had attached some sort of luck to this particular blade. "In the city?" he asked.

"Wherever you can find them. This friend of yours— Simon. He said he was an ironsmith. Get them from him."

Daniel remembered that Simon and Rosh did not see eye to eye. "You mean I should buy them from Simon?"

"Buy? He is a Zealot. He can give a scrap of metal for the cause."

Daniel woke next morning hoping that Rosh had forgotten, but he saw at once that the leader was more determined than ever. He gave Daniel no money. All the way to the village Daniel tried to think of an argument that would convince Simon. The metal parts that he needed were costly. Rosh seemed to think he could snatch them as he might a squash from a village garden. It occurred to him that perhaps, unknown to Rosh, he could offer to do a day's work in Simon's shop.

The smithy was closed, a bar and padlock across the door. Strange, for if Simon had gone off about the village to fit a lock or repair a plow, he would have left the shop open to customers. Daniel sat down on the stone doorstep to wait. After a time he felt uneasy. The unoccupied feel of the place grew on him, and he was not surprised when a passing villager called out to him.

"If you're waiting for the smith you'll have a long wait. Shop hasn't been open for a month."

"Where is Simon?" Daniel called back.

"Left town. Heard he went after a preacher, one who came through here awhile back. There's a new smith in Chorazin, if you want some work done."

Gone after a preacher! All at once Daniel remembered

the Sabbath morning and the strange look in Simon's eyes. "I don't know what he means," Simon had said, "but I intend to find out."

What could Simon have found that would keep him for a month?

Daniel had not lived with Rosh for five years without learning that there was no use going back without the rivet. He knew well enough, too, what Rosh would expect. But Simon had been good to him. He refused to break into Simon's shop and help himself. There was nothing to do but find Simon, and with the thought he knew a deep satisfaction. He knew that all along he had hoped for an excuse to go to Capernaum.

Would he be recognized in the city? Daniel thought not. He had a hunch about Romans. To him every stupid Roman face looked alike. He had an idea that to the Romans every Jew would look alike too. He was sure they seldom bent their stiff necks to take a good look at one. There was little likelihood that the soldier on horseback would remember the boy at the well. At any rate, it was worth the chance. He got to his feet and set out for Capernaum.

He reached the city in the early afternoon and made his way straight to the harbor. If anyone knew where the preacher could be found, it would be those fishermen and their wives. They had taken the carpenter's coming for granted. Surely they must know where he spent the rest of his day

There was no bustle at this hour. The Jews jested that no one worked in the heat of the day but dogs and soldiers. The heavy barges bumped each other lazily, waiting for the next day's cargo. But farther along the shore he saw a few slow-moving figures, men lazily preparing their fishing boats for the night's work.

Daniel approached a fisherman who was folding in a long net. "I am looking for a preacher," he said. "I heard him talk here one morning."

"You mean the carpenter." The man nodded. "He's back in town again. He'll be here tomorrow without a doubt."

"Do you know where I could find him now?"

"That would be hard to do. Sometimes he goes about preaching. Sometimes he takes a woodturning job. But at night you could find him at the house of Simon bar Jonas in Bethsaida. He sleeps there."

Bethsaida was scarcely two miles the other side of the city, and there were many hours to spare before nightfall. Daniel had the excuse he wanted. He climbed the hill to the house of Hezron. He located the hinged door, and it swung open at his touch. He picked up a sharp pebble and scratched the shape of a bow on the mud wall, and looking carefully up and down the street, crawled through the door and along the passage.

He waited for a long time. Twice he cautiously pushed open the door and peered out, knowing by the shadows on the street that he must soon be on his way. When he had almost given up hope, Joel came crawling along the passage.

"I've checked every day," he greeted Daniel. "I didn't think you'd come so soon."

"It was just luck." Daniel explained about the dagger.

"Are you all right, Daniel? Thacia said your wound was not healed enough. You should have stayed here." With his usual thoughtfulness, Joel had brought a small loaf of bread, which Daniel munched gratefully.

"I must find Simon," Daniel said. "It's time I started

95

for Bethsaida." He hesitated. "Could you go with me? This Jesus—I'd like to know what you make of him."

Joel considered. "There's talk about him everywhere," he said. "Do you think he's a Zealot? Father says he is dangerous. I'd like to see him myself. Yes, I think I'll risk it."

At dusk the two boys emerged from their hiding place and Joel led the way through unfrequented streets till they came out on the path above the lake. Below them four men were sliding their boat into the water. As they watched, three of the men climbed aboard, one took the heavy oars in hand, the last man gave a shove, and the boat drifted slowly out from the shore, its image wavering on the glassy surface. The oarsman began to sing, and the others took up the melody. For a long time, as the boys walked on, the song floated back over the water with a strange sadness.

The village of Bethsaida was a tumbled mass of fishing shacks in the gathering darkness. Smoky light glimmered from the open doors of the huts. They followed the one narrow street till presently they overtook a man and woman who walked slowly to keep pace with a small boy who stumbled between them. Before Daniel could speak, the man looked back and questioned them instead.

"Do you know which would be the house of Simon the fisherman?"

"We're looking for it ourselves."

The man nodded. "With so many looking it shouldn't be hard to find. But the boy is getting tired. We've walked all the way from Cana today. They told us in town that the preacher would be at the home of Simon tonight."

Daniel glanced at the child, noting the way he hugged

one arm close to his body, wrapping it in his mantle.

"It's his hand," the woman explained. She reached out and pulled the mantle aside. Both boys started at the glimpse of red swollen flesh. The child flashed them a look of fury, jerked the mantle back into place and trudged on, his eyes on the road.

"Bit by a camel," the man said. "Two months ago and it won't heal. I'm a weaver, and so the boy must be after me, and a weaver needs two good hands."

"We only heard about the preacher yesterday," said the woman. "We have not wasted any time."

Daniel was puzzled. "This preacher—is he a doctor as well?" he asked.

"Where do you come from, that you haven't heard about the preacher?" the man demanded. "Our neighbor who came back from Capernaum said that they talk of nothing else. My neighbor saw him heal a man who had been lame for twenty years. The man ran, he told me, ran like a young boy. If this preacher can do that, he can heal my son."

Daniel glanced at Joel uneasily. "Have you heard of this?" he asked under his breath.

Joel hesitated. "There is talk. Father says—" He checked himself, and the two walked on silently, keeping their doubts to themselves. It seemed a shame to have made a child walk all the way from Cana.

Presently the murmur of many voices came to them. The sound drew them away from the street into an alley, at the end of which they made out the outline of a house.

The square of light that was the doorway was choked by dark figures. People crowded the room inside and overflowed into the courtyard, blocking the path to the door. Some sat crosslegged on the ground or leaned against the gate. They seemed to be waiting. Daniel saw that many of them were ill. Some had been carried here and lay on the ground on crude litters. All about him he saw canes and crutches and the glimmer of bandages. From one corner of the yard smoke rolled from a clay oven, carrying a pungent odor of frying fish.

The two boys stepped around the litters, and Daniel plucked the coatsleeve of a man who leaned on the doorpost. "Peace," he said.

"Peace," responded the man. "There's no room inside. The master will be out when he has finished eating."

"I'm looking for a friend of his," Daniel said. "Simon the blacksmith, from Ketzah. Do you know of him?"

"The Zealot? He's inside." The man leaned into the door and called out. "Simon! There's one here asking for you."

The figures in the doorway shifted. Framed against the square of light Simon peered out into the dim yard.

"Here, Simon. It's Daniel, from Ketzah."

"Daniel!" There was genuine pleasure in the man's voice. "I'm glad you found the place. Come inside. Have you eaten?"

They pushed their way into a small room, smoky, airless, overfull of dark bearded men. The smell of fresh bread, of fish and burning oil made Daniel's head swim. He introduced his two friends to each other.

"By the look of you, you've walked all the way from the mountain," said Simon. "But first you must meet the master." One hand on each boy's elbow he steered them across the room.

Daniel stood face to face with the carpenter. The man's eyes, looking straight into his, blocked out every other thought. Filled with light and warmth, those eyes, welcoming him with friendship, yet searching too, disturbing, demanding.

"I am glad you have come," Jesus said. Daniel could say nothing at all. For a moment he was afraid. Only when the man turned away and his eyes no longer held his own, could he breathe freely again.

Simon found a place for the boys between two burly fellows who reeked of fish and garlic. Someone had led Jesus to the seat of honor at the head of the table. Several women were moving now among the men, carrying wooden platters of bread and lettuce and small fish fried in oil. They placed the dishes on the mat before Jesus, and he looked up with a warm smile.

"You must have worked long, my daughters," he said, "to provide a feast for so many."

The women glanced sideways at each other, smiling, their brown faces flushed. Jesus reached out and took a wafer of bread from the plate.

A voice spoke from the end of the table. "Teacher," a man said, "no one has provided for us to wash our hands. In this house do you not observe the Law?"

The woman of the house gasped, hand against her mouth in dismay. All her pride and pleasure was wiped out in an instant. "Was it needful?" Her eyes pleaded with the carpenter. "I did not think—so many—"

"Do not be distressed," Jesus answered her gently. "It was not needful." He looked down the long mat toward the man who had spoken. "In this house the food has been given us with love," he said slowly. "Let us make sure that our hearts rather than our hands are worthy to receive this gift." He stood up, his long white robe holding the light, and spoke a blessing over the bread. Then he passed the platter to the one beside him.

Daniel glanced at Joel. With a pucker of confusion between his brows, Joel had taken a small morsel of the bread and was putting it to his lips. Perhaps this was the first time in his life, Daniel realized, that Joel had deliberately broken the Law. He too must have felt the carpenter's words as a reproach.

When the short meal was done, Jesus rose from the table, gave thanks again, to God and to the woman of the house, then moved slowly through the crowded room to the door. Instantly a clamor rose from the courtyard, a frenzy of wailing, shouting, pleading voices.

"Let me touch you, Rabbi. Let me only touch the edge of your cloak!"

"My son, Rabbi! He has had the fever for seven days!"

"Over here, Master! Look this way! I cannot move for the crowd!"

Jesus stood on the threshold for a moment, looking out over the wailing people. Daniel, who had pushed close behind him, almost reached out to hold him back. Those people out there—so frantic—they could tear a man to pieces! But Jesus stretched out his hand and spoke, and the clamor died away. A few voices kept on pleading, the moaning could not all be stilled, but once again the crowd waited. Then Jesus stepped down into the courtyard and moved, with serenity, among them. Feeble hands reached out to him, stretched and grasped at his clothing. Some of the sick dragged forward, and when they could not reach him, kissed the ground behind him. Before one after another Jesus stopped. Sometimes he spoke quietly. Sometimes he touched a man briefly, or a child. What he said no one could hear.

Suddenly a scream rang out. "I am well!" a woman

cried. "He has cured me! I am well!" The clamor rose again, drowning her out.

The women who had served Jesus moved now among the crowd with the platters of food, and the bearded fishermen helped them. Hands snatched the food as it passed, cramming it into mouths, spilling it in frantic greed. Daniel understood now why those in the house had eaten so sparingly. There would never be enough to satisfy this starving horde. He shuddered, looking at them. Where had they come from, these wretched creatures who had dragged themselves to this place in the hope of a morsel of bread?

Then Daniel saw the man and woman he had met on the road, standing almost within the reach of Jesus' hand. As Jesus turned, they pushed the child in front of them. The woman went down on her knees and hid her face. The man stood, his eyes fixed on Jesus. Then four men carrying a litter blocked them from Daniel's view, and when he saw them again the three were going rapidly through the gate in the hedge. He sprang after them.

"Did you see him?" he demanded, catching up with them. "Did he speak to you?"

Tears were streaming down the woman's face. Her eyes were dazed, and she could not speak. The man had the same dazed look. "The boy is healed," he said.

"How do you know?" Daniel demanded. "Have you looked at it?"

"No. I have not looked. Show him your arm," the man ordered his son.

The boy shook off the mantle and held out his hand. "It doesn't hurt anymore," he said, puzzled. Daniel felt a sudden chill. He leaned closer.

"It is still swollen!" he accused the man.

The man did not look. "The pain is gone," he said. "The swelling will go too."

"What did he do? Did he touch it?"

"No," the man said. "I don't think he touched it. I started to tell him what was wrong, and I couldn't get the words out. I could only look at him. And then I knew that the boy was all right."

Suddenly Daniel was furious. "You are lying to me!" he cried. "There is some trick—"

"Why should I lie to you?" The man looked back steadily. "I tell you, the boy's hand is healed, and now he will make a weaver."

Back in the yard Simon stood with Joel. Daniel clutched at the older man. "That boy!" he stammered. "Simon—he said his arm was healed!"

Simon did not ask what boy or seem surprised. "Yes," he said quietly.

"But I saw it—we both saw it—not an hour ago. The boy says it doesn't hurt."

"Several people were healed tonight," said Simon.

"It's impossible! Is it some trick?"

"You say you saw the arm yourself. What do you think?"

"I don't understand."

"Nor do I," Simon answered. "But I must believe my own eyes. I have seen it happen, over and over."

Joel spoke thoughtfully. "Is he a magician?"

"No magician could do the things he does. He claims that his power comes from God."

"But these other people—all these—?"

"I don't know why they are not all healed. It seems to require something from the person himself, a sort of giving up. The child you saw, or his parents, must have had that sort of faith."

"Perhaps the arm would have healed anyway."

"Perhaps," said Simon. He put a silencing hand on Daniel's arm. "Wait now, he is going to speak."

For the third time, something in Daniel leaped to answer that voice. It was not a joyous voice tonight or a commanding one as it had been on the sunlit shore. This time its gentleness rested on the suffering people like a comforting touch. But strength still poured through its calm tones, and utter sureness.

"Do not be afraid," Jesus said to them. "For you are the children of God. And does not a father understand the sorrow of his children, and know their need? For I tell you, not even a sparrow falls to the ground without our Father seeing, and you are of more value than many sparrows. Try to bear your suffering with patience, because you know that God has made a place for you in His Kingdom."

The kingdom! Daniel looked about him. What good would it do to speak of a kingdom to these miserable wretches? What could it mean to them, when not one of them could lift a hand to fight for it? But he saw their faces, white, formless blots in the darkness, all lifted toward this man. He heard their harsh breathing all around him, stifled in their straining not to miss a word. They listened as though his words were food and they could never get enough.

"But you must be kind to each other, and love each other," the voice was saying. "For each of you is precious in His sight."

The figure in the white robe swayed slightly. In the dim light from the doorway the man looked very weary.

Instantly one of the fishermen was at his side. Another came from the house with a lighted lamp. Together, shielding him from the people, they persuaded their master across the garden. The crowd watched them, quieted, almost stupefied, by the spell of that gentle voice. The three climbed the outside staircase of the house and entered the shelter on the roof.

Daniel straightened his shoulders, trying to shake off the spell that seemed to bind him close to the silent crowd. At the same time he remembered the errand that had brought him to this place.

Simon listened, showing little interest in Rosh's demands. Daniel was sure that Simon was going to refuse his request, but instead the man looked at him keenly.

"This Rosh," he said thoughtfully, "you have a lot of faith in him, haven't you?"

"Of course I have."

"All right. I don't have these things to spare in my own shop. But there is a shop here in the city, on the Street of the Ironworkers. You will know it by the bronze horseshoe over the doorway. I work for the owner sometimes. Samuel is his name, and he owes me wages. Tell him to give you what you need."

"But your wages?"

"I have little need for money just now. Take what you need."

Daniel could not leave his friend without some answer. "Are you staying with Jesus, Simon?"

"If he will have me."

"Is—is he one of us?"

Simon smiled. "A Zealot, you mean?"

"Isn't that why you came? Have you asked him to join us?"

"I had some such idea when I came," Simon admitted. "But it has not worked out just as I expected. No, I have not asked Jesus to join us. All I hope and long for now is that he will ask me to join him."

Daniel saw that he would get no more certain answer from Simon tonight. The two boys went back along the road in silence. Presently Joel spoke, his young voice troubled.

"How can he call those people children of God?" he questioned. "They have never heard of the Law. They are unclean from the moment they are born."

Daniel could not attach too much importance to this. He was too far outside the Law himself. "Perhaps it does no harm for them to hope," he suggested.

"But they have no right to hope!"

Joel was silent again, struggling, in some way Daniel could not share, to reconcile what he had heard with his lifelong training. "I think Father is right," he said at last, unwillingly. "This man is not a true rabbi. He practically said it was all right to eat without washing our hands. Perhaps it's dangerous even to listen to him. And yet—"

Some unfinished question, only half formed, filled the darkness around them as they made their way back to the city.

FIVE MORNINGS LATER, Daniel sat at the foot of the mountain trail waiting. Though the sun weighed down on his head like a vast hammer, the palms of his hands were cold and damp. Any moment now the man he waited for would come into view. This was the first job he had ever had to do alone. He must not bungle it.

Of course, there was little likelihood he could fail, or Rosh would not have sent him. He understood that in a way this was a peace offering on Rosh's part, to repay him for mending the dagger. It was also, he knew, a test, the easy sort of test that Rosh often devised to try out a man's usefulness.

"He'll be alone," Rosh told him. "Always travels alone, the old skinflint, by the back roads. Pretends to be a beggar, whining at everyone he meets for a mite of bread for his next meal. He could buy the tetrarch's palace if he wanted to. He lives like a pauper, and every month he carries a bag of gold across the mountains to the coast and smuggles it to a friend who's buying property for him in Antioch. One day he'll disappear and spend the rest of his life living like a king. But he reckons with me first. This bagful comes to me."

This was Rosh's idea of justice, and the kind of sport that most delighted him. He made it sound like a privilege that Daniel should have the chance. Daniel agreed with him on principle. Why should one greedy old miser live like a king in Antioch while his fellow Jews toiled and starved? Moreover, the thing would be done quickly. A lonely stretch of road, a moment's bluffing, and the man would go on his way unharmed—but not until he had made a contribution to his country's freedom. Fair enough, Daniel reasoned. Still, his stomach was uneasy.

After nearly an hour's wait, he spotted the man on a bend of the road just below. He slid behind a rock and waited. The man climbed slowly, with a wheezing sigh at each step. He would have fooled anyone, with his rags and his tottering gait. The deceit of the man made the job he had to do seem easier. When the miser was fairly opposite the rock, Daniel pounced.

The man did not resist him. He cringed and sank to his knees. A poor man, he moaned, with not a thing that anyone could want. Daniel jerked him back to his feet and reached for the girdle. Then, like a snake, the man struck. Daniel caught the gleam of the knife barely in time to grip the man's wrist. He saw the cold glitter of the man's eyes. For a moment they struggled in deadly silence. Who could have guessed that that bony frame would have so much strength? Then Daniel saw the second dagger, this time in the man's left hand. With one mighty unthinking thrust, his own fist came up, and the man crumpled back across the path. Daniel stood breathing hard. Then he stooped and felt for the man's girdle. The moneybag was there all right, a fat one. He stuffed it into his own girdle and turned away. The thing was done.

At the turn of the road he looked back. The man lay sprawled on the road, and suddenly a long-forgotten memory hit Daniel's stomach with the thud of a blow. For a moment he stood, feeling wretchedly sick, and then he remembered. How many times in his childhood had he waked in the early morning and seen his grandfather lying just like that on the mat beside him, cap slipped sideways off the pinkish scalp, scrawny neck muscles stretched like a half-grown chicken's?

Curse Rosh! Daniel knew what the orders were. He should get away from this place as fast as possible. He looked behind him up the pathway at the rocky hillside. If anyone were watching, he would be laughed out of camp. But he could not leave an old man who looked like his grandfather lying helpless on the road. He went back and knelt down, his throat suddenly like ice, and fumbled in the rags over the man's chest. With relief he recognized an uncertain beat of life under the bony ribs. He picked the man up, carried him to the side of the road and laid him down in the shadow of a rock. Then he sat down and waited.

It was some time before the man regained consciousness. Finally he blinked and turned his head, and Daniel was suddenly angered by the terror that leaped into the old eyes.

"Lie still," he said roughly. "I'm not going to touch you. Wait till you're able to walk."

But the old man would not wait. He jerked to his feet and backed away.

"Wait," said Daniel. "Take this. You may need it." He held out one of the daggers that less than an hour ago had threatened his own life. Then he stood watching till the man, in a tottering course, dragged around the turn of the road by which he had come.

Back in camp he flung the moneybag at Rosh's feet.

108

Rosh snatched it up, weighed it rapidly from one horny palm to the other, jerked open the strings and poured out the coins onto the stone. Talents, a glittering heap of them. He slapped them down as they bounced and rolled.

"Yah!" he gloated. "A good morning's pay. He's got something to whine about now, the old camel."

Daniel said nothing, waiting.

"Did you get his dagger too?"

Daniel threw the dagger down. He knew now what was coming. Someone had already brought back a report.

"The other one?"

"I gave it back to him," said Daniel. "He wasn't fit to travel without it."

Rosh shot a derisive glance from under the black brows. "So he took you in with his whining! I gave you credit for more sense."

Daniel held his tongue.

Rosh rubbed a coin between dirty thumb and finger. "You think he'll thank you for your pains? You'll find out if he ever sets eye on you in the city. You should have finished him off."

"You didn't order me to kill him," Daniel said sullenly.

"I expected you to use your head. What ails you? Afraid of a drop of blood?"

"It is Roman blood I want!" Daniel burst out. "Do we fight against Jews?"

Rosh tossed the coins back into the bag, pulled the string tight, and got to his feet. His eyes looked dangerous, but his voice was level.

"You fool! You'll have your fill of Roman blood! Have you wasted your time with me? Are you still a stupid villager who wants to rush at the Romans with your bare hands? It will take men and arms and food.

And they have to be paid for with money. And get this through your head once and for all—we take the money where we find it!"

Daniel's lips were tight, his eyes on the hard-packed earth.

"Would the old miser have given his money to free Israel?" Rosh went on. "He'd have parted with his life first! A decent death for his country was better than he deserved. And what loss would it have been—one old man more or less?"

Suddenly, with one of his lightning reverses of temper, Rosh stepped forward and laid a hand on the boy's shoulder. "I know what's in your mind," he said gruffly. "It's better to do without killing when we can. But there's a flaw in you, boy, a soft streak. I've seen it over and over, these years. Like a bad streak in a piece of metal. Either you hammer it out, the way you'd hammer out a bubble, or you'll be no good to us. When the day comes there'll be no place for weakness."

Daniel's head went back.

"Wait a minute!" Rosh warned, bearing his hand down as if to hold down the boy's leaping anger. "I didn't say cowardice. You think I don't know you inside out? But softness can be just as dangerous. And by all the prophets, I'm going to hammer it out of you, if it's the last thing I do. Someday you'll thank me for it!"

Rosh took his hand from the boy's shoulder and held it out, waiting. Daniel stared at the bearded, weather-pitted face, the fierce black eyes of the man who had been his hero for five years, and his defenses gave way. Was it Rosh's logic, or the rough friendship in the man's hand and voice that had won him back? In relief he reached out, and he could sense the man's pleasure when his own hand, trained to the anvil, returned without flinching his leader's iron clasp.

Rosh was right, he thought later, taking up his work. More right than Rosh himself suspected. Would the man be so patient if he could read Daniel's mind? Rosh knew about his passion for the day to come. Rosh did not know about the other things that bound him like cobwebs when he woke in the night. Leah. His grandmother. Thacia! A flush came up over his face. There was no room for such weakness. He raised the anvil and struck the softened metal, blow after powerful blow, beating out his weakness. He put the metal back into the fire and watched it heat to a glowing red, drew it out with tongs, and hammered on it again, till his arms ached. He would get rid of this flaw in himself!

Yet, like a treacherous bubble that fled under the hammer and formed again, a doubt returned. Was there a flaw too in Rosh's argument? He could not put a finger on it, but he felt it just the same. He wished he could talk to Joel about it. Could Joel find the answer in those scriptures of his? Somewhere, Daniel had been taught in his childhood, there would be an answer in the scriptures, for Moses had handed down in the Law an answer for every situation a man could encounter in this life. Thou shalt not kill? But that did not apply to war. And what difference would it make if he had an answer, chapter and verse, on his tongue? Rosh was his own law.

Suddenly words were echoing in his mind. "For each one of you is precious in His sight." Not scripture, but the words of the carpenter. That was what had confused him. Rosh looked at a man and saw a thing to be used, like a tool or a weapon. Jesus looked and saw a child of God. Even the old miser with his moneybag?

111

He hammered more violently, till the sparks flew wild and the iron squashed down on the stone like clay, and he had to heat it again and begin all over. Samson, kneading the bellows, watched him broodingly.

EBOL, THE SENTRY, brought the message to Daniel one sultry August morning, a single sentence scratched on a fragment of broken pottery, "Your grandmother is dying," and signed "Simon." The message had been in Ebol's pocket for three days; no knowing how many times it had changed hands before reaching him. Better if it had never reached him at all, Daniel thought fiercely, thrusting it deep into his girdle pocket. For half the day he carried it about with him, saying nothing, the bit of clay weighing heavier and heavier till it dragged at him like a stone. Finally he showed the message to Rosh and set off down the mountain to the village.

The door of his grandmother's house was bolted, and only silence answered his knock. As he stood uncertain in the road before the house, two women, and then a feeble old man came hurrying from the nearest house.

"About time you came," one of the women scolded. "They've been locked in there for ten days. We don't know whether the old woman is alive or dead."

"Why didn't you break in?" Daniel asked.

"The girl is possessed of devils," the old man answered. "She will let nobody come near her."

"We tossed bread through the window," a woman

113

added. "But I'll have no more to do with it. Suppose the devils were let loose?"

"My sister is harmless," Daniel told them impatiently. "She could hurt no one."

But probably none of them had even glimpsed his sister in all these years. He could see that he could expect no help from them. He looked up at the small high window. Then he wrenched a portion of the ladder from the wall, braced it, and tried to peer into the house. He could see nothing but a patch of floor. There was no sound, but just as he turned away he thought he caught the flicker of a shadow.

"Leah," he called, softly at first, then insistently. "It's Daniel, your brother. Let me in." The shadow did not move again.

Panic crept over him. What horror did that room contain? With all his heart he longed to run from this silent house. Yet the fearful, demanding eyes of the three neighbors goaded him on. He had no choice. He would have to break down the door and go in.

At the second thrust of his powerful shoulders the hinges burst from the rotting frame and he fell forward into foul-smelling darkness. Sunlight poured in behind him, lighting up a crouching figure with a mass of tangled yellow hair. For an instant Leah's eyes stared wildly from an ashen face. Then she darted away and coiled into a tight ball of fear against the wall. Where the girl had crouched, on a pallet of straw, lay a shrunken gray shape. Dread froze Daniel on the threshold. Then, to his shattering relief, his grandmother slowly turned her head.

"Daniel—you've come," she whispered. They were the last words he was ever to hear from her.

Daniel drove away the two curious women and sent the old man for a doctor. He kicked the door all the way open and let fresh air into the damp, fetid room. He threw out the rat-gnawed loaves of bread that littered the floor.

The doctor bent over the old woman and shook his head. "Only her will has kept the life in her," he said. "She has waited till you came. Let her go now, poor soul. Look to your sister instead, and see that she eats."

Daniel had no knowledge of nursing. Clumsily he spread a fresh bed of rushes and shifted the weightless old body. He walked to the well and filled the jar with water, and bathed the hands, thin and dry as shriveled leaves. One of the neighbors called from the roadway, and handed him a bowlful of broth, and a clay dish of hot coals to light a fire. He piled straw into the hollow in the floor and built a fire against the damp. He tried to coax the old woman to take a sip of the broth.

In all this time Leah had not moved from the wall. Once or twice, from the corner of his eyes, he noticed that she had very slightly turned her head, and he suspected that she watched him from behind the tangled hair. He tried not to look at her, to crowd back the fear that rose in him at the sight of her disheveled figure. She had been shut in here in the dimness for ten days. Had the devils taken possession of her altogether?

Daniel went out into the garden and milked the little goat, awkwardly, the feel of it gradually coming back into his hands. He carried the jar of milk into the house and set it on a shelf. The goat followed him through the broken door, sniffing timidly at the unfamiliar smell of him. Daniel was reminded that the door must be mended before it was too dark to see. The goat circled the room and found Leah, and he saw her hand go out and her fingers grip the black fur.

Night was coming on. He mended the door after a fashion and propped it against the frame. Then he discovered that there was no oil in the lamp. How many nights had they gone without a light? He had not thought to ask Rosh for money, and though it was too dark now to search the room, he doubted there would be a single coin hidden there. Just as darkness fell, there was a timid knock on the door. The second neighbor, the one who had most feared the devils, held out to him a small saucer of oil with a flaming wick. He accepted the lamp with shame. Through all these years when he had thought of the village, he had remembered the poverty, the dinginess, the quarreling and meanness and despair. He had forgotten there was kindness too.

He put the lamp on the floor and sat down near his grandmother's mat. He was all at once very tired, more tired than after a day at the forge or a long hunt over the mountain. Dread began to creep along his nerves again. He knew he was terribly afraid to spend the night in this place. Rosh was right. There was a weakness in him. That devil of fear that held his sister helpless—was it cunning enough to find out his weakness? If he could run, out into the street, back to the mountain, it could never overtake him. But he could not run. He could only sit, while the fear reached closer and closer, hemming in the small circle of light that held it at bay.

Sometimes his grandmother stirred, the thin wrinkled eyelids opened, and the faded eyes groped toward him. If he spoke to her, she closed her eyes again, satisfied. How had she been so sure that he would come? What had he ever done for her that she would dare to believe he would come back? He wished now he could tell her why he had run away. He wished that he could explain about Rosh, could let her know that it was for her too that he worked on the mountain. But it was too late for that. The only thing he could do was to sit here beside her, to let her be sure that he was there.

Perhaps if she could hear him, she would not have to make such an effort to see. He began to talk, as he had talked that night to Samson while he filed off the chains, not knowing whether anyone heard or understood, but out of some need in himself.

"You thought I had forgotten," he said. "But I remember how it used to be when Leah and I first came to live with you. Your hair was still so black, Grandmother. You worked in the ketzah field that summer. But at night you used to tell us stories."

There was no sound, not from the still figure or from the corner. But was it his imagination that a faint softening, almost like a smile, relaxed the thin tight lips? He went on talking.

"You were the one who told me the story of Daniel, the prophet I was named for. How when Daniel refused to stop praying to his God, Darius cast him into a den of lions, and how God sent an angel and shut the lions' mouths and Daniel was not hurt. And about the three men who walked in the fiery furnace and not a hair of their heads was singed. I can remember their names still —Shadrach, Meschach, and Abednego. I used to like the sound of them. You made me feel proud of being named Daniel."

There was a faint stir in the corner. Daniel did not turn his head. He went on talking.

117

"At night, before we went to sleep, you made us repeat a psalm after you. I have forgotten them now, but there's one I think I could remember, the one you liked best."

He fumbled for the words, and they came, slowly, from the depths of his memory.

" 'The Lord is my shepherd; I shall not want; He maketh me to lie down in green pastures: He leadeth me beside the still waters. He restoreth my soul: He leadeth me in the paths of righteousness for his name's sake.' "

There was a hesitant footstep beside him. Not knowing what to do, not daring to look up, with the cold prickle of fear along his skin, Daniel held out his hand. He felt Leah's fingers touch his own. He forced himself to go on.

" 'Yea, though I walk through the valley of the shadow of death, I will fear no evil: for thou art with me; thy rod and thy staff they comfort me. Thou preparest a table before me in the presence of mine enemies: thou anointest my head with oil; my cup runneth over. Surely goodness and mercy shall follow me all the days of my life: and I will dwell in the house of the Lord for ever.' "

Leah sank down beside him. Side by side, without speaking, the brother and sister sat and listened to the breathing of the old woman. Leah's hand in his own was like the hand of a small child reaching out to him in trust and helplessness. It was a sign that even now the devils did not have complete dominion. Fear retreated into the shadowy corners.

There were only the small sounds, the hiss of the wick in the saucer of oil, the wheezing and sighing of the sleeping goat, the ceaseless rustling in the thatch overhead where countless small creatures nested in the molding straw. Once the thin thread of a snake swung down, twisted back on itself, and disappeared. A rat came out of the shadows, sat on its haunches, and glared at them. Leah looked at them both without surprise or alarm. Sometime in the night he was aware that one sound in the room had ceased. His grandmother was no longer breathing.

NEXT MORNING a meager funeral procession straggled
through the village toward the burial ground outside the
gates. There were no flutes, no hired mourners, only a
scattering of neighbor women wailing halfheartedly, and
the trundling cart that carried the body of the old woman.
Leading the procession was the lone mourner, a broad-
shouldered young man with a fierce, forbidding scowl.

After the burial was over, Daniel, turning homeward,
saw a hurrying figure coming from the village, and presently, with a burst of gratitude, he recognized his friend
the blacksmith.

"I am sorry, my friend," Simon said, wringing his hand.
"I tried to get here in time for the burial. I'll go back to
your house with you, if you don't mind."

Simon was the only guest at the funeral feast, which the
neighbors spread outside the house. They ate in silence,
and when the women had cleared away the dishes and left
them alone, Simon turned to Daniel.

"What now?" he asked.

"Is there more to be done?" Daniel asked wearily.

"I meant tomorrow. What are you going to do?"

Daniel looked away. Since he had received Simon's
message he had managed not to ask himself that question.

"I had another reason for coming today," Simon went

on. "I told you in Capernaum that I intended to follow Jesus. But it weighs on my conscience that the smithy is closed. The money does not matter. I've learned to do without that. But it worries me that the tools lie idle while the men have no one to mend their plows. It has been on my mind for some time that you might help me. If you could take over the shop while I'm gone—keep the place from going to seed, I'd be very grateful to you."

It was like Simon to make it sound like a favor! Daniel stared down at the road and kicked up a spurt of dust with his bare foot. He was almost at the point of tears. Yet in the same instant such a fierce resentment sprang up in him that he dared not look his friend in the face. They had it all worked out for him. Everyone—the doctor, Leah, the neighbors, and now Simon, took it for granted that he had come home to stay. Did he have nothing to say about it? What about his life on the mountain? What about Rosh and Samson, and the work that must be done in the cave? Wasn't that more important than a few farmers who wanted their wheels mended? Everything he loved, the wind on the mountain top, the irresponsible life, the excitement of the raids, rose up and fought off the shackles that Simon held out to him in kindness.

The battle did not last long. He was trapped. Simon knew he was trapped. Though he longed to defy them all and fight for his freedom like a mountain wolf, the weakest one of them had defeated him. He could not leave Leah to sit alone in a house with the door barred. Simon, who had waited without speaking a word, was carefully looking off down the narrow street when Daniel finally raised his eyes.

"Will they bring their business to me?" the boy asked miserably.

"That will depend on you," Simon smiled.

"If I can find someone to care for Leah while I work—"

"I had thought of that too," Simon said. "My house is connected with the shop. No use having it empty. Why don't you both move in there and use my things? Better to have her where you could keep an eye on her yourself."

Not a word about the crumbling mud or the sagging roof or the gaping door which Simon could see plainly from where he stood. Daniel's throat suddenly ached.

"Thank you," he managed. "It is good—"

"It's just good business," Simon said crisply. "I'm sure of your work. I know my reputation is in good hands."

He went on, in a practical tone, explaining some of the problems of the trade, the work that this or that man was likely to demand.

"One more thing," he added. "From time to time—not often—one of the legionaries comes into the shop for something, a broken harness or clasp. They have their own forge at the garrison, of course, but sometimes a man needs a repair done quickly."

Daniel bristled. "I will never serve a pig of a Roman!"

"Yes," said Simon levelly. "You will serve him, and civilly too. There is something you will have to learn, my friend. An outlaw may think he is accountable to no one. But in a village every man holds his neighbor's safety in his hands. If a legionary is in a mood for trouble, any excuse will do. A single insult could cost half the lives in the town in the end. This is one thing I must ask of you."

To Daniel it seemed the final blow that struck his shackles into place.

Simon laughed. "It's not so bad as all that. After all, a horse deserves a comfortable bridle whether he belongs to a Roman or no. Besides, a good Zealot does not bring down suspicion on his roof."

Daniel looked at his friend sharply. Did Simon mean—?

"Did you think you had to give up serving your country? All the patriots don't live in the mountain. There are Zealots in blacksmith shops too. Do what you will—the place is yours now. So long as no harm comes to my neighbors. Can I count on you for that?"

"You can count on that," the boy said, feeling a measure of hope and a great gratitude toward his friend.

"I'm going back to Capernaum tonight," Simon said. "Perhaps you can find a neighbor to help you move your things."

Before dark Daniel climbed the mountain and explained to Rosh that he must stay in the village. Rosh heard him out in silence. Then he spoke.

"This witless sister is more important than your country's freedom?"

Daniel flushed. "No. But I cannot leave her alone."

"They boast of charity in the synagogue, don't they? Let them care for her."

Daniel remembered the untouched loaves of bread tossed through the window. "She would starve," he said.

"I have said it before," Rosh said with scorn. "You're soft."

This time Daniel did not look away. He faced his chief levelly. "I will prove you are wrong," he said quietly. "I will work for the cause in the village. You will see. I belong here on the mountain. I'll never forget that. But now I am going back, and tomorrow I will move into the house of Simon the Zealot."

Next morning he cleared out the little house. There was practically nothing worth taking. Surely there had been more than this in the days when he had lived with his grandmother. He remembered very clearly a blue glazed dish she had cherished, and a red woolen rug that had hung against the wall. Probably she had sold them for food. The decent and usable things he could salvage from the whole house went into a very small pack.

Since his grandmother had died, Leah had sat quietly, waiting, her hands folded. Like a small child, she did as she was told, ate what he brought to her.

"Will Grandmother be hungry?" she asked once.

"No," Daniel answered.

"Is it cold where she is?"

"She will never be hungry or cold again," he promised her. Now he explained to her as gently as he could that they must move.

"Simon's house is much nicer than this. It will keep out the rats and the rain and the cold in winter. You will have a mattress to sleep on like a rich girl."

She listened with wide unfathomable blue eyes, and he thought she understood. But when the moment came to leave, he saw he was mistaken. As he opened the door she shrank from the sunlight as though it were a sword. Outside in the roadway a handful of neighbors had gathered to watch his departure. One glimpse of them sent Leah cowering against the wall. Nothing Daniel could say persuaded her to move a step. Daniel's impatience mounted. He was tempted to pick her up and carry her, without any nonsense. But some instinct told him that if he laid a finger on her by force he might never win her back again. Finally he went out to speak to the neighbors.

"It is no good," he told them. "She can't abide being looked at. We could never get across the town. I will have to leave her here alone while I'm working."

"Better tie her up," one man advised, keeping the width of the road between him and the house. "Kin of mine has a daughter is possessed. They've kept her on a chain all her life."

Daniel shook his head. He'd seen such people, poor raving creatures tied to trees like dogs. Before he put a rope on Leah he would stay in this house till it crumbled to pieces around them. He went back into the house and slammed the door behind him, sending a shower of dust and clay across the floor.

In the afternoon he answered a cautious knock. Just outside the door stood a vehicle so extraordinary that he stood peering out at it, not realizing what it could be. An aged carpenter who lived a short way down the road stood beside the thing, grinning.

"It's a litter," he explained. "Like those fancy Roman ladies ride around in. Lift your sister in and she'll be as snug as in her own bed. My wife sewed all our cloaks together to make the curtains. There's four men ready to carry it for you, but we'll stay out of sight till she's inside."

A lump pushed up against Daniel's throat. Once again he felt shamed. Why should they show such kindness to a stranger and an outcast?

When every neighbor had tactfully vanished from the street, Daniel inveigled Leah into taking one look through the door.

"That's the way queens travel," he told her. "The way the Queen of Sheba came to visit King Solomon. You will sit inside it and we'll pull the curtains tight around you. In no time at all we'll be at the new house."

She shook her head. He did not hurry her. He could see that her curiosity was piqued. From time to time the blue eyes slanted toward the door.

125

"No one can see me in there?" she asked finally.

"Not so much as your little finger."

"Do I have to go away from here, Daniel?"

"I want you to be near me when I work. Wouldn't you like that, Leah?"

After a long time she seemed to give in. She moved toward the door and stood, still terrified. Then before she could refuse again, Daniel picked her up. She hid her face against his shoulder, whimpering, but she did not scream. He lifted her gently into the little box and drew the curtains around her shuddering figure.

So Leah traveled across the village like a queen. Behind her strode Daniel, carrying the sack that held all their belongings and leading the small goat by its tether. A neighbor boy carried the loom, the only valuable thing Leah possessed.

There was so much work to do in the new house that he scarcely had time to think of the cave. Very early in the morning, before the women and girls were likely to be about, he carried the water jars to the well. This was not a man's job, nor was the sweeping or the cooking or the washing of clothes. Still, these things had to be done, after a fashion. He had learned to take care of himself in the cave, where there had been no women to wait on them. But everything was more complicated here in the village, and in addition there was Leah to provide for.

The moment the shop door was open, villagers appeared with work they had saved for Simon's return. They watched the strange young blacksmith with suspicion, waiting to see what he could do. Daniel took up the challenge. He could not deny that it was a satisfaction to step every morning into Simon's tidy shop, stocked with bars of iron and hung with rows of tongs and chisels and hammers. For five years Daniel had smelted his own ore and fashioned it with clumsy makeshift tools. He had never realized that he was learning to make up in skill what he lacked in equipment. After a little practice he discovered that he could make Simon's tools do just what he wanted them to do. The work he turned out was true and light and strong. Word went round that the new smith was a good worker, for all his fierce, unapproachable scowl.

With money in his pocket for the first time in his life, he was able to buy meat from the butcher and round flat loaves of barley bread from the baker. He did not eat as well as he had on the mountain, where meat from the farmers' flocks had been free for the plundering, but he suspected that Leah had never known such plenty.

Once the shock of the journey and the terror of the new house wore away, Leah settled down unprotestingly. She began to take pleasure in very small things, in combing her long fair hair, in arranging the row of jars along the shelf, in watching the pattern of sunbeams along the plaster wall. She reminded him of Samson, the way she did not want to let him out of her sight. Odd, he thought, how he had shaken that great black shadow only to be chained now to a little gray one, scarcely bigger than a mouse, but inescapable. Leah insisted that the door between the house and shop be left open. For hours on end she sat and watched him through the opening. When customers entered the shop she would disappear, waiting concealed in a corner till they had gone. Sometimes he suspected that she watched them too from behind the long yellow hair.

Daniel was concerned that she was idle all day long. He urged her to work at the loom, but though she was willing she had no notion where to procure the thread. Her grandmother had brought her thread and taken away the

127

finished cloth; that was all she knew. One morning, however, a man called at the ___ not with a tool to be mended, but with skeins of fine linen. He was the servant of a wealthy widow in Chorazin, who, it appeared, had bought all the cloth that Leah had woven. Daniel had assumed that charitable people had bought Leah's work out of pity. He was astonished to learn that this woman knew or cared nothing about his sister and desired the cloth for its fine quality. The servant was much relieved to have tracked down the weaver. Daniel set up the loom in the corner, so that sitting before it Leah could see through the open door into his shop. Then he watched with amazement as she threaded it with expert fingers.

One morning when business was slack, Daniel discovered a measure of wheat flour on Simon's shelf and decided to try his hand at bread-making. He lighted a fire in the clay oven outside the door, measured out a little pile of the flour, stirred in some water, and began to pat the lumpy mixture into a flat cake, trying to remember how his mother had once done it. Absorbed in the work, he was startled when two small hands suddenly thrust themselves into the mixture. "That's not the way," Leah said softly. She patted the lump on a flat stone, rolled deftly with a flat roller which she took from the shelf, and handed him the thin circle of dough, ready to plaster against the wall of the oven. It gave off a delicious fragrance as it baked, and came from the oven crusty and satisfying. After that they made their own bread together and saved the money that had gone to the baker. She taught him how to save a bit of dough for leavening for the next day's baking.

An even greater surprise was to come. Behind the house Simon had planted a small plot of vegetables, enough to

supply his own solitary table. Through the luxuriant
tangle of weeds which had sprouted untended, Daniel had
glimpsed the shiny green of a cucumber, and one evening
after he had closed his shop, he went out to clear away the
weeds and see what else might be hiding there. He had
worked for some time, liking the feel of the green plants
and the smell of the earth, when he heard a soft footstep
behind him, and suddenly Leah knelt beside him, thrusting her hands into the green leaves as she had thrust them
into the dough.

"Don't, Daniel," she said, "you are pulling up all the
carrots!"

He watched her, almost afraid to speak.

"See," she showed him, "these red leaves are beets, and
these are onions. All the rest are weeds."

After that Leah spent many of the daylight hours in the
garden, hidden by the high surrounding wall. Her pale
cheeks took on a faint golden tinge. Blowing up his fire
in the shop, Daniel pondered. Without the faintest idea
what had really gone on in that dim shuttered house behind the cheesemakers, he had taken for granted that Leah
had lost her wits on the terrible night of her childhood.
Was he any better, he thought now with shame, than the
neighbors who would have tied her with ropes? Nor
could he blame his grandmother. She had been grief-
stricken and worked to the bone, terrified by the child's
screaming spells, afraid to trust her with any household
tasks. Now he saw that Leah remembered accurately
almost everything she had watched her grandmother do.
Praise be, she could take over most of the work of the
house from now on, and he would feel more like a man.

Yet as the days went by he saw that he had been too
quickly encouraged. The weaving progressed at snail's

pace. The slightest effort exhausted the girl. She was often fretful, complaining of the horrid men who came into the shop and demanding that he lock the door against them. He could not get it through her head that he had a business to carry on. At a moment when she seemed most contented, a knock at the door, a shout in the distance, the most trivial sound could reduce her to utter helplessness, and it might be hours or even days before she would so much as pick up a spoon. On other days she swept out the house, combed her hair, and sat passing the shuttle through the threads for hours. Daniel gave up trying to understand her and accepted her, as he had accepted Samson, as a burden he was doomed to carry.

Late one afternoon Daniel looked up to see a legionary standing in the doorway. He had almost forgotten Simon's warning, but even as his hammer arm stiffened he remembered and laid down the hammer on the stone. He did not spit, but there were other ways of showing his contempt. He bent over his work, absorbed in it, sanding over and over an imaginary flaw on the surface of the smooth metal. Finally, in his own good time, he raised his head. He saw that he had made his point. The soldier's face had flushed an angry red, but he said nothing. Doubtless he too was under orders to preserve the peace.

"My horse has a broken bridle ring," the soldier said, in stilted, reasonably good Aramaic.

Daniel reached for the thing as though it were a scorpion. "It will take some time," he muttered. "Come for it tomorrow."

"I need it at once," the Roman answered. "I will wait for it now."

Daniel studied him, trying to assess how much delay the man would tolerate. Then, with a shrug, he set to work.

The sooner the job was done the sooner his shop would be rid of the man.

The soldier did not sit down on the bench by the door as ordinary customers did. He hesitated, through pride—Daniel would not admit that it might be decency—waiting to be asked. Let him rot away on his feet, Daniel thought. He would get no such invitation in this shop. Turning his back, Daniel seized the bellows and blew up the fire.

When he straightened again, the Roman was pulling off his helmet, revealing crisp fair hair. He wiped the back of his hand across his wet forehead where the metal had left an uncomfortable-looking crease. With a shock Daniel saw that he was very young, certainly no older than Joel. The beardless cheeks and chin scarcely needed a razor. His skin was white, mottled and peeling from exposure to the sun, so that he could not have seen service long under Galilean skies. The eyes that stared back at Daniel were a clear bright blue. He looked as though he might be about to speak, and Daniel turned his back and resumed his work.

He took a ridiculously long time for the simple job. When finally he turned again, the soldier still stood, looking hot and uncomfortable, swinging the bronze helmet from one hand. He was no longer looking at the anvil, and Daniel, swinging to follow that intense blue gaze, suddenly stiffened with horror. The door to Simon's house stood open. Leah, who had surely not known the man was there, was coming through the little rear door from the garden, her hands full of green lettuce. The long golden hair streamed around her shoulders, lighted up all around her head from the sunlight behind her. Her eyes, blue as the ketzah blossoms, were empty with surprise.

Before she could shrink back, with one lunge, Daniel

131

slammed the door between them. Murderous hate boiled up in him. How dare the man look at his sister? The very touch of his eyes had defiled her, as surely as though he had touched her with his hand. Daniel was quivering as he handed over the bridle ring. It took every ounce of his will not to hurl the coin back into that blond face.

That night he began again to think of the mountain.

LATE ONE AFTERNOON a village boy came into the shop with a scythe to be mended. He had a bony, weather-toughened face under a shock of straight black hair, a defiant, touchy alertness, and a blackened eye that roused Daniel's curiosity. As Daniel examined the blade, the boy paced the length of the smithy floor.

"Sit down," Daniel suggested, jerking an elbow toward the bench near the door. The boy, unable to sit for more than a moment, resumed his nervous pacing. Daniel set to work, blowing the waning fire with the bellows, heating and pounding straight the blade, then applying the sandstone to the nicks that the pebbly land had left. From time to time he glanced at the boy. Daniel seldom had words to spare for his customers. He did the work they required of him and took their money, not caring that he had a reputation for being surly. Today, for the first time, he was prompted to speak. For one thing, the boy was about his own age, and for another, he looked like a fighter. When he could make himself heard, Daniel attempted a joke.

"Must have been quite a scrap you were in."

There was no answering grin, but Daniel tried again. "What did you give him in return?"

There was a pause. Then, "What could I?" the boy

burst out. "There were five of them."

Daniel's eyebrows lifted. He bent over his work.

"My own friends!" Bitterness rasped through the boy's voice. "Waited and jumped on me coming home from the field last night."

"Why?"

"Because my father has gone to work for Shomer the tax collector."

No wonder the boy looked defiant. It was a contemptible business for a Jew to hire himself out to collect the taxes the Romans did not stoop to collect for themselves. "There are better ways of earning a living," Daniel observed.

"He's worn out trying. Last year it was the locusts, and this year some cockle seed got into the grain and the crop isn't worth harvesting. He could never meet the taxes."

Daniel said nothing.

"He could have sold my sister. There would have been no shame in that. But he's too softhearted."

"That's a hard choice," Daniel agreed.

"They force it on us, the cursed Romans. The land would feed us well enough if we were rid of them."

Daniel leaned closer to the stone and carefully ground out a slight roughness.

"But it's not true what they said," the boy went on. "My father would never put one penny of the taxes in his own pocket."

Daniel did not answer. A tax collector might start out honest enough, he reflected. But a man weak enough to take the job at all would find it hard to resist the easy pickings. He felt embarrassed. It was a bad thing for a boy to have to be ashamed of his own father.

"I guess this will do," he said, rubbing his thumb along

134

the blade. He knew the boy did not want his sympathy. The boy paid him and moved toward the door, hesitating. Daniel guessed the shrinking with which he looked out into the twilight street.

"Any chance they'll be waiting again?" he asked.

The boy shrugged, but his eyes looked sick.

"Hold on a minute," Daniel suggested. "When I close the shop I've got to deliver an axhead. We can go along together."

"I can take care of myself!" the boy flashed.

"I don't doubt that. What's your name, by the way?"

"Nathan."

"Then come along with me, Nathan. There's something I'd like to tell you about."

There was not much use talking, however, to one whose ears were straining for every sound on the dark roadway. Daniel could almost feel the tensed muscles of the boy beside him, but he observed with approval that the nervous stride did not falter. He gave up any attempt to talk, and walked on in silence, savoring with keen pleasure the thought of the coming attack. He had not realized how much he had missed this rising prickle of anticipation.

The rush came quickly out of the darkness. Six or seven, Daniel noted, even while his fist sent the first comer sprawling. With a shout of sheer enjoyment, he caught two others, one with each hand. In the dark there was a shriek. "The blacksmith!" A frantic wrench and the sound of tearing cloth, and one of his captives darted off in his tunic, leaving his cloak in Daniel's hand. The other, teeth rattling from a shake and a kick that would be remembered, stumbled after him. Then Daniel stood watching while his new friend dealt efficiently with two young attackers.

"Not bad," he commented, when the whole pack had slunk into the shadows. "You need to tighten your guard. Now, that's over, and you can pay attention to what I have to say. How would you like to use those fists of yours for a good purpose?"

So Daniel won his first recruit in the village, Nathan, son of the new tax collector.

As though Daniel's very eagerness had somehow acted as a signal between them, a few days later Joel walked into the smithy, bringing with him a recruit of his own.

"How did you know where to find me?" Daniel demanded, eying with curiosity the slender scholarly boy who accompanied his friend.

"I ran into your friend Simon," Joel told him, after just the slightest hesitation. "He told me you were looking out for his shop. He suggested I come to see you."

"A good thing," Daniel said. "I was wondering how I could get to Capernaum. There's busniess enough for two men here." He tried to sound matter-of-fact, but he could not keep the pride out of his voice.

Joel showed a flattering interest in the shop. He wandered about, picking up the tools, weighing bars of metal from one hand to another. He was impressed with the shining gleam of a newly finished blade.

"I've brought someone who wants to join with us," he said. "Kemuel feels as we do."

Daniel looked uncomfortably at the newcomer. The boy was plainly wealthy, and used to having his own way. There was an edge of disdain in his voice, and in his proud, handsome face. Yet there was something else too. The new boy whirled suddenly round at him.

"Do you mean to fight them?" he demanded. "Or are

you playing a game? I came today to see if you are serious."

"We are serious," said Daniel levelly. "What right have you to ask?"

"Because I am tired of words!" the boy answered. "Everywhere men talk and argue, while Israel lies helpless at the feet of Rome. Where is our courage? Why does no one dare to step forth? If you mean to fight them, then I am with you. But I have no use for children's games."

A feverish light burned in his dark eyes. He reminded Daniel of a panther, lean and dark and fiery, and his own fire leaped up to meet this boy's. He forgot his suspicion.

"You're welcome here, Kemuel," he said. "You'll find we're not playing a game." Yes, Joel had chosen well. Strong arms and muscles were easy to find. A fiery spirit was not so common.

Presently Nathan stopped by on his way home from the field, as he had formed a habit of doing. Already Nathan had lost his resentful air. At first awkward in the presence of the city boys, he soon surrendered to Joel's friendliness. Daniel disconnected the bellows, banked the fire for the night, bolted the door, and the band of four held its first meeting. Certain of Simon's approval, Daniel offered the smithy as a gathering place. They agreed to meet on the third day of each week.

"If you want members," Nathan offered, "I could name you ten here in our village who would give their right arms to join you."

Daniel hesitated. "I've thought about that," he told them. "I know there are plenty. If word went out tomorrow half the village would probably be with us before night. Some because they love Galilee, or hate the Romans, and some just because they love a good fight. But would they lose heart? The trouble is, we can't fight tomorrow. We've got to work slowly, and it may take a long time."

"How long?" Kemuel demanded.

"We must be strong enough so that we cannot fail." Daniel tried to remember how Rosh had talked to them in the cave, whetting their impatience, but always holding it back, leashed for the day to come. He saw how much he had still to learn from Rosh.

"Right now we need members who will be willing to work without any reward," he went on, not looking at Kemuel, but speaking chiefly to him. "We've got to be absolutely sure we can trust them, no matter what happens."

"Then we shouldn't take too many right away," Joel said thoughtfully.

"We should not make it too easy," Kemuel spoke. "We only value the things we pay for."

"Who has money to pay?" Nathan bristled. "That would keep out all the villagers."

"I was not speaking of money," Kemuel answered, with a touch of scorn. "I meant we must be committed altogether, without any reservation. Only that way can we be sure."

"We will each take the oath," Joel reminded him.

His friend was not satisfied. "An oath can mean one thing to one and something altogether different to another," he argued. Daniel suspected that he argued habitually and enjoyed it, like the Scribes who debated the fine points of the Law.

"I know!" Nathan sprang to his feet. He seized a rod

of iron from the wall near him. "We can brand ourselves! That way we would know—"

"Are you forgetting the Law?" the scholar cut in icily. "You shall not print any marks upon you!" It was exactly as though he had pulled his cloak tighter to avoid contamination. Peasant! his tone said unmistakably. Daniel's heart sank. Already his little army was behaving like the men in the cave.

"We don't need a brand," Joel spoke quickly, in the reasonable friendly way that made everything he said so convincing. "If we choose carefully we can trust each other. We will carry the sign of the bow in our minds. You know—from the Song of David: 'He trains my hands for war, so that my arms can bend a bow of bronze.' That is our password."

Within three weeks the four members had increased to seven, then to nine—twelve—sixteen. Young men would meet each other on the village streets, in the school at Capernaum. "Did you ever see a bow made of bronze?" they might ask, in passing. Or they would drop in at the smithy and pick up a lump of metal. "It would make a good bow," they would say. The password gave them pride and pleasure. They were bound together by the sign. On the first day of Ab, twenty-one boys crowded the smithy. Daniel looked around at them with a surge of elation.

"When can we tell Rosh?" Joel demanded, eager for another glimpse of his hero.

"Not yet—" Daniel answered. He could not tell even Joel how he dreamed of the moment when he would tell Rosh. Now, while Joel read aloud to the listening boys the thrilling accounts he had shared with Daniel in the passageway, of David and of Judas Maccabeus, Daniel thought how he would lead Rosh down the mountain and confront him with an army, ready for his command. Then Rosh would no longer be an outcast. Then everyone would recognize the leader they had longed for, and the day would be very near.

On the morning after the third meeting, the fair-haired Roman soldier appeared again at the smithy. This time he had a broken stirrup to be mended. He paid no attention to the sullen scowl that showed that his business was unwelcome. He stood, his feet planted well apart in that Roman pose they seemed to learn young, looking deliberately about the shop, at the shelves of metal bars, the tools hanging along the wall, the door that Daniel had instantly shut between them and the inner room. Daniel kept his eyes on his work, fighting down a compulsion to find out what the man might be looking at. Could there possibly be a sign of last night's meeting? He did not draw an easy breath till the Roman, taking his time about it, finally clanked through the door, mounted his horse, and rode off. Then, searching the room frantically, he could find nothing that could possibly have drawn the man's suspicion. Had it been his imagination that the man was looking for something?

The Roman returned. Sometimes on the very day of a meeting, often on odd days between. He came now with work for his fellow legionaries, or with ridiculous excuses to have some perfectly sound bit of harness checked for a flaw. Once or twice Daniel, hearing the hoofbeats in the street, looked up to see the man ride slowly by his door, and then, almost immediately, so soon the man could scarcely have turned his horse, ride slowly back again. He discovered the prints of a horse's hoofs in the soft earth of the alleyway that ran along the garden wall where

140

there was no possible reason to ride a horse. No question now, the house was being watched. The meeting place would have to be changed.

A new recruit, son of a farmer in the village, offered a solution. He led Daniel to an abandoned watchtower in his father's cucumber field, a small round stone house in which the whole family had once lived during the time of harvest to watch lest thieves despoil the ripening crop. Below the tower a shaft had been cut, designed, Daniel suspected, for hiding part of the crop from the count of the tax collector. It made a fine place to store the weapons they planned soon to have. The tower could be approached from many sides, across the field of vines. It was an ideal meeting place.

Abruptly, almost as soon as they shifted the meeting place, the Roman stopped coming. Warily, they stationed a guard near the new headquarters, taking turns at the duty. Not a sign of the soldier was ever reported. Luck was with them, Daniel decided. Still, there was something about it that made him uneasy.

DANIEL'S CHIEF DOUBT about the new meeting place, that
it would take him from home for long hours at a time,
resolved itself more simply than he expected. Leah listened
to his explanation and seemed to grow accustomed to his
absences as she had once accepted the fact that her
grandmother must work in the fields. Leah was gain-
ing confidence. She did not tire as readily at the
loom. She had even completed a length of cloth which
had been paid for by the servant of the widow of Chorazin.
When Daniel had laid the shining silver talent in his
sister's hand, she had been bewildered. He realized that
she had never before known any recompense for her hours
at the loom. He showed her how to sew the coin into her
head scarf, where every village girl, even the poorest,
boasted the jingling coins that would be her dowry. Leah
was as enchanted as a child. Now she always wore the
headdress as she worked, and from time to time her hand
stole up to touch the coin. Underneath the scarf the long
yellow hair was always combed and carefully arranged.
Was it the work in the little garden that had brought a
faint flush to her pale cheeks?

One afternoon, looking through the door of his shop,
Daniel saw two figures coming slowly along the road in
the shimmering waves of heat. One, he soon saw, was

Joel. The other he was not sure of. A new recruit? The two figures were almost at his door before he recognized, with a shock of pleasure, that the one who had come with Joel was his sister Malthace. She wore a yellow mantle with a green embroidered girdle, and a green and white striped headdress that showed just the edge of the dark sweep of her hair.

"I've never been in a blacksmith's shop before," she exclaimed, sweeping back the headdress in the impulsive gesture Daniel always remembered first when he thought of her. "I've been begging Joel to let me come to see it."

Embarrassed, Daniel wiped his sooty hands and brought a jar of water from the house, wishing he had more to offer.

"I'd like to ask you to come into my—into Simon's house—" he began.

"It doesn't matter. It's lovely here in the shop," said Malthace quickly. The two visitors sat on the bench and watched him complete the lock that he had promised to deliver before sunset.

"I'm glad you came today," Daniel told Joel, when the work was done. "There's an apprentice I want you to meet over in the Street of the Weavers. I think he wants to join us, but he has some foolish ideas in his head that the rabbi has taught him. I can't talk him out of them, but you could."

"Go along and see him," Malthace suggested. "I don't mind staying here alone. I'd rather start back when it's cooler."

"Are you sure? It would take only a short time."

It took a considerably longer time than Daniel had reckoned, because Joel and the young weaver lost themselves in the intricacy of a theological debate. It was

143

nearing sunset when they started back toward the smithy.

"He's going to be one of the best we have," Joel said. "But you should have stopped us. When I get started on an argument I forget what time it is."

He did not seem to want to hurry, however, and shortly it appeared that he had something else on his mind.

"I've put off telling you this," he said finally. "I don't know just why. I saw your carpenter again."

"Was Simon with him?"

"Yes. As a matter of fact, when I told you that day that I'd run into Simon, that wasn't altogether true. I went back to Bethsaida on purpose. I went back several times. Lately I've been getting up early to hear Jesus when he talks to the fishermen."

Daniel was surprised. "You think he will help us?"

Joel hesitated. "He has helped me. He has explained several points of the Law that have always puzzled me."

"Explained them to *you?* You're the scholar. He is only a carpenter."

"I don't know where he got his training," Joel said. "But he knows the scripture. Some of his ideas are the same as Father's, only he seems to go beyond somehow. He has a way of making something very clear and— uncomplicated—so that you wonder why you never thought of it that way before."

"The first time I heard him," Daniel said, "I thought that if only he and Rosh could join together—"

"I've thought so too. So many people follow him. Some mornings there are more than a hundred. If anyone could persuade them—But then again I'm not sure. I wish you'd come to listen to him, Daniel. Every time I hear him I wish you were there. We both think—"

"Does Kemuel go with you?"

Joel laughed. "Not Kemuel. I persuaded him to go once. He was horrified. He's too much like Father. No, Thacia goes with me. She—oh my word! I forgot Thacia! She'll be furious at me."

The girl was not in the smithy. As the two boys stood uncertainly in the doorway, a soft murmur of voices drifted through the inner door. Surely it could not be—? Then Daniel heard the quick light peal of Thacia's laughter.

"Wait here!" he told Joel.

There was no one in the inner room. Beyond, in the small garden, two girls sat side by side on the bench.

"Oh Daniel!" Leah cried, catching sight of her brother. "Thacia came to see me!"

Dumfounded, Daniel stared from one to the other.

"How—?" he stammered, and then caught the warning in Thacia's eyes. Don't spoil it, her look cautioned him quite plainly. He could think of nothing at all to say, could only stand stupidly. How had she managed it, when no one, not a neighbor or an old friend, had been allowed to see Leah's face for almost ten years?

"We've been having a lovely visit," Thacia said, as casually as though it happened every day. "Leah has been showing me her vegetables. The time has gone fast. We had so much to talk about."

These two—so utterly different! "What could you talk about?" he burst out before he could stop himself.

Mischief danced in Thacia's eyes. "You," she said.

He felt his ears redden. He knew he would never know how she had accomplished it. Girls were strange creatures. He could not understand them. But he could see the change in his sister's face. She was fragile and pale beside Thacia's vivid beauty, but smiling with a smile so like their mother that it caught at his throat.

Joel, impatient and curious, came through the inner door. It was too much to hope that the miracle should include him too. At the first glimpse of him, Leah's bright face grayed with fear. Thacia motioned him out of sight.

"My brother and I must go home now," she said gently. "But I will come back soon. You won't forget me, will you, Leah?"

There was no answer. Leah's head was bent. The folds of the scarf that hid her face were trembling.

"Here's something to remember me by," said Thacia. She undid the green embroidered girdle from her waist and laid it gently across Leah's knees. The gold threads twinkled in the afternoon sun. "God be with you," she said quickly, and not waiting for any answer, moved past Daniel through the smithy, too quickly for him to stop her or to try to thank her. Daniel stood looking down at his sister. He saw one finger slowly move out from the veil and touch the girdle, tracing the scarlet and blue and purple threads as though they might vanish at too heavy a touch. It was the first beautiful thing she had ever owned.

Thacia's visit caused Daniel to look at his sister with new eyes, and one thing that he had never noticed before suddenly shamed him. She spent all day weaving fine cloth for a wealthy woman, and she herself was dressed in a faded gray rag. Next morning he took down the jar in which he kept the money his customers gave him, counted out a handful of coins, and made his way to the market.

It was a confusing place, the kind a man did well to stay away from. The booths of the weavers were surrounded by women, chattering like a woods full of sparrows, fingering the lengths of scarlet and purple, bargaining with sharp, accusing screams. He gathered his courage and approached, trying to ignore their derisive glances. Presently he found what he wanted, a length of smooth cotton the clear fresh blue of the ketzah blossoms.

"How much?" he growled.

A girl with gold earrings studied him shrewdly. "Blue dye is rare," she said. "Two shekels."

He knew it was too much. He had no way of knowing how much too much, and he had no knack for bargaining anyway. He paid the money, and cursed himself when she did not hide her contempt.

"Thread?" He glared at her. When she had found it for him, "Do you have a needle too?" he asked.

The girl laughed. "We don't sell needles. Surely your wife must have a needle."

He said nothing, but the flush creeping up his cheeks made the girl laugh again. "Oh," she said, "a present, is it? Wait a minute." She delved beneath a pile of odd articles. "Here. Take one of mine. I won't charge you for it." The fine gesture, he could see, was an apology for the scandalous profit she had made on the cloth. He took the package and walked away, his ears red.

Leah could not believe that the cloth was hers. Just to touch its smooth surface seemed to give her such joy that Daniel did not dare to suggest that it had a useful purpose. He waited for two mornings before he brought out the needle and thread. Leah watched his clumsy experiments, fascinated. Suddenly a squeal of laughter broke from her, so startling that he dropped the needle. He had never heard her laugh before! The breathy little sound died away as he stared at her.

"Oh Daniel! You hold it like one of those great iron things. Give me that."

"Can you thread a needle?" he asked, astonished.

"Anybody can thread a needle! Daniel, do you think —would you be angry with me if I made a dress out of the blue cloth?"

Through the door of the smithy he watched Leah spread the cloth on the floor, marveling at the capable way she turned it this way and that as she cut. Praise be! Perhaps she could even make him a new cloak!

IT STARTED with an innocent question.

"Daniel, what is a wedding?"

Across the mat with its earthen dishes, Daniel looked at his sister. They sat late over their morning meal. He knew that the shop door should be open, but he was in no hurry about it. Well into the morning hours he had celebrated the wedding of his new friend, Nathan, son of the tax collector. He felt heavy-limbed and slow-witted. He wished Leah would stop prodding him with questions.

How pitifully little the girl knew of the world outside their walls. Had their grandmother never talked to her? In the early days here in Simon's house, he and Leah had eaten their meals and done the work with few words. Then, out of his own loneliness, he had begun to talk, as he used to talk to Samson, sorting out his own thoughts aloud, not expecting any response. Leah had listened in silence, as Samson had done, but later she had astonished him by remembering. She had begun to ask questions, odd, childish questions that revealed an incredible ignorance. Lately, since Thacia's visit, there had been altogether too many questions. She wanted to know about the girls he saw in the village, what they wore, what they did in the town, what they talked about. He did his best to answer her, because he could understand how his words

149

were like a window through which she could peek out at a world of people she did not dare to meet face to face. Now, scowling in the effort, he tried to tell her about a wedding.

"It's a feast," he said slowly. "On the day a man takes a bride into his house. When all his friends come to celebrate with him and wish him happiness."

"Does the bride have friends too?"

"Oh yes, all making a fuss and talking at once."

"Did many people come to Nathan's wedding?"

"Well no, not so many as usual, I guess. Of course this was the first wedding I've been to since—" Since that far-off night when he had carried a torch in his uncle's procession! He hurried on. "You see, Nathan is ashamed because his father is already making money from the tax collection, so he refused to let his father give the feast for him. I guess as weddings go it was a pretty poor one, but Nathan was satisfied."

"Did you have good things to eat?"

"Yes. Cakes and lots of fruit and grape wine." Curse his selfishness! Couldn't he have brought her a morsel?

"Tell me about it, Daniel!" Her blue eyes sparkled. He wished he had Joel's gift for words.

"First we went to the bride's house. Her family had made garlands out of flowers. Nathan and Deborah stood in the garden behind the house, because the house was too small to fit in so many people."

"Was the bride pretty?"

"I don't know. I guess Nathan thought so."

"As pretty as Thacia?"

For a moment he was disconcerted. Then he remembered that Thacia was the only girl she knew.

"No," he said honestly. "Not so pretty as you, either."

"What did she wear?" Leah looked pleased and flushed.

"Oh—" he floundered. "A dress—white I think it was. And a veil over her head, and the flowers. Then we all made a procession to Nathan's new house. There were some little boys who played on pipes, and we all carried torches, and the older people threw rice and grain at the bride."

"Why?"

"Oh—it's a custom. To wish her a fine family. And everyone sang songs and shouted and clapped their hands and stamped their feet."

He stopped at the alarm in her eyes. Even the mention of noise terrified her. She could not imagine that noise could be merry. He got to his feet and began to clear away the meal. But Leah did not move, only sat brooding over what he had told her.

Finally she asked, "Will Nathan's bride live in his house with him all the time?"

"Of course. Just as our mother and father lived in our house."

"Daniel," she said slowly. "When you bring a bride here to live with you, what will happen to me?"

He was completely taken aback. "That's a silly question," he snapped. "I'm not going to marry."

"Why not?"

"Because I have no time for such foolishness. Not till the last Roman is gone from our land."

"Is Nathan foolish because he has a bride?"

Daniel felt his good humor sliding away. "It is another matter for Nathan. I have taken an oath. I live for just one thing—to rid us of our Roman masters."

His voice sounded loud in his own ears. Was he shouting at Leah—or himself? Angrily he began to pull on his

151

cloak. He felt sore, as though she had unexpectedly probed a wound he had not even been aware of.

"Are the Romans our masters?" she asked, her soft voice sounding puzzled.

"Don't you even know that?"

She sat silent. But as he opened the door of the shop he saw that another question was beginning. He did not intend to listen. He had had enough for one morning. But the words caught him like a suddenly flashing net.

"That soldier—the one who comes into your shop sometimes—the one who rides on the horse? Is he a Roman?"

"Yes. May his bones rot!"

"Is he your master, then?"

"Ask him! He would say he is!"

"Oh Daniel—how silly! He is only a boy, not half so big and strong as you. And he is homesick."

A fury of impatience seized him. "What does it matter how strong he is? He carries a sword. He has the whole Roman army to protect him!"

"Daniel—why are you so angry at the Romans?"

In a rage of frustration he glared at her. Because they did this to you! he wanted to shout at her. Because they robbed you of your parents and a decent life and a chance to drink out of the marriage cup like that girl last night. Because they robbed you of everything—all but one thing. A brother to avenge you!

Suddenly all he wanted was to get away from her. He felt choked. A heavy weight he could not understand dragged at him. But as he stumbled through the door he turned back.

"What made you say he was homesick?"

Her eyes looked up at him, misty blue. "I think he is

152

homesick," she said. She bent and began to roll up the mat.

Furious, he slammed the door behind him. Homesick! That stiff-necked son of a camel!

But where had she learned the word?

He could not put his mind on his work. His head throbbed. Without warning, Leah's childish questions had unleashed all the rebellion he had kept so carefully chained. All day at the forge he thought of the mountain. Twice he laid down the hammer and went to stand in the doorway of Simon's shop, looking up at the line of hills shimmering in the heat against the unbroken blue of the sky. Up till now he had been able to deal with his restlessness, push it down out of sight, hammer it out with great blows on the anvil. Today it seized him with the strength of a hundred demons. All day he stuck to his work, trying to hammer out his longing on the metal, trying to keep his eyes from the distant hills. In the late afternoon he laid down the hammer, banked the fire carefully with earth as for the Sabbath, and bolted the door of the shop.

"I must be away tonight," he told Leah. "There is food and water, and oil enough to burn all night."

"You will come back?" Could she sense the demons that were driving him?

"Of course I'll come back. Bar the door when I have gone."

He took the road toward the hills. With every step the tiredness went out of him. As he began the long climb he could feel the air growing cooler. A light breeze moved the tops of the cypress trees. With every breath he drew in freedom.

153

How many nights, lying on Simon's rooftop, had he imagined the moment when he would walk again into camp? For a few moments it was just as he had pictured it—the shouts, the surprise, the good feeling that he had come home. But the brief excitement soon died down. Rosh, after a sharp demand for news, went back to an oath-studded argument with two of the men. No one else had much to say to him. Daniel wandered about the camp, noticing a few new faces, trying hard to experience the elation he had expected to feel. Then he knew what was missing. He had been watching, all the way up the trail, for a motion on the hillside above, for a familiar welcoming figure to come bounding down to meet him. Ridiculous. The black man had something better to do than to sit watching for him after all these weeks. But why wasn't Samson somewhere about? The forge had been heated. He could feel the warmth of the stone when he laid his hand against it.

"How's the village?" asked Joktan, coming in with a load of thorns which he flung down near the fire. There was a hint of hostility—or was it envy—in his voice. "Did you b-bring anything to eat?"

Daniel looked surprised. He had come away empty-handed without a thought.

"We've had trouble getting meat lately," Joktan explained. "S-some of the shepherds made an ambush. You'd think they'd taken lessons from us. Two of our men got beaten—bad. The shepherds are in a mean humor, and Rosh ordered us to lay low for a while."

Daniel was suddenly uncomfortable. Up here on the mountain he had taken for granted that the flocks that grazed on the slopes were free for the taking. Now he knew by name the men who owned those flocks. They were not wealthy men.

"Oh well," Joktan said. "Rosh won't be patient long."

Daniel laughed, pushing away his uneasiness. "Where's Samson?" he inquired.

Joktan shrugged. "That's anybody's guess. Samson has his own rules."

"Rosh lets him?"

"Rosh l-leaves well enough alone. If you ask me, he's sorry he ever got the brute. But Samson earns his keep. Look! There he is now. G-goodness, look what he's brought!"

The giant stood at the head of the path. Over his shoulder, as easily as a rabbit, was slung the carcass of a sheep that must have weighed more than a man. Swinging it from his shoulders, dropping it to the earth, he stood grinning, looking from man to man, waiting for their praise. With a shout Daniel sprang forward. At the vast white-toothed smile that split the black face, his own spirits gave an answering leap. For a moment the two stared at one another. Then Samson stepped over the carcass of the sheep. When he would have gone down on his knees, Daniel reached out both hands and grasped the powerful arms and held on hard. They stood grinning at each other wordlessly.

Two men had pounced on the carcass and were worrying off the skin with the ferocity of jackals. Others heaped thorn branches on the fire and made ready the spit. Men poured from the cave into the clearing as word of a feast spread. Rosh, glowering from the door of the cave, shrugged his shoulders and said nothing.

While the meat was cooking Daniel debated with himself. Was this the time to tell Rosh about his band? But he did not want to spoil the moment when he could confront Rosh with a real army. Besides, he had chosen a poor day to come back. Rosh was obviously out of sorts.

"Your friend Joel," Rosh inquired once. "Ever see him again?"

"Yes," said Daniel. "Quite often."

"Keep an eye on him," Rosh growled. "I'm going to need him soon." He said no more, and only half listened as Daniel tried to tell him about the move to Simon's shop.

Later in the night Daniel sat watching the thorn fire leaping and crackling. He felt satisfied, full of roasted mutton. He leaned back against the rock, feeling with his shoulder blades for the remembered niches. "It's good to be back," he said.

"G-good to be full," Joktan commented, wiping a hand across his grease-smeared chin. "We've got you to thank for it."

"You mean you've got Samson to thank."

"Samson only did it for you. He knew you were coming all right. He j-just knows things. He's deaf, maybe, but he hears things that aren't there. Look at him sitting there s-staring at you. You'd think you were one of his gods. You think it's an accident we've had the only good meal in a week?"

Someone else, too, knew that the meal had been no accident. Glancing at Rosh, Daniel saw the small eyes, above the unkempt tangles of black beard, glittering at Samson. The dislike in them startled him. Rosh had gorged himself on the forbidden mutton, but he hadn't forgiven the one man in the camp who had dared to flout his orders.

Later still Daniel lay awake. Overhead the stars were

big and close. The cool air was clean, free of the mists and taint of the town. He lay filled with meat and wine, his old comrades stretched out beside him. It was all just as he had imagined it on those endless steaming nights in the town. Yet sleep did not come. He turned over, twisting his shoulders to fit a hump in the rocky ground. In these few weeks his body had forgotten the feel of pebbles. In the same way, his mind shifted uncomfortably, trying to find a resting place.

Pictures began to form in his memory. Leah alone behind a bolted door. Joel reading aloud from the scroll. Thacia standing in the doorway of the smithy in her striped headdress. Simon looking away down the road, waiting for Daniel to accept the offer of all he owned.

Simon had chosen a different leader. Daniel thought now of the one meal he had shared with Simon's comrades. He remembered the silence as Jesus had stood to bless the meager feast, and how each one had taken less than he needed so that those outside could be fed. A closeness had seemed to draw them all together. Tonight, who but Samson had cared that he had come back?

All at once he thought of Leah's little black goat. Would some child in the village be hungry because of tonight's feast?

At the first gray glimmer he got up. Instantly Samson was awake. Daniel put a hand on his shoulder. For a moment he stood, shaken by the question that stared from the dark eyes. Then he shook his head and made his way among the sleeping figures to the top of the trail. Samson did not try to follow him.

He wished he could take the black man with him. But how could that huge figure fit into the narrow cage of his life at the smithy? Samson would alarm the villagers and terrify Leah into a corner forever. No, Samson belonged to the free life on the mountain.

Where did he himself belong?

The fire in Simon's forge had almost gone out. He raked back the ashes, blew on the coals and coaxed it back to life. Then he opened the inner door to the house. Leah looked up at him, her blue eyes as lifeless as the fire. She had not combed her hair or bothered to get herself breakfast. With irritation he saw that the water jar was empty and that he would have to stand in line at the well with the snickering women. He bent and picked up the jar, and the bars of his cage slid into place around him.

FROM THE MORNING when Daniel went back to hear Jesus on the shore of Capernaum, life in the village began to seem less burdensome. Though he would have been surprised if he had stopped to realize it, the long hot days of the month of Ab came to be the happiest he had ever known.

He went first because Joel had asked him to, and because he was still curious to find what it was about the preacher that had drawn first Simon and then Joel. Two days later he went back again, because he could not get the words of the carpenter out of his head. After that, nearly every morning in the week he rose before dawn and walked three miles to the city to join the little crowd that always waited at the shore. Though it meant that his shop would be late in opening, Simon encouraged his coming, and seemed glad to see him. Daniel could meet Joel and talk with him freely, and often he had the added reward of Thacia's flashing smile. Even the fishermen came to greet him by name.

It was harder to explain to himself why he sometimes was drawn to Bethsaida at night, when he could not expect to meet Joel, and when he could only sit in the little garden of Simon's house and listen to the words of Jesus. He did not always understand the words, and often he walked home puzzled and impatient, but a few nights later, almost against his will, he would go again. He was still not sure what Jesus intended to do, but day after day the hope and promise in Jesus' words drew him back.

At mealtimes he told Leah the stories he had heard. Sometimes he thought that if the long walks to Capernaum and the hours away from his work had accomplished nothing else, they had at least given him something to talk to Leah about.

"Was Andrew there?" she would ask. "Did he have a lot of fish in his net? Did the rich women come and bring food for the poor people?"

She would sit with her own food untouched, wanting only to listen. Often when he returned late at night she would bounce up on her mat, her eyes shining with wakefulness, and hug her knees with her arms. Even when he was too tired to think he would manage some bit of news before he climbed to his bed on the rooftop, or the disappointment in her face would nag at him,

It puzzled him that this timid creature who had never dared to venture beyond their tiny garden patch should now be so curious about the busy life of the city. How could he possibly make her see it, when she had never even glimpsed the little crossroads and the well and the small flat synagogue that made up the center of their own village?

"I like to go in the morning best," he told her. "When the fishermen are just coming in with their night's catch. Some of the families have been bringing their boats in at the same spot for years, so that everyone takes it for granted that certain places belong to certain men. That's why no one really dares to interfere when Jesus sits and talks, because everyone knows that that spot belongs by right to Simon and Andrew.

"Why should they want to interfere?"

"The overseers think he keeps the men from starting their work. Not the fishermen. They have been out all night and their work is done. It's the men loading the trading boats who stop and listen when they should be working. And people like me with work waiting to be done at home."

There was so much he could never find words to make her see. The lake, gray and still at sunrise, the hills beyond like huddled sheep, the first lines of camels and donkeys coming sleepily to the water's edge. The crowing of a cock somewhere in the town, and the first busy chirping of sparrows, and, abruptly, the swifts, coming from nowhere, filling the air, darting over the water. And then suddenly the sun, leaping over the hills, warm and yellow, so that the mists melted and the lake shone blue and sparkling. The boats coming in, dragging the nets with their heaving burdens of fish. The smoke of little fires quickly lighted, and the fragrance of roasting fish. Worth getting up in the dark, even when his tired muscles pleaded for a little more rest; worth the long walk to the city and the waiting. But how could he put it into words?

And how could he tell of the people? The women who came down to help their men spread the wet nets on the shore. The almost-naked men, their shoulders glistening, dragging the heavy baskets up from the boats, spreading the fish on flat stones to be salted and dried. The never-ending lines of men with sacks of grain and baskets of fruits and vegetables.

"Jesus stands on the shore and talks to them all," he

told Leah. "His friends to start with, and people like me. And then there are the beggars and cripples. Heaven knows where they sleep, but every morning they drag themselves down to the shore, partly to hear Jesus and partly because Simon and Andrew and the women always give them some fish. Then there are curious people who come because they see a crowd. It drives the overseers crazy when their men stop to listen. Sooner or later they break in and drive the men away. Sometimes Jesus gets into one of Simon's boats and goes out from shore a little. That way they can't order him away, but the crowds on the shore can still hear him."

"What did he say to them today?" she would ask. And Daniel would do his best to remember. He would try to call back the lakeside and hear the lap of the water and the shouts of the workmen and even the breathing of the men and women packed close around him. He could hear their stillness, and that deep, steady voice. Sometimes he could remember almost word for word, because Jesus had left an unforgettable picture in his mind.

"He told us a story about a traveler who fell among thieves who beat him and left him half dead beside the road. And a priest and a Levite came by and saw him and passed by on the other side, but a cursed Samaritan stopped and bound up his wounds and took care of him. I wish the story had been about a Jew instead. If Jesus means that Jews and Samaritans should treat each other like neighbors, that is foolish. It could never happen."

Often the words themselves eluded him, and only the memory of the voice struck troubled echoes deep within him. It was true, he did like best to go in the morning, not only because he loved the lake at dawn and the bustle of work beginning, and the walk back through the fields

162

fresh-washed from the night dew, but also because then, in the clear bright sunlight, nothing seemed impossible. He could truly believe that the kingdom of God was coming nearer, and he could almost hear the sound of trumpets in the distant hills.

When he went to the city in the evening, everything seemed different, and he was not so sure. A sadness seemed to hang over the world. At night people came flocking to the home of Simon the fisherman, where Jesus lived in a booth on the rooftop. There the workers would gather, weary from a day of hard labor at the forge or the wharves or the vineyards. They would crowd into the small room, spilling out and filling the narrow yard, sprawling on the trampled earth, so close-packed that one could scarcely find a way between the bodies. It was at night that the hungry, who had not eaten all day, came to be fed, and the down-and-out and worthless. It was at night that they brought their kinfolk on litters. The air was thick with the day's heat and the stench of bodies and the smell of fever. The eyes of the ill and lame, which looked up with hope in the new morning, were glazed at night with a long day's suffering. Daniel was disgusted at the way they jostled each other and tore at the food, and snatched bread from the helpless, and at the way no one bothered when some poor creature who could only crawl on hands and knees was passed over or even trodden on.

At night Jesus too looked weary. His brilliant flashing eyes were dark with pity. Yet he never turned away, never refused to speak to them. While he talked, they all forgot for a while. You could see their faces, turned upward to the light that streamed from the open door. And you could see that his words touched their minds and hearts like some healing ointment, and that the scars on their spirits that came from being beaten and kicked and turned away all day long, lost their smart and for a short time did not matter. Often a man's body was healed, and he leaped up, full of new strength; and then a new hope coursed through them all.

But as Daniel went home, with the black heat pressing him down, all the misery he had seen dragged at him, clinging like burs to his spirit, and he did not hear any distant trumpets. On these nights it was difficult to find anything to tell Leah. When he lay down and tried to sleep, the same question went on and on in his mind. When—when? How long must the world go on like this?

There was one story he almost wished he had not told Leah, because she asked for it over and over again.

"Tell me about the little girl who was sick," she would beg. Daniel would repeat the words that he had said so often that they were like a lesson memorized in school.

"Jesus went to her house and—"

"No, begin at the beginning," she would demand like a child. "When you were waiting on the beach."

So he would begin, knowing that nothing but the whole story, just as he had told it so many times, would satisfy her.

"We were waiting on the beach. Jesus had been across the lake to visit some of the villages, he and some of his followers, and they were coming back in a boat. People had been waiting for him since before dawn, and they were hungry and hot, but they were bound they wouldn't leave before they had seen him. Finally someone saw the boat coming, and they all stood up and strained their eyes, and as it got nearer they went wild. You'd have thought he was a prince, the way they screamed and cheered. It was all Simon and James could do to make room for him

164

to step on shore. I think Simon was trying to persuade him to get back into the boat again, the way he sometimes has to do, because for all they call him master and teacher, they lose their wits and have no regard for him at all. But just then there was a shout behind the crowd, and everyone turned around. Those in the back were pushing to make room for someone, and we saw a man trying to get through to Jesus.

"Joel whispered, 'It's Jairus,' and then people began to step on each other's toes to get out of the way. Some of them tried to hide behind the others for fear Jairus would recognize them. Jairus is one of the rulers of the synagogue. I think even Joel looked a little scared. Jesus' friends moved up close around him. No one was quite sure what was going to happen. But Jesus made a sign for them to stand aside, and he just stood quietly and waited. Jairus passed very close to me. His cloak was twisted sideways, and he was panting as though he had been running, and no one need have bothered to hide, because he did not see anyone or anything except the one man he was looking for. What happened was the last thing we expected. Jairus went down in front of Jesus like a beggar, and stretched out his hands, and his voice was so low and hoarse that only those who stood very near could understand what he said. But the word went through the crowd. His daughter was dying. The only child he had. Then Jesus said—"

"No—tell me first what Joel said."

"Oh, Joel said, 'The only child he has, poor man. She is the apple of his eye.'"

"'The apple of his eye,'" Leah would repeat softly, caressing the words.

"Of course I felt sorry for him, but I thought too, what

a chance it was for Jesus. An important man like this—a ruler. I thought if Jesus could bargain with him—but of course he would never think of that. He only reached out his hand and helped the man up and started straight for Jairus' house. The crowd let them through and then flocked after like a bunch of sheep, and me along with them, because when a crowd like that starts to move you don't stop to think. I was curious as anyone to see what would happen.

"But halfway to the synagogue we saw a man hurrying along the street, and he met Jairus and Jesus and stopped them. I could not hear what he said, but I could see his face and I knew that he had bad news. They told me afterwards that he said the girl was dead and not to bother the teacher any more. But before Jairus could speak, Jesus put his hand on the man's arm and said something quietly, and they went on again, and all of us after.

"Then we heard the women wailing, and the flutes playing, and the women in the crowd began to howl too, out of sympathy, and Jesus turned around to us and said, 'Do not weep, she is not dead but sleeping.' And none of us knew what to think. The women at the door of the house were weeping and jeering at him, both at the same time. Then Jesus told the crowd to stay back, and he gave a sign to Simon and John and James, the three who are always nearest to him, and he took them into the house with him. And in a moment all the mourners who had been wailing in the house came out. Some of them were angry and some of them were frightened, but Jairus shut the door behind them."

"I wish you had gone inside," Leah would say now.

"Well, I couldn't, and neither could any of the others, except those three. We have only their word for what happened. They said the child lay on her bed, and they would have sworn too that she was dead. But Jesus did not hesitate at all, he just walked up to the bed, and reached down and took her hand and spoke to her."

"Tell me," Leah would whisper. "Tell me exactly what he said."

"He said, 'Little girl, get up.' Just as though she were asleep. And she woke and got up and walked.

"And then Jesus said, 'Give her something to eat,' and he went away, before her father or mother had a chance to say anything. When he came out to the street no one dared to ask what had happened because there was something about his face—I can't describe it, but I have seen him look like that at other times, as though he had come to the very end of his strength. Simon and John understand when he looks like that, and they got him through the crowd and back to their house, and everyone knew better than to try to follow."

"The little girl—she was really well?"

"Yes. I have seen her walking with her father. You'd never guess she had been ill."

"Is she pretty?"

"Yes," Daniel would say, although he had not actually noticed, because it seemed to please Leah to have her pretty.

"Yes," Leah would sigh. "Of course she must be pretty. And she must be very happy."

Daniel wished she would not keep asking for the story. It had seemed wonderful to him at the time, but it had a puzzling aspect as well. It hadn't seemed to make any difference. Some of the followers thought that Jairus had offered to pay Jesus and that Jesus had refused, and Daniel could not understand this when all those people were clamoring to be fed every night and Jairus would never have missed the money. At any rate, the thing had been hushed up, by Jesus' own order, they said. Some of the disciples had grumbled about it too. Simon, who had been in the house when it happened, would not talk about it at all. But Daniel noticed that Simon seldom went out in his boat now, that he stayed close to Jesus wherever he went. The fisherman watched his teacher more carefully than ever, protecting him from the carelessness of the crowd, and when Jesus spoke, Simon's eyes never left his face.

One day, as Daniel finished the story, Leah sat silent for a long time. "Do you think Jesus will ever come to our village?" she asked finally.

"He did once, and he may again."

"If he came here would there be a great crowd of people?"

"There always is, wherever he goes."

"Like the people who watched the day we came here?"

"You think that was a crowd? That was only a handful. Where Jesus is they come by hundreds." He could see she had no way of imagining people by hundreds.

"Do women come?"

"Of course."

"Do the people—crowd together and push each other?"

"It's all you can do to stay on your two feet sometimes."

She was silent so long that he thought she had stopped thinking about it. Then she asked, "Are there children too?"

"Oh yes, usually some children."

"Do they hurt the children?"

"Of course they don't. What gave you such an idea?"

"Jesus wouldn't let them hurt the children, would he?"

"He won't even let them send the children away when they're a nuisance. He insists on talking to them, and finding out their names, and listening to their foolishness. It makes some of the men furious—as though he thought children were important."

She sat silent for a long time, and this time Daniel asked, very carefully, "If he comes, will you go with me to see him?"

Leah did not speak, only lowered her head and hid her face behind her veil.

How changed she is, he thought, filled with hope as he looked at his sister. It must be Thacia's visits. For Thacia came often now, walking out from the city with Joel to stay with Leah while the boys met in the watchtower. Each time she brought some small gift, a lily bulb to plant in the garden, a tiny alabaster jar of perfume, a skein of scarlet thread. She had opened for Leah a whole new world.

After Thacia's last visit, he had come into the house and found Leah peering into the tiny hand mirror of polished bronze that had been Thacia's latest gift, peering so earnestly that she had not even heard him come in. There had been something in her face, a searching and a wistfulness that still haunted him. Sometimes, when he talked, she did not seem to hear him at all, but seemed to be listening intently for some expected sound. Often there was a dreaming look in her blue eyes. Twice when the first patter of early rain had passed like footsteps along the street outside, she had flown to the garden door and flung it open and stood looking out into the dark damp garden. Girls were strange creatures. Would Thacia understand all this? Perhaps it was only his imagining, but it stirred in him an odd uneasiness that he could not put into words.

There was another satisfaction in these days. As Daniel grew confident of the skill in his own hands, his work became a source of pleasure. It was satisfying to give a villager a pair of hinges for his house, and to know that they were not only strong and well balanced, but exactly matched and pleasing to look at as well. He became aware that something more than usefulness could take shape under his hammer, and he began to experiment.

One sultry afternoon when the work was slack, he picked from the floor a bit of bronze which had dropped from a molten mass. Seeing its dull shine between his fingers, he had an idea. He heated it carefully, pulled it from the fire with the smallest tongs, and tapped it gently with Simon's finest hammer. After several tries he achieved a stroke delicate enough so that it would not flatten the small lump, and presently he managed to beat out a fine wire. He heated it again, and twisted it between his fingers, and watched it slowly take the shape of a tiny slender bow, no longer than his little finger. For a moment he stared at it with pure pleasure. Then he had a further inspiration. He rolled out and sharpened a slender bronze pin which could pass down like an arrow between the bow and the fine wire of its string, so that the bow became a brooch such as he had seen the city folk wear to fasten their cloaks.

Then he hid his experiment away, half ashamed of it and half proud. He would keep it to remind him of his purpose.

He trains my hands for war,
    so that my arms can bend a bow of bronze . . .

170

He thought again of Jesus, and his hopes flared anew. Surely this man, like David of old, had the strength of God in him. If he willed, he could bend the bow of bronze. But was Jesus training his hands for war? Daniel was not sure. He must go back again that night to the garden in Bethsaida.

For Daniel the month of Ab was a time of waiting. It was only afterwards that he remembered these days as a time of quietness and hope.

I'll do anything, Daniel. You know that—anything!"
Joel's voice shook with earnestness. His eyes in the flickering lamplight were fixed on his friend's face. The three sat crouched in the narrow passageway of Joel's home.

Earlier that day Daniel had received a summons by messenger from Rosh. He had climbed to the cave, and then, after a brief conference, had gone straight to the city. Shortly before dark Joel and Thacia had crept through the passageway to join him.

Daniel brought with him the long awaited orders from Rosh to Joel. At first, waiting in the dark passageway, Daniel had battled with his own jealousy. That Joel should have the first chance to act, while he himself, the one who had brought Joel in as a recruit, should stand aside and wait! But now he was beginning to see the thing reasonably. This was only the beginning.

"Rosh needs some information," he told his eager friend. "You're the only one who can get it, Joel. You know your way around the city and everyone is used to seeing you. None of the rest of us could get near."

"What does Rosh want? I'll get it, whatever it is!"

Daniel told him, his voice echoing the contempt with which Galileans always spoke of the tetrarch—the half-Jew, Herod Antipas, who had been appointed to rule over them—and of the extravagant city he had built on the sea. "Herod is entertaining a special legation from Rome. While they're at Tiberias they plan to come up to Capernaum for a day or so to inspect the garrison here. For some people, the rich ones who toady to Rome, that will be a great occasion. Mattathias, the banker, is giving a banquet for the whole legation, and some of the richest men in Capernaum will be there."

"Mattathias would do anything to gain favor with the tetrarch," said Joel with scorn. "How does Rosh know about the banquet?"

"Don't ask me how. He has his own ways. What he wants to know is what others will be there. The names of all of them, and the day and the time when the banquet will take place."

Joel nodded. "I can see why. It would give us a good idea which men would be against us. Any Jew who would eat at the tetrarch's table—"

"That's it. We need to know our enemies as well as our friends."

"Is that all I have to do? Just find out those things?" Joel looked disappointed.

"You may not find it so easy. Rosh didn't have any idea how you'd go about it. He left all that to you."

"How will I get the word to Rosh?" asked Joel, looking flattered.

"I'll take care of that. Bring what you find to me, or send it by one of the band, someone we can trust. I'll see that it gets to Rosh."

Joel's eyes began to sparkle at the thought of intrigue. "Let's see," he began. "It doesn't really help that people know me here. That kind would hold their tongues because of Father. I don't think I'd find out a thing. Besides, Mattathias and father don't speak to each other. No, the servants are the ones to talk to. If I could get in to the servants—If I could sell something—"

"Fish!" Thacia broke in. "You could get all the fish you want from Simon and Andrew." At moments like this, caught up in the same excitement, the brother and sister were unmistakably twins.

"Good idea!" Joel flashed. "I'll get a basketful of extra fine ones, and peddle them for a good price. I can say I'll take orders for any special occasion. You know how the kitchen slaves talk about a party. I'm sure it would work!"

Struggling with envy again, Daniel sat silent. Joel was too excited to wonder why he, the youngest of the group, should have been given this assignment. The truth was, Daniel knew, Rosh had no one else to send. The band in the mountains boasted more muscle than wit. How far would he himself get, with his smith's shoulders and his country manners? Joel had to be the one.

Then, watching Joel's rapt flushed face, Daniel felt not envy, but unexpected misgiving. If anything went wrong? He glanced at Thacia. Her eyes met his, and in them he saw his own doubt suddenly mirrored.

"Joel," he said. "You don't have to do this. Rosh has no right to order you."

"Why hasn't he? If he asked you—?"

"It's different with me."

"Why is it different?"

"I'm a nobody. You have your future to think of, and your father and mother—and Thacia."

"No," said Thacia quickly, "not me. I took the oath with you, remember? Only—Daniel, is this a dangerous thing?"

"Stop fussing, both of you," said Joel, with new im-

174

portance. "Let me think. I can get the fish early, before it's light. But suppose Father finds out I'm not in school? Perhaps I could ask him for a holiday."

Thacia leaned forward. "Joel—I have an idea! What if you and Daniel were seen going out of the city tomorrow morning? Suppose you passed the guards and even spoke to them, so if we needed, people could swear they had seen you? Wouldn't that leave you free to do anything you like?"

Joel stared at his sister, and then his face came alive like hers. "Thace! Why didn't I think of it? Would you do it—honestly?"

"You know I would."

As always, Daniel was baffled by the swiftness with which these two caught up each other's thoughts and left him stumbling behind. "I don't see—" he said, annoyed.

Joel laughed. "We've done it plenty of times in the past just for the fun of it. When we were little and her hair was short we sometimes even fooled Father. Once Thace took a beating for me and never even opened her mouth. Of course, she's shorter now, but unless we stand side by side, who would notice?"

Daniel caught on. "You mean—?"

"Of course." Joel interrupted him as he did his sister, without realizing it. "Thace wears my clothes, and with her hair back under the turban I'll wager she could fool even you. Then you two go about together. "I'll arrange for a day off. You could go—oh—somewhere out of the city would be best."

"We'll go to visit Leah. I've been wanting to for days."

In the face of their enthusiasm, Daniel's scruples melted. Before he crept out of the passageway, and set out for the village, the three had agreed to meet next morning by the boats of Simon and Andrew.

Before dawn Daniel joined the farmers on the road to the city. At the harbor the usual crowd waited hopefully by the fishing boats. As he drew nearer, two boys moved from the rest and came to meet him. One was a sturdy barefoot fisherman in a rough cotton tunic, his throat and arms bare. The other made Daniel gasp. Beneath a close-bound turban was half hidden a second Joel, younger, smooth-faced, more finely-drawn, but with the same lustrous eyes. Thacia tipped back her head for Daniel's scrutiny in a gesture that reminded him of Leah.

"It's not quite so perfect as it used to be," she admitted cheerfully. "We'd better keep away from the market-place. Once out of town I'll be safe."

Both brother and sister were relishing their conspiracy. Their high spirits made his own doubts seem niggardly. Joel had already arranged for a consignment of fish and had them hidden under a half-upturned boat, packed under fresh green leaves in a woven basket. Presently he set off with a swaggering step and a wide grin. Then Thacia took control with a brisk efficiency that surprised Daniel.

"We'll go this way," she directed. "We won't be so likely to meet anyone."

"Aren't you going to wait?" Daniel asked, surprised. "Jesus will be here soon."

A slight cloud darkened her face. "No," she said. "Not this morning. I'd rather get out of the city."

"I thought you meant to be seen."

"Yes—well—I don't want to meet anyone face to face."

She hurried him along unfamiliar streets toward the gates of the city. For a time they walked in silence, and then Thacia spoke. "It isn't really that I'm afraid to be seen," she said honestly. "I didn't want to wait for Jesus. I didn't want to see his face when he saw me like this."

Daniel was surprised. Then he remembered, dimly, the ancient law that forbade a man and woman to wear each other's garments. "Are you worried about the Law?" he asked. "I don't think Jesus—"

"Oh—the Law!" she replied. "Joel and I have broken so many laws lately that one more wouldn't matter." She paused, embarrassed, because he must know that any laws she and Joel had broken had to do with their visits to Daniel's house. Then she hurried on. "It's just that I don't want to face Jesus with a lie. I couldn't bear the way his eyes would look at me."

"If he understood the reason he wouldn't blame you."

"Yes, I think he would," she said thoughtfully. "I think that for Jesus a lie is impossible, no matter what the reason."

"In war a lie is a weapon," said Daniel. "We have to use what weapons we have. Even Jesus must see that."

"I don't think he would see it at all," said Thacia. She walked on a little way, then she spoke again. "Daniel, what makes you and Joel so sure that Jesus means to make war?"

"He says that the kingdom is at hand. What else can he mean?"

"Did you ever think he might mean that the kingdom will come some other way? Without any fighting?"

"You mean just wait—forever—like your father says?"

Thacia's forehead wrinkled in an effort to put her thoughts into words. "Not exactly. You see, Jesus has made me see that we don't need to wait for God to care for us. He does that now. Every one of us. Jesus says

177

that God sees into our hearts and loves us. If everyone understood that—every man and woman—"

"Would that rid us of the Romans?"

"Suppose—the Romans too could understand?"

He stopped in the road and stared at her. "*Romans?* You think God loves the *Romans?*"

Thacia sighed. "That's impossible, I suppose. Then why does he say that we must love our enemies?"

"He is talking to men. A girl can't understand such things!" He said it rudely, and too loudly, because Thacia's words had come close to his own secret doubts. So loudly that two passers-by turned to stare at them, and Thacia lowered her head and hurried her steps. When she spoke again she changed the subject.

"This thing that Joel is doing—is it dangerous? I don't quite understand it. Why does Rosh want those names?"

"I don't think it's dangerous," he told her, not quite truthfully. "Joel thinks fast. Don't worry about him." The last part of her question he did not answer. He did not want to admit that he could not see why Rosh wanted the names.

Thacia was only too willing to accept his assurance, and at once she was confident again. They left the stone houses behind them, passed through the wall of Capernaum, taking special care to greet the sentries, and took the broad road that led north into the hills.

All at once Daniel's muscles tensed. He had seen, just ahead, two figures in the familiar metal helmets. Two soldiers rested beside the road, their heavy packs in the dust. One of them sat on the stone wall, his spear leaning beside him. The other was adjusting the strap of his sandal, but he glanced up now, and Daniel saw that it was too late even to consider turning back.

178

"They're sure to speak to us," he cautioned Thacia under his breath.

"What if they do?" she asked. "That's what I came for, to be seen."

"All the same, you let me do the talking."

The two soldiers watched their approach with interest. "The gods have done us a favor after all," one of them said. "Didn't I predict it?"

"It's more than you deserve," said the other. "But who's to question the gods? Here, boy!"

With a snap of his finger he indicated the two packs. A quick upward jerk of his elbow made his orders clear.

Black anger rose in Daniel. He knew well enough the law that allowed a Roman to command that a Jew carry his burden for one mile. But the man didn't live who could make him shoulder a Roman pack! He looked squarely at the soldier. Then he spat, deliberately. The blow across his mouth came instantly and staggeringly, but he did not lower his head. The second soldier got to his feet, easily, carelessly, his eyes watchful.

There was a stifled gasp. Then Thacia very quietly stepped forward and lifted one of the packs. It was heavier than she expected and she paused a second, then made another try, and hoisted it awkwardly to her shoulders. The soldiers waited. Daniel stood in helpless fury. Then, for the first time in his life, he bent his neck to the Roman yoke and picked up the second pack.

He wanted to weep for shame. The blood pounded in his temples. He did not know which he hated more, the two soldiers or the girl who walked beside him, who had tricked him into this humiliation. He looked at her from the corner of his eye. She was walking at a fair pace, only a slight stagger betraying the effort. Let her stumble. Let her fall, and see if he cared! In a moment he looked side-ways again. He saw the drops of moisture that clung to her forehead and trickled down her chin. Suddenly shame for her flooded over his own. Thacia!

"Put it down," he muttered, shifting closer to her. "I'll take mine on and come back for it."

"—nothing of the kind," she panted. "Keep quiet. Don't talk."

The two soldiers ambled behind them, chatting good-naturedly to each other, as though the two packbearers were mules. Finally they reached the milestone. By rights the soldiers could have made them go on, since they had taken the burdens well within the limits of the last stone. But Thacia's pace had become irksome, and it was obvious that though willing she could do no better. So the owner of her pack shouldered it himself, and less willingly the other let Daniel off also, with a parting blow on the ear for his sullenness. They strode ahead along the road, and Thacia sank down on the grass, rubbing her shoulder.

"Are you all right?" Daniel asked finally, not looking at her.

"No thanks to you. What possessed you, Daniel?"

Daniel scowled down at the road. "The very sight of them makes me lose my head. Filthy foreigners! If you hadn't been with me—"

"You'd have lost your silly head for good. How would that serve your country?"

"All right!" he burst out. "I made a fool of myself! Do you want to go back now?"

"Certainly not!" She sprang to her feet. "I want to see Leah."

They went on, Daniel keeping his eyes on the road

ahead. But presently, stealing a furtive look at the girl beside him, Daniel discovered that she was looking directly at him.

"I might as well be honest, Daniel," she said unexpectedly. "Back there—I was proud of you. Scared to death, but proud too. If I were a boy, I hope I'd have the courage."

The frank words took Daniel by surprise. He could feel the pleasure of them spreading, warm as wine, along his veins. He had never had much praise in his life. He didn't know what to make of it.

As they climbed the first rise from the plain, a breeze stirred their hot faces. On every side the land stretched, brown and parched under the summer sun. Here and there a solitary thresher still moved in a field, tossing the grain in great forkfuls into the air, letting the breeze catch the chaff while the heavy grain fell back to the ground.

Presently they reached the village. Outside his own door Daniel knocked and called out, and presently the bolt inside was quietly drawn back. As Daniel pushed open the door, Thacia stood back.

"I have brought a friend of yours with me," Daniel announced.

Leah, from the corner where she had retreated at the first glimpse of an unfamiliar figure, stared out into the road. Then her face lighted. "Thacia!" she cried. "Why are you dressed in Joel's clothes?"

Thacia came into the room laughing and pushing back the hot turban with relief. "It's lucky everyone doesn't have your sharp eyes," she said. "You won't give me away, will you? It's a—a sort of game we're playing."

Leah came forward slowly. "Daniel never plays games," she said soberly.

"What a pity," said Thacia lightly. "Joel and I pretend all sorts of things. But I'll tell you a secret. Your brother does know how to smile. Quite nicely, actually. He doesn't always hide behind that fearful scowl."

Unexpectedly, Leah giggled, and then both girls were laughing. Scowling more fiercely than ever, Daniel stamped into his shop. But he left the door open behind him.

In Thacia's lighthearted presence, Leah was a different girl altogether. As he worked, Daniel caught, between the hissing of the forge and the blows of his hammer, the sound of their voices, and over and over again Leah's soft laughter. When he crossed the room for a tool he could see them, the two heads, dark and fair, bent over a bit of sewing. He found a good many excuses for walking across the shop that morning.

At noon they ate their meal together. Leah spread out with pride the hard bread and the olives and the inferior dates, not knowing how meager the fare really was. With every bite Daniel remembered the fine white cloth, the damask couches, the wine in alabaster cups. But Thacia seemed to have forgotten. What was there about her? he wondered. A sort of naturalness that made her seem without the slightest effort to belong, no matter where she happened to be—on the mountain, in the luxury of her own home, among the fishing boats? Her gaity touched with a special grace everything around her.

Leah had begun to clear the dishes when some sound distracted her. Daniel, leaning back on his elbows, only half awake in the heavy heat, caught first the look on his sister's face. She was staring through the open door of the shop, and a deep flush was rising slowly from her throat to her pale temples. Daniel sat up. Then he caught the flash of sunlight on a helmet. The pleasure of the moment exploded like a bubble. In an instant he was on his feet, had flung himself into the shop, and slammed the door shut behind him.

He had thought he had seen the last of the blond Roman. What had brought the man back? Curse him too, for choosing to bring his work in the heat of the day. In a black humor, he blew up the fire.

When the shadows began to lengthen in the little room, they all knew with regret that the visit must end. Before they set out for the city, Daniel took Thacia into his shop.

"You have brought so many gifts to Leah," he said, trying to choose his words carefully. "Would you let me give one to you?"

He reached into a deep niche in the wall and drew out a small object wrapped in a fragment of Leah's blue cloth. Awkwardly, he laid in Thacia's hand the little brooch. "I made it with a bit of scrap," he said.

Thacia stood looking down at it. "A bronze bow!" she whispered.

"Do you remember? It was you who thought of it, that night—that the bronze bow might mean some impossible thing—the thing we could not do alone? I never forgot it. I don't know how to say it, but it came to stand for everything we are working for. For our oath. For the kingdom."

He had never seen Thacia before when she could not speak. He would remember as long as he lived the look that sprang into her eyes, and was quickly hidden as she bent her head.

Then her words came hurrying out. "To think that

you made it!" she exclaimed, her voice shaky. "Why, you ought to be a silversmith, Daniel. You shouldn't be working with these great chunks of iron!"

"I'd like to try," he confessed. "Perhaps some day, when we are at peace." It was the first time he had ever voiced his ambition, even to himself.

They set out together along the road, Thacia with the turban snugly about her head once more.

"Every time I come, Leah has changed," she told him. "It's like watching a flower opening very slowly. From week to week I can hardly wait to see how it has opened since I saw her last."

"It is due to you," Daniel told her humbly. "She has never had a friend before. After you leave, I see her trying to do things the way you do them."

Thacia smiled at him. "Little things," she said. "Her hair, and the way she folds her veil. That's not what I mean."

"She does almost all the work in the house now," he went on. "But there are days when she—goes back." He was grateful for a chance to speak of this to someone. "Days when she doesn't pay any attention. It's hard for me to have patience enough."

Thacia smiled again. "No, no one would ever take you for a patient man," she said. "But do you think Joel and I do not know what you have done for Leah?"

Daniel's gratitude went out to her. He would like to think he had done something to make up for those years.

"She is so lovely," Thacia went on thoughtfully. "I can't believe there are really any demons in her. Have you ever asked a physician?"

"The one in the village said there was no cure for her. Once there was a man traveling through the country who had magic power to heal, and my grandmother paid him to look at Leah. He could not do anything, either. He said that the demons that make a person afraid are the hardest to cast out. He said something queer. Leah was only a child, but he said that she did not want to be made well."

Thacia was silent for a moment. "I have heard Jesus say something like that, when people ask him to cure them. Once there was a lame man on a litter. Jesus bent over him and looked right into his face, and asked him, 'Do you want to be whole?' It seemed such a queer question. Why would anyone want to stay crippled?"

Daniel hesitated. This was something he had thought about, walking alone on the dark silent road from Bethsaida. He was not sure of his own thoughts. "Haven't you ever wondered," he attempted, "what good it is for them to be healed, those people that Jesus cures? They're happy at first. But what happens to them after that? What does a blind man think, when he has wanted for years to see, and then looks at his wife in rags and his children covered with sores? That lame man you saw— is he grateful now? Is it worth it to get on his feet and spend the rest of his life dragging burdens like a mule?"

"I never thought of it that way," said Thacia, her eyes clouding. "Is that why, do you think, that so many of them aren't cured?"

The thought was troubling to them both. They walked on in uncertain silence. Then Thacia's naturally happy spirits reasserted themselves.

"Have you thought, Daniel, of taking Leah to Jesus?"

"Yes, I've thought of it. But I don't see how I could get her to Capernaum without frightening her to death. She asked once if Jesus would ever come to our village. But I don't suppose she would really have the courage."

"When he comes, if she will not go to him, then you must ask him to come to your house with you. He often goes with people, you know."

"To the centurion's house, or to some rich man's."

"Do you really think that would make the slightest difference to Jesus?"

"No. No, I guess it wouldn't. But somehow I wonder. It's the same as the lame man. It's not much of a world, is it? Is it worth trying to bring Leah back into it?"

Thacia stood still in the road. "Yes!" she cried, and Daniel was astounded to see that tears had sprung into her eyes. "Oh Daniel—yes! If only I could make you see, somehow, that it is!"

"All this—" she exclaimed, the sweep of her arm including the deepening blue of the sky, the shining lake in the distance, the snow-covered mountain far to the north. "So much! You must look at it all, Daniel, not just at the unhappy things." Suddenly she reached out and touched his hand. "Look!" she whispered.

He lifted his head and followed her gaze. Overhead, barely discernible against the blue of the sky, a long gray shadow hung suspended. Cranes, hundreds of them, were passing in a great phalanx. They wheeled and caught the sun, flashing light from banks of white feathers, with a shimmering like the snow on the mountain. Motionless, the two watched till the line slowly melted into the distant air.

Thacia let out her breath. "How beautiful!" She sighed. "It is beautiful just to be alive in Galilee!"

Daniel looked down at her. Her head was still thrown back, her lips parted. He could see the pulse beating under the smooth ivory skin, and somehow the line of her throat was one with the long slow arc of the birds in flight.

She was aware all at once of his look, and then that their hands were joined. Red surged up into the smooth cheeks, and she drew her hand away. For a moment neither of them moved, and then they both began to hurry, almost to run.

At the junction of the road they passed two more Roman sentries, but this time the men did not speak or even take notice of two dusty boys. For once Daniel felt almost grateful to a Roman. Tonight he could not have born to watch Thacia shoulder a pack.

T HIS TIME," the villagers said, as Daniel halted the blows of his hammer, "Rosh has gone too far."

"How do you know it was Rosh?" Daniel inquired, keeping his eyes on the ax he was mending.

"Is there any other man in Galilee who would dare such a thing? Five of the wealthiest houses in the city robbed last night! But how would he find out? That's what I can't see. How would he know, off there on the mountain, that Mattathias was giving a banquet? Or which men would have taken half their slaves to make a showing? None of the rest of us even knew the tetrarch was coming."

"Then how can you think it was Rosh?"

"I don't have to think. The legionaries found out. Rosh might have got away with it, if he'd been satisfied with the loot from the houses. But no, he had to make a night of it."

Daniel started. Was there more to the story that had not yet reached him? Hand on the bellows, he waited.

"They tried the house of the centurion himself. He might have known the centurion wouldn't leave his house unguarded. Most likely the cutthroats got careless when they found the other houses such easy picking. Two of them were captured—both escaped convicts anyway, they say. One died as soon as they started to question him, but the other told, before they finally made an end of him."

Which? Daniel wondered sickly. Which of the men he had lived with side by side in the cave?

"I say they deserved what they got. Nothing but a pack of thieves up there, for all the fine talk we used to hear."

Not for a moment could Daniel let such a statement pass in his shop. "Rosh is no bandit," he said. "When he robs it is for a good purpose."

"So I've heard. Rob the rich to feed the poor. I'll be glad to see the poor that gets one penny of what he took last night."

"There may be more important needs," said Daniel.

"Like filling his own stomach? We'll see if he's satisfied now. We'll see if he lets our crops alone. I'll believe you when we can trust our sheep on the mountain."

Daniel started up the bellows and cut off the rest of the man's complaint. This was the third man since morning who had brought the news that had slithered out from the city like a swarm of snakes to every village round about. Some men praised Rosh's daring, elated to see the rich men defrauded. But more, like this man, were indignant.

At the first news, Daniel's spirits had soared. Then on the heels of rejoicing had come doubt. Now, at the end of the day, he felt dull and let down. This, then had been the reason for Joel's enterprise? A wholesale looting of rich men's houses. Somehow both boys had expected something more noble, more worthy of the cause. What did Joel think of it? Was it worth the hours lost from his study, the danger?

No question what Joel thought. That night the meeting in the watchtower was jubilant. Bit by bit the boys from the city had garnered every crumb of news to relate to the village boys. Joel was a hero twice over. Not only had he furnished all the information that had made the raid possible; he had even returned this morning to the very doors of the robbed houses, to listen to the full story from the unsuspecting kitchen slaves.

"I'm going to keep at it," he boasted. "It would be a shame to give up such an opening. I've got a special order from the centurion's head steward—two-dozen fish every second and fourth day of the week. There's no telling what I may chance on!" He was far too elated to notice Daniel's silence.

"Is Rosh in danger?" one of the boys asked. "The yellow rat who was caught—"

"Yellow?" another boy objected. "Do you know what the Romans do to a man? How long do you think you could keep quiet?"

There was an uncomfortable pause. This was a doubt they all faced in the night, in their own secret thoughts; they did not often speak of it.

"Don't worry about Rosh," Daniel assured them. "The Romans have had a price on Rosh's head for years. It's another matter to lay a finger on him."

Questions broke out again. What would Rosh do with the money? Would he buy arms with it? Would he divide it among the farms, maybe pay back for some of the sheep he had killed? There were so many needs for money. Daniel sat silent while they debated passionately the greatest needs for the stolen goods.

"Leave that to Rosh," he broke in finally. "It is for the cause."

The argument ended. They were perfectly satisfied. Looking at the circle of intense swarthy faces, at the flashing eyes, feeling the unquestioning loyalty that bound them all to Rosh, Daniel cursed his own heavy misgivings. Why could he not be satisfied with his own answer?

Nor were the villagers satisfied. Every day in the shop, in the marketplace, at the door of the synagogue, one heard the name of Rosh, sometimes bitterly condemned, sometimes as hotly defended. At last Rosh's name was on every lip, as he had once predicted. Some swore he was the defender of the Jews. But others pointed out that he had turned against Jews. But though they muttered, most men clung with blind faith to Rosh. They still looked to the mountain as the stronghold of freedom and hope.

The relay of messages which had succeeded so well, was now intensified. Joel threw himself into the role of fish peddler, and with experience he grew more shrewd in interpreting the bits of gossip, the signs of activity that he picked up in the doorways and kitchens of the city. Because he could not often leave home in the evening, other members of the band brought the messages to Daniel's shop. At night Joktan crept down the slopes like a jackal, across the cucumber field to the watchtower, and back to Rosh with the day's report. A mounting excitement filled the watchtower, where boys met nearly every night in the week. Here at last was something to do. Now they could see the results of their work.

For the results were never far behind. Rosh had acquired at last the link with the city for which he had waited. The boys had given him a weapon he needed, and he struck far and wide, with suddenness and cunning. Joel learned of a Galilean merchant who was expected to deliver seven cruses of oil to the centurion's household on the morrow. Though the merchant set out from his vineyard before dawn, neither he nor his oil was ever seen again. A bridegroom, son of the wealthiest elder in the synagogue, left the city with a gala party of his friends, laden with gifts, to claim his bride in Sepphoris. The bride waited in vain. Next day the whole party returned to their homes, clad only in their tunics, bereft of their handsome cloaks, their gifts, almost of their senses. A holiday party, returning late by torchlight from the games in the theater at Tiberias, was routed, stripped, and badly beaten.

For none of these victims did the boys feel the slightest pity. Any traitor who sold his goods to the Romans did so at his own risk. Those who flaunted their wealth or patronized a Roman theater were fair prey. And every cruse of oil, every silver talent swelled the fund that would soon maintain the army of Israel.

As Rosh grew bolder, caravans and travelers increased their protection. The mountain outlaws also suffered losses. Two more men fell into Roman hands, three were secretly buried after night attacks, and four more nursed wounds in the cave. Rosh needed more recruits. Thus it came about that the boys were admitted at last into Rosh's active service, and came to see the action they had craved. Not the trained army that Daniel had dreamed of marching to confront Rosh. Only a guerrilla force of nineteen eager boys. They met at the the watchtower, coming one by one, crawling on hands and knees through the tangled vines, to wait, on fire with impatience, for a summons from Rosh. Throughout the village there was a sudden rash of bandages. Boys limped with a swagger, leered smugly through purpled eyelids and grinned through swollen lips.

To harrass the Romans was their real delight. A pilfered bit of Roman equipment, a spur, a leather gauntlet, was a prize worth risking one's neck for. One city boy, who

192

had made off with a helmet even while a legionary who had laid it aside stooped to take a drink at the well, was almost as great a hero as Joel himself.

Much of all this Daniel watched with dismay. It was not for this sort of skirmishing that he had dreamed of raising a band. To him many of the exploits they boasted seemed childish. It had been his plan to wait, to train, to grow strong, and then to strike. This activity was like a fire lighted too soon. Would it burn itself out before the day had come?

But even he was proud of the catapult. Two boys brought word of it one evening, rushing into the shop out of breath.

"Right on the road they've left it!" one of them panted. "Only two guards. It's one of the big engines they used in the siege of Sepphoris. A wheel crumpled and they've had to leave it there till morning."

"I'll tell Rosh," said Daniel, laying down his hammer.

"Wait! Let's take care of this one ourselves," the other boy suggested. "What could Rosh do with a catapult? Come on, Daniel. We discovered this. Why can't we have some of the fun for ourselves?"

"We can stuff it with oiled rags and set fire to it! What a bonfire that would make!"

"Enough to be seen for miles," Daniel reminded him. "No use to burn good wood. We're in need of supplies, not bonfires."

"We'll take it apart, then," they decided. Before he could make up his mind, they had taken the lead out of his hands. The word went out. Hurriedly they scrambled together weapons, files from the shop, chisels, and mallets. One at a time, by various routes, they made their way to a point overlooking the Via Maris and looked down at the monster that crouched there like an unearthly beast in the darkness.

"What do you suppose they're moving that thing for?" someone whispered.

"I've a good idea," Daniel answered. "It's the kind of thing Herod used against the caves at Arbela."

"You think they'd dare to attack Rosh?"

"If he makes enough trouble for them."

"All the more reason," said the boy. "We'll do away with it."

"Wait," cautioned Daniel. "The guards are not to be killed. It would mean death in the village. I'll take one of them, Nathan takes the other, the way I've taught him."

Before the guard knew that anyone was near, Daniel had one arm about his throat. When the man lay, stunned and gagged, Daniel relieved him of spear and dagger. A moment later a sharp whistle announced that the second guard also was overcome. One by one, shadowy figures crept from the rocks and surrounded the monster. They worked silently, muffling under their cloaks the rasp of the file and the chipping of the chisel. Bit by bit, plank by plank, the monster shrank and crumpled. Over and over, during the long night, the boys retraced the devious path to the watchtower, staggering under heavy planks and crossbeams. When the sun rose next morning the catapult had disappeared without a trace. Nor did Roman offers of reward or threats of reprisal produce a single hint of its whereabouts.

The boys were wild with success. They swaggered through the village, taking little pains to hide their barked shins and blistered palms. Daniel tried to warn them.

"You will ruin everything," he urged. "This is only the beginning."

"Why?" they demanded. "Why can't we strike now? Look at the people. Would one of them give us away? They are just waiting. One word and they'll be with us. Why doesn't Rosh give the word?"

Joel sent warnings from the city. The Romans were strengthening their forces. A detachment of footguard had come up from Tiberias to join the garrison. The road patrol had been doubled. Even in the village unfamiliar soldiers strolled, apparently without purpose, their eyes alert under their helmets. Daniel insisted there would be no nightly activity for a time. The boys, chafing under the restraint, went scowling about the village. There was an explosive quality in the air.

One morning a shepherd hurried into town with word that three of the town flock had been snared and slaughtered. That morning two men visited Daniel's shop.

"They say you can get a message to Rosh if you choose," one began.

Daniel did not answer.

"If you can, tell him this: he is to leave our sheep alone."

"Do you begrudge a sheep now and then," asked Daniel quietly, "to the man who would give his life for your freedom?"

"We have had enough of his brand of freedom. He's free up there. Free from the taxes that bleed us dry. Free to play with the Romans while we stand and take the punishment. By the prophets, if you have any fondness for this savior of yours, warn him now. We have had enough."

Two days later a farmer, about to move with his family to man the watchtower in his field, came upon his near-ripened crop and found it plundered, trampled, wantonly ruined.

Dismayed, Daniel climbed the mountain to take the warning to Rosh, only to have Rosh laugh in his face.

"They are afraid of their own shadows," Rosh jeered. "What good are they but to raise food for men who will fight?"

"They are desperate," Daniel urged. "You know they cannot carry arms themselves. They are going to appeal to the centurion for protection. They want him to send legionaries."

"Let them come!" Rosh boasted. "Let them get a taste of the mountain. They will only break their teeth on it."

Daniel went back to the village sick at heart.

We must hurry, he thought with despair. The whole village is turning against him. If the day does not come soon, they will never follow him.

Late in the afternoon on the last day of the month of Ebul, Daniel, looking up from his work, saw a figure hurrying along the road, an unfamiliar figure, muffled in a heavy turban and moving with a haste that warned him of trouble. He put down his hammer and waited. It was only when the stranger entered the shadow of the doorway and pushed back the turban that he saw it was Thacia. Who could have imagined that Thacia could look like this—stricken, gray-faced, the wet hair clinging to her forehead?

"Oh Daniel!" she gasped. "They have taken Joel!"

"The soldiers?"

"Yes. Oh I knew—I knew from the beginning that this would happen. What can we do?"

I knew it too, he thought, with a wave of sickness. "Where is he?"

"In the garrison. He didn't come home all night. This morning I went to the harbor and couldn't find him. I didn't know what to do. So I went to Kemuel and he managed to find out. They have been suspecting the centurion's kitchen slaves. Yesterday five slaves were flogged, and when Joel came to the door they took him."

"Did Kemuel find out any more?"

"They're sending some prisoners east in the morning. They've sentenced Joel to go with them. Does that mean the galleys? Daniel—Joel could not live in the galleys—he—"

Through his own horror Daniel saw that the girl was close to collapse. Numbly he reached out and touched her shoulder.

"Rosh will have planned for this," he said. "He will know what to do."

At his touch she began to weep wildly, her hands covering her face. She has borne this all night, he thought, and all day. Has she eaten or rested?

Through the open door to his house he saw Leah, standing behind her loom, staring. How much had she understood? With one arm across her shoulders he led Thacia to the door.

"Take care of her," he said to his sister. "I'm going up the mountain."

Leah came from behind the loom and held out her arms, and Thacia stumbled into them. The golden head bent gently over the dark one.

In two hour's time Daniel reached the cave. The thorn fire was blazing, and the fragrance of roasted mutton hung in the air. The men who sprawled on the ground barely glanced at him. At the mouth of the cave Rosh sat, rubbing at a fine ivory-handled dagger. He listened, giving more attention to the blade than to Daniel's distraught message.

"He was getting too confident," he grunted.

"They can't know who he is," Daniel urged. "Joel would never let them know his father's name. They'll think he's only a fisherman. They won't be looking for an attack."

"Attack?" Rosh repeated coldly. "What are you talking about?"

198

"If we move fast, we can surprise them on the road."

"We?"

"All of us will help you. You can count on us."

"Speak for yourself," Rosh said. "It's not my affair."

Anger exploded in a red blaze before Daniel's eyes. "Joel was following your orders!" he shouted. "You're responsible for him."

Rosh still rubbed at the steel. "On this mountain every man is responsible for himself. That holds for Joel."

Daniel held back his rage. "Listen to me, Rosh." He struggled to speak reasonably. "Eight of us took Samson."

"From the Romans? Use your head. We took Samson from some scurvy traders. Roman soldiers—that's another matter."

Desperately Daniel tried a different tack. "Joel is important to us," he argued.

"Important? He was stupid enough to get caught. You think I can spare eight men—or one man—for that?"

Daniel's control gave way. "You'd just use him and then let him go? Without even a try—?"

Rosh squinted up at him. "I've warned you before," he said, his voice ugly. "There's a soft streak in you. Till you get rid of it you're no good to the cause."

The red mist of anger cleared suddenly from Daniel's mind. He looked at the man who had been his leader. He saw the coarsened face with its tangle of dirty beard. He saw the hard mouth, the calculating little eyes. He saw a man he had never really looked at before.

"The cause!" he said with despair. "How could you know what it means?"

Fury mottled the man's face. "Take care, you—"

"Don't threaten me," Daniel said. "I am not one of your men. Not any longer."

Rosh coiled back. "You fool!" he spat out. "How far could you get without me?"

Daniel looked steadily into the narrowed black eyes. In another moment Rosh would spring at him. At the prospect his hands clenched with savage pleasure. But his mind was in control now. He could not fight with Rosh. The very strength of his hands he owed to this man. And what good would it do Joel? He turned away without speaking, and passed through the ring of silent, wary men. He knew that he was through with the mountain for ever.

As he went down the trail footsteps came pounding after him. "Daniel—w-wait!" It was Joktan. "W-what are you going to do?"

"I'm going to get Joel."

"By yourself?"

"No. There are nineteen of us."

"T-twenty," said Joktan. He had drawn himself up to his last skinny inch. "Let me go with you!" he pleaded, before Daniel could refuse.

Daniel decided quickly. "Come then," he said. "You can't be worse off."

Even in his haste he felt a sharp disappointment and regret. He had hoped that the footsteps were Samson's. He would have liked to say good-bye to the big man, to clasp the man's hand, to try to tell him not to watch anymore. But this too he must put behind him.

He and Joktan had the trail to themselves. But as he went down, the uncanny feeling grew on him that someone was behind. Had Rosh sent someone to follow him? Time and again he whirled about, but he could see nothing. His skin kept prickling. He quickened his stride till Joktan was running to keep pace.

In the watchtower twelve boys waited in the darkness,

Before dawn the boys had found their position. In the darkness they had followed the shore road south past Magdala, striking inland to a place where the Via Maris, the road the Romans must follow to the coast, wound between steep, almost unscalable banks. There they worked their way painfully upward and hid behind rocky projections to rest. With the first light they ventured out, only one boy showing himself at a time, to collect the stones that would be their weapons. A very few carried spears and daggers. By the time the sun was fully risen, every boy was well fortified and concealed.

Even during the night there was traveling on this main road to the sea. During the early morning they counted five large caravans, with long files of burdened camels. Families, tradesmen, sometimes small detachments of soldiers passed beneath their hiding place. This had long ago been a dangerous section of road, but now travelers passed with confidence because, more than fifty years before, the great King Herod had wiped out the robbers who dwelt in the caves of Arbela, and now a Roman wall flanked the heights. So long had it been since bandits had inhabited this place that now Daniel dared gamble that the Romans would have no suspicion of attack.

On the steep cliff below where the boys were stationed,

making no sound. One by one others crawled through the field to join them. Kemuel had summoned every boy in the city.

"What is Rosh going to do?" they greeted Daniel, their faces sober.

They read the answer in his silence.

"Nothing?" Nathan cried out, incredulous. "After Joel has—" His voice broke.

The others stared at Daniel, too stunned and angry to speak. I have failed them all, he thought. They trusted me!

"What does it matter?" Kemuel suddenly lashed out with scorn. "We don't need your Rosh—your great leader! We'll do without him."

Tumult exploded in the watchtower, anger flaring instantly into new hope.

"Wait," Daniel silenced them. "Let's have one thing clear. Maybe some of you think as Rosh does—that every man answers only for himself."

"We answer for each other!" Nathan spoke swiftly. A dozen voices echoed him with passion. Kemuel cut sharply across the clamor.

"Do you have a plan?"

"Yes," said Daniel. At once every boy was quiet.

"For nineteen against a Roman force?"

"Twenty," said Daniel, his hand on Joktan's shoulder. "If we use our heads, we can make twenty count for a hundred. We won't try to fight them. We will only get Joel."

"How?" Confidence had come back to their voices.

"On the road." Daniel's mind was working clearly now. "We can't break into the garrison. We can't afford to meet the Romans face to face. We can go south, beyond

Magdala, and wait in the pass near Arbela. On the cliff we can spread out and throw down rocks so that they won't know how many we are. The Romans have no reason to expect an attack. When we have stirred up as much confusion as we can, then we take Joel."

"How?" they questioned. "He will be chained."

"That's a blacksmith's job."

There was a silence. "One cannot do that alone," said Nathan. "I'll go down with you."

"Before we go on," said Daniel, "we must have a leader. Up till now we have all been equal."

"We have already chosen," said another boy. "You have always been the leader."

"Not by a vote."

"There's no need to vote," said Nathan. "Does anyone here question who is our leader?" Not a whisper challenged him.

"Then you will obey my orders," said Daniel sternly. He felt no pride or glory that he was their leader, as he had once dreamed. Only a cold heaviness.

"The time has not come to fight the Romans," he told them. "We have no right to waste lives that are needed for the cause. Even for Joel. You are to stay on the cliff and distract the soldiers while I free Joel from the chains. Then you will all retreat as fast as you can. I don't think the Romans will follow. They'll be leery of a trap."

This time they kept silent, not questioning his command.

"Take all the weapons you have," he ordered. "We'll start now and find our place." He hesitated, feeling awkward but compelled to speak. "Joel is the one who has always read us the scriptures. Now we'll have to remember the things he has read. Judas and Jonathan and Simon

202

went out with a few against the enemy. We can do it too. The same God will strengthen us."

In the darkness each boy reached out and clasped the hand of the one nearest him. "For God's Victory," they said together solemnly.

203

Daniel found the spot best suited to his own purpose. A fissure in the rock extended in an oblique line down the face of the rock, wide and deep enough in some parts to hide several men, ending on a narrow shelf barely ten feet above the road. In the crevice that dipped below the level of the rocky shelf he posted Nathan and Kemuel.

"I'll free Joel and lift him up to you," he told them. "You reach down and pull him up. If any soldiers follow, use your spears. Only one can climb up at a time, and I think the second will think twice before he tries."

"How do you get back?" Nathan asked, looking closely at Daniel.

"When Joel is up, then give me a hand," Daniel answered. He had no real expectation that he would get back up the bank, but he meant to see, with the last ounce of his strength, that Joel did. Nathan opened his mouth, then closed it, seeing in Daniel's eye a reminder that they had chosen a leader.

Through the noonday heat they waited, their energy draining away bit by bit under the merciless sun. As the hours went by, Daniel's foreboding deepened. This waiting was not the same as the times he had crouched behind a rock eager for Rosh's signal. It was no flimsily-guarded caravan they awaited. And behind him was no tight-knit band that would move with precision and cunning, only a cluster of untried boys. Even now, as he glanced up, the flutter of a coatsleeve betrayed one of them. Still, he could count on them. He knew that every boy in the band was prepared to give his life. It was up to him, the one they had chosen leader, to see that none of them had to.

But how different this was from the glorious battle they had hoped for! Would the day ever come when together

205

they could pit their strength against the Romans for God's Victory? Daniel put that thought aside. A more immediate worry was the uneasiness that had persisted all night, the feeling that he was followed and watched, even in the darkness. Could it be that in setting a trap for the Romans he had led his band into some other trap? Almost, he was tempted to call them back. But there was Joel.

At midafternoon Joktan brought the warning. He alone, of all the band, was trained to this kind of attack. He wriggled and dodged his way along the roadside and skinned up the cliff into the crevice.

"Horsemen!" he gasped. "About e-eight. Then footsoldiers. Then the prisoners."

"Did you see Joel?"

"No. Too far away. But they've come a distance. The horses are lathered."

Daniel gave two sharp whistles, the alert they had arranged, and looked up at the bank.

"Climb up there, will you?" he growled to Joktan, pointing. "Tell whoever that is to pull in his rump before he gets a javelin in it." That would get Joktan also above the danger line, he reckoned.

The first horsemen swung into view, moving slowly to keep pace with the footmen. The cavalry rode in pairs, their spurs almost touching in the narrow pass, erect, silent, the plumes of their helmets rising and falling with the horses' pace.

Would the others remember? The horsemen were to go through. Daniel tensed. He felt a vast relief as not a sound or motion betrayed the boys on the cliff. Behind the horsemen came the footsoldiers, in a double line. He watched them pass, one steely face after another. He counted sixteen. Then shuffled the prisoners, chained to-

206

gether by the ankles in a long line. Joel was the fifth, barefoot, disheveled, his feet dragging. Between him and the rock marched a guard with a heavy whip. Behind the prisoners there would be more footsoldiers.

Daniel held his breath. When Joel was nearly below him he gave the signal. The first rock hurtled through the air and found a mark. A footsoldier stumbled. Instantly the air was flecked with rocks. An order crackled back across the line. As one man, the Romans raised their shields above their heads. Four men broke from the rank and charged up the almost vertical rock. A stone caught the first in the chest and sent him reeling back. A spear struck the second cleanly. But the line behind them resealed itself into an unbroken, purposeful unit. Daniel's heart sank. He had guessed wrong. The Romans were going to charge the bank, and the boys could not possibly hold them back for long.

But in the same instant as his shout for retreat, a thunder drowned out his voice. Jerking back his head, Daniel saw with horror the great rock that teetered on the opposite bank, ripped from the cliffside, and crashed down, gathering speed and force, carrying with it a roar of dirt and stones. Stupified, he watched the leaping, frenzied soldiers. There had been no one on the other bank. What had dislodged the rock?

Then he glimpsed a shape, huge, crouched like an animal, dodging on all fours along the bank. For one flash he saw the powerful arms, the massive dark head. Samson! But how——?

Abruptly he came to his senses. Now was his chance. With a thrust of his arms, he pulled himself up to the shelf of rock and leaped. As his feet found the path, he sank his dagger below the shoulder of the guard, and as the man crumpled, dropped to his knees before Joel, pulled out his chisel, and reached for the chain. The first blow of the sharpened tool left a nick in the iron. He struck again, and saw the nick deepen.

Confusion swelled around him. The prisoners were screaming now. He heard a second thudding roar, but he did not look up. As he raised his arm for a third blow, he felt himself seized from behind, in a paralyzing grip, lifted clear off the ground, jerked upward like a helpless sack. For an instant he hung in the air, and then he struck against the rock. Pain whirled him in crazy circles, and through the pain he felt hands clutching and pulling, scraping his flesh along the rock. A heavy body struck squarely on top of him. Legs thrashed about his head, and blackness crashed down on him.

He came out of the blackness into the blinding sun. There was rock under him, and pain zigzagged through his body. He blinked, trying to focus through the glare. Near him he made out a figure—Joel—sitting with his knees drawn up, his face buried in his arms.

"Don't move!" a voice warned. Kemuel's face blocked out the sky. "They've about cleared out."

Memory came back suddenly. He jerked up, and sank back again, helpless against the pain. He saw now that he was in the crevice of rock, but higher up the bank.

"Careful!" Kemuel warned. "You've got a broken shoulder bone, I think. Maybe a couple of broken ribs. Joel was luckier. He landed on top of you. He's got hardly a scratch."

Daniel's hand groped for his head. It had an unfamiliar shape.

"My irons hit you," Joel said, his voice sounding weak and dull.

"Good thing," Kemuel spoke to Joel. "How could I have got him up here?"

Daniel pulled himself up. "The soldiers—?"

"Gone. But there may be a guard."

"They didn't come up the bank?"

"No. I think the leader went down with that rock. They never got organized again."

The rock! "Samson!" Daniel cried out, remembering. "I saw him up there!"

Joel and Kemuel looked at each other.

Daniel tried to shake his mind clear. "How did we get up here? We were on the road—"

Neither boy spoke for a moment. "You didn't see?" Joel asked finally.

"Not after they jumped on me."

"Not the soldiers," Joel said. "It was Samson. I thought at first it was another slide coming down, and then he was there. He threw you onto the rock. Right over his head. Then he got hold of my chain and twisted it open with his bare hands, and he pulled me free and threw me up on top of you. Nathan and Kemuel pulled us down inside."

It was Samson who had lifted him. And Samson who had been following all night, not knowing what they were going to do, but knowing that they could not do it alone. And Samson—the stupid one—who had hidden on the other bank and routed the soldiers. Daniel stared sickly back at Joel. He made himself ask, "Where is he?"

Joel's eyes met his squarely. "They took him. He was wounded. A spear hit him even before he had the chain open."

"He might be still—"

"No," said Kemuel. "They dragged him with them.

209

He didn't even fight them. He was—you don't need to worry about the galleys, Daniel. He won't live to reach the coast."

Daniel turned his head away. Then he saw Nathan, sprawled with his face against the rock, the blood gathered in a blackened pool beneath him.

"He leaned too far out to pull you down," said Kemuel.

Nathan, whose bride of a few weeks waited in his new house!

A sob suddenly twisted Joel. "Why did you do it?" he choked. "I'd rather—you should have let me—"

"How many others?" Daniel asked.

"We couldn't see the others. Can you walk, do you think? We can climb back to where we planned to meet."

"I can walk," said Daniel.

Crawling, wriggling along the crevice, pulling themselves by fingers and toes, they finally reached the top of the cliff. Daniel lay panting, almost blinded again by pain. When he was able to look about him, he saw that five gray-faced boys lay flat on the cliff's top.

During the next endless hour, twelve more slowly wriggled their way to the meeting place. Finally they were all together, all but Nathan. They lay in hiding till sundown, not talking much. After the darkness fell, four of them went down to the crevice for Nathan's body. They could not hope to take him home with them, so they made a grave on the cliff and left him there. Then slowly, wearily, one at a time, they crept down to the road and made their way north like ordinary travelers. They shared a deep thankfulness that Joel was with them. But the might of Rome, seen close at hand, had shaken them. They knew that without Samson they would have failed, and the eager confidence of the night before would never be regained.

THE MONTH OF TISHRI brought the first autumn rains.
The parched brown fields drank in the moisture. The
soil fell back, dark red behind the plow, rich for the fall
sowing. In the roads, after a sudden shower, the puddles
shone like pools of melted lead.

There were no meetings in the watchtower now. The
boys of the band moved cautiously, not daring to be seen
too frequently with each other. Soon, they whispered as
they passed, they would begin again. They would build
up once more their store of weapons. They would make
ready for the day to come. But there was no eagerness in
the whispers. They knew in their hearts that the day
would not be soon. They had lost faith in the mountain.

In the steaming dimness of his shop, Daniel labored to
the limits of each day's strength. Unable to lift the hammer, he filled his time with light tasks, filing, smoothing
and polishing, trying to ignore the pain in his shoulder.
He cursed the pile of untouched work. He longed to
beat a wall of furious sound against his own thoughts. At
night, in the roof shelter he now shared with Joktan, he
drew his cloak over his head and fell into an exhausted
slumber. But always, during the long hours, he woke to
the slashing of rain, and then the pain could not be ignored, and the thoughts were louder than ever.

In the darkness the same words echoed over and over. "They who live by the sword will perish by the sword." At first he could not recall where he had heard these words. They did not sound like Joel's scriptures. Then he remembered. Jesus had spoken them on a hot summer morning under a blue sky. Daniel had not questioned the words. To live by the sword was the best life he knew. To take the sword for his country's freedom and to perish by it—what better could a man hope for? But something he had not reckoned on had happened. He had taken the sword, but Samson, instead, had perished by it, who had no freedom to gain, and Nathan, who had left behind a bride. Their deaths were on his head. And freedom was farther away than before.

Without the help of Joktan he could not have managed. The boy, who had come back to the village with him, could not do enough to prove his gratitude. Having never in all his memory had a house to live in, Joktan was not at all troubled that he could not enter Simon's house. He was content to eat his meals in the shop or on the doorstep where he could greet the passers-by. Far from missing the freedom of the mountain, he took naturally to village life. He went cheerfully every morning to the well for water, shrugging off the good-natured jibes of the girls. He delivered the work, making new friends everywhere with his jagged-toothed grin. Daniel's customers took the boy for a new apprentice and praised his willingness, though they doubted that with his puny arms he could ever make a blacksmith.

Nine days had gone by since Joel and Thacia had returned to Capernaum, and no word had come from them. Day after day his friend's silence grew heavier to bear. Was Joel in danger? What were Joel's thoughts in the night? Did he regret now the vow he had taken? Had the feel of the Roman chains shaken his purpose?

Late one evening, as he was about to climb to the roof-top, there was a knock on the door of the shop. Lighting a second saucer of oil, Daniel went through the house door, and drew back the bolt. A stranger, heavily muf-fled in a dripping cloak, pushed in quickly, and shut the door behind him. With a rush of thankfulness Daniel saw that it was Joel. He could only clasp his friend's hand without speaking.

"Did you think I wouldn't come?" Joel asked with sur-prise. "It seemed wiser to wait."

"You are watched?"

"I'm afraid so. I've been out only once, on the Sabbath. Coming home from the synagogue with Father I met a steward of the centurion's. He recognized me, but I think he was not sure. So Father wouldn't let me go out again."

"Your father knows?"

"I couldn't keep it from him any longer. I told him everything, about the passageway, and the meetings, and my part in Rosh's work. I owed Father that, Daniel. When I saw how he had grown older in those two days—"

Joel had grown older too. His face had a new purpose.

"How he must despise me!" Daniel said with shame.

"For saving me? He sent you a message. He says you are not to hide in the passageway again. You're to come to the house whenever you like. In a way I wish he hadn't tried so hard to forgive us. It would have been easier tonight."

"Tonight?"

"I left without telling him. I'm not going back. If I

214

can't stay here with you I'll go to the mountain and join Rosh."

In a burst of relief and joy, Daniel forgot every doubt. How could he have thought that Joel would forget his vow? Now, working together, they could accomplish anything. The band would go on again, stronger than before. But almost at once a new doubt clouded out his pleasure.

"Why did you leave home, Joel? The band has never asked that of anyone."

"I can't stay at home. Father is terrified to let me go out the door. I knew he was making some plan. Then today he told me I was to go to Jerusalem—tomorrow morning—with a friend of his. He's arranged for me to study in a school there. So I had to get away quickly."

Daniel stood looking at his friend, his mind troubled. "School in Jerusalem?" he asked soberly. "Isn't that what you always wanted?"

Joel did not quite meet his eye. "I used to," he admitted. "That was before we started the band."

"Don't you still want it?"

"I want to work for the Victory. I've vowed to. If you can't have me—if it isn't safe—then I'll go to the mountain."

"Rosh is no longer our leader," said Daniel.

Joel hesitated, then said very earnestly. "You must not break with Rosh because of me."

"It would have happened anyway," Daniel answered. "I've had a lot of time to think these past days. Somehow we've been going in the wrong direction. The things we've been doing for Rosh weren't what we planned when we started the band. Attacking people on the road,

215

especially our own people, isn't going to bring the day any closer. We haven't weakened Rome at all. We've only weakened ourselves instead. We have lost Nathan and Samson. We almost lost you."

Joel was silent a moment. "A new leader will come," he said. "We must go on making ready."

"Yes," said Daniel. Hearing Joel say it had given him back the hope he had almost lost. Now he was able to say the thing he knew he must say. "But until he comes, Joel, you must go on studying. That's what you are suited for. When the day comes, we're going to need more than farmers and laborers. We'll need the priests and the scribes too, and you can win them over because you understand them."

Joel had never been able to hide his thoughts. Now he could not conceal the hope that sprang into his eyes. "That's what Thacia said," he admitted. "Are you sure you mean this, Daniel?"

"I'm sure."

"What will the others think?"

"They have chosen me leader."

Joel thought for a moment. "I'd like to do it for Father's sake too," he admitted finally. "He's a good man, Daniel. You can't know how good he is, because you've only seen his narrow side. I know that I have hurt him. He wanted to be proud of me. A son who died for Israel—even a Zealot—he could be proud of that. But that day on the road—with the chains on—I knew that I had left him nothing, nothing at all to be proud of. Now you—you and Samson and Nathan—have given me another chance. I'll never forget that. I'll do my best to make up for it."

"Can you get back safely tonight?"

"I think so. But there are some things I must say first. For one thing, I brought a gift from Thacia to Leah. She won't be able to come here alone. Right now she's forbidden to leave the house at all."

"Leah will be grateful," Daniel managed, trying to hide his dismay.

Joel hesitated. "Do you think Leah would let me give it to her myself?" he asked.

"You can try," Daniel answered doubtfully. "She has seen you often through the door."

He opened the door to the house. Leah, sitting in the lamplight, raised her golden head. "Joel has brought you a gift from Thacia," he said. He waited. Behind him Joel stood quietly in the doorway. Leah seemed to shrink into a tight mold of fear. He could see her quiver, but she did not move, only watched with terrified blue eyes.

"Thacia sent her greetings," Joel spoke very gently. "She asks you not to forget her, and she will come to see you as soon as she can." He reached out and softly laid a packet on the chest near the door. Then he backed into the shop and Daniel followed him.

"You realize," Daniel said with wonder, "that you're the only person who has been inside that door, ever, except for your sister?"

"Thacia told me to try. Leah is very lovely, Daniel. I wish—Thacia sent you a message too, by the way."

Daniel felt his cheeks grow hot.

"Four days from today is the Day of Atonement. First the fast, of course, and then the service at the synagogue. Why—I never thought—I'll see it at the Temple in Jerusalem! I can't believe it! But I'll miss the festival here in Capernaum. The girls will dance and sing in the vineyard. Will you come to town for it?"

217

"I wouldn't know how to behave," Daniel protested.

"Think it over. It would please Thacia. Now, the other thing is about Leah. Thacia and I want you to know that you never need to be worried about leaving her, because we will take care of her. When the day comes, if you ever have to go away, Thacia will come—or even better, we would like to have Leah safe in our own house."

He hurried on, while Daniel groped for words to thank him. "Thacia is very fond of Leah. She'll miss her. Thace is going to be lonely, I'm afraid."

Daniel looked down at his hands.

"Father regrets now that he's allowed her so much freedom to go about with me. Thace is spoiled. She isn't used to staying at home the way most girls do."

It will be like caging a wild bird from the mountain, Daniel thought.

Joel looked away then, into a far corner of the shop. "Father wants to arrange a marriage for her," he said.

Daniel was not even aware that his hands reached out or that his knuckles whitened around a hammer handle.

"There is an old friend of the family," Joel went on. "But Thacia won't hear of it. It puts Father in a hard position, because, no matter how he regrets it, he is bound by his own promise. You see, it's different with our family. When our mother was only eight years old she was betrothed. But when she was fifteen my father, who was a poor student, came to do some work in her father's library, and they fell in love. It caused a terrible uproar. Her father was furious. He had to get divorce papers from the boy she had never even laid eyes on. She and Father promised each other then that they would never arrange marriages for their children against their will,

218

that they would let us choose for ourselves."

Daniel did not dare to look at his friend.

"The trouble is," Joel said. "Thacia is sixteen years old, and she refuses to choose."

Still Daniel could not look up. He knew that Joel had spoken straight from his heart, with the impulsive frankness that would always be Joel's way. But he knew too that his friend's loyalty had always blinded him to the truth.

"She must choose," he burst out now, too harshly. "Someone of her own kind. Your father is right. And you will have to choose too, before long."

"And you?" Joel asked quietly.

"I have no choice. How can a man who is sworn to vengeance and death take a wife?"

The angry words echoed in a silence that neither of them could seem to break.

"One more thing," Joel said finally, with an effort. "It is Jesus. Somehow he must be warned. He has enemies everywhere."

"You mean Herod's men?" asked Daniel, relieved that Joel had turned to a safe subject.

"He knows about those. I mean the elders of the synagogue. The rabbis and the scribes. They can't understand him. They're furious at the things he says and does. He is too free with the Law. They say he is trying to destroy all the authority of the Temple. Some of them even say he is in league with the devil."

"Does it matter what they say? Jesus pays no attention."

"He must pay attention now. Some of them hate him so much—I think they would kill him if they could. Will you try to warn him?"

"Simon says he has been warned, time and time again."

"Go to see him, Daniel. I wish—but it's too late for me now. Perhaps we made a mistake. Maybe Jesus is really the leader we're waiting for."

Then he straightened his shoulders and held out his hand. "Don't forget the festival, anyway," he said. "Thace will be looking for you."

The two clasped hands. "For God's Victory," they said. Then Joel drew his cloak about his face and went out into the darkness.

It is the end of everything, Daniel thought, looking at the closed door. The end of everything we worked for. For the first time he despaired that the day would ever come.

It was good of you to come, Daniel. But do you think Jesus does not know all this?"

Annoyed, Daniel looked back at Simon. He had walked all the way from the village at the end of a long day's work. Twice a slanting rush of rain had drenched him to the skin, and the night air, heavy with fog, had only chilled him and not dried the clothing that clung to his body. He had fought his way through the tattered crowd in the garden, and now that he had reached the door they refused to let him approach Jesus. The teacher, they explained, was conferring with important men who had come all the way from Jerusalem to question him. Now Simon brushed off Joel's urgent warning with no more than a shrug.

"Forgive me, Daniel," Simon said now, seeing that he had offended his young friend. "We are worried too. These priests from Judea—they haven't given him a moment's peace for three days. They pretend to be so respectful, and they're only trying to trap him into saying something they can prove is blasphemy. It keeps us all on edge."

"Why does he stay here if he knows he is in danger?

Why doesn't he hide till he's strong enough?"

"The people need him. Come another time, Daniel. I cannot talk tonight."

With the door shut against him, Daniel stood in the crowded garden. He wanted desperately to see Jesus. He knew now that the warning had been only an excuse. If he could have one word, one sign from Jesus, he might find the strength to go on working.

For a long time he waited, lost in his own misery. Finally Andrew came to the door of the house and looked out. "No use to wait," he called to the wretched crowd. "The master is very weary. He can see no one else tonight."

A wailing filled the garden. Then gradually the sick and the lame, convinced that the man had meant what he said, began to hobble back toward the road. A few simply settled themselves on the damp ground, having no other place to spend the night. Presently the door opened again, and Simon and Andrew and Jesus came out into the garden. They moved slowly and Jesus spoke kindly to those who obstructed the way, touching them sometimes with a pitying hand. Firmly, the two disciples pushed a way for their master to the outside staircase that led to the upper room. They stood watching till Jesus, carrying a small night light, ascended the stairs, went into the shelter, and closed the door behind him.

It was dark in the garden. When the disciples had gone back into the house, Daniel moved forward and stood at the foot of the staircase. He could not bear to go away.

He was sure he had not made any sound, but over his head the door opened. "Who is there?" Jesus spoke. He raised the lamp.

Daniel did not dare to speak, but almost without thought he moved into the small circle cast by the lamp and raised his head till the light fell upon his face.

"Come up, my friend," said Jesus softly.

The upper chamber was completely bare and clean. On the floor was unrolled the thin mattress on which Jesus was to sleep.

"Sit down," said Jesus, and he himself sat, opposite Daniel, on the floor of rolled earth. "Why are you troubled?" he asked.

"I came to warn you," Daniel hurried into his errand. "Joel says you are in danger. He says they have turned against you in the synagogue. He's afraid they will try to kill you."

"Thank you," said Jesus gravely. "It is kind of you and Joel. Now, tell me, why are you troubled?"

Shamed, aware that he should not disturb the master's rest, Daniel sat struggling with his conscience. Then his misery spilled over. "Because I don't know where to turn. Everything has failed. Everything I hoped and lived for."

"What did you live for?"

"Just one thing. Freedom for my people. And vengeance for my father's death."

"Two things," said Jesus. "Not one."

"They are the same. I will strike for both at once."

"Are you sure?" Jesus asked.

The familiar tightness pulled at Daniel's mouth. He had come for help, not questions.

"All I wanted was a chance!" he went on. "I thought it had come at last, and I worked and planned for it. Then it all went wrong somehow. All I have is another debt to pay—Samson."

223

Jesus was silent for a moment. "This Samson," he asked, "he was your friend?"

The question surprised Daniel. He had thought of Samson as a burden, as a symbol of his own weakness. He had never thought of Samson as a friend, but now he saw that it was true.

"He died for me. He didn't understand about Israel or the kingdom. He just died, without any idea what we were fighting about." Then, heedless of the master's weariness, forgetting everything but the guilt that had tormented him every moment since the day of the rescue, he poured out the story of Rosh, of the betrayal on the mountain, of Nathan's death, and the debt that Samson's sacrifice had laid upon him.

"Yes," said Jesus slowly. "An eye for an eye. A tooth for a tooth. It is so written. We must repay in kind. But Samson has given you all that he had. In what kind can you repay him?"

"By vengeance!"

"He did not give you vengeance. He gave you love. There is no greater love than that, that a man should lay down his life for his friend. Think, Daniel, can you repay such love with hate?"

"It's too late to love Samson. He is probably dead." Then, as Jesus waited, "Should I love the Romans who killed him?" he asked with bitterness.

Jesus smiled. "You think that is impossible, don't you? Can't you see, Daniel, it is hate that is the enemy? Not men. Hate does not die with killing. It only springs up a hundredfold. The only thing stronger than hate is love."

The boy lowered his head, scowling at the floor. This was not what he had come to find. With terror, he pushed away the words that struck treacherously into his own weakness. When he looked up again, Jesus sat with his head bowed, one hand across his eyes. Every line of his body showed his urgent need to rest. Daniel felt a stab of conscience. But his own need was too great. He had to speak.

"I don't understand," he pleaded. "But I know that you could save us all if you would. Master! Why will you not lead us? There are so many—hundreds—thousands—in Galilee, who only wait for a word. How long must we wait?"

Jesus did not seem to have heard. He did not move. Slowly Daniel got to his feet. As his hand touched the latch, Jesus spoke. He had risen too, and stood looking after the boy.

"Daniel," he said. "I would have you follow me."

"Master!" A great burst of hope almost swept him to his knees. "I will fight for you to the end!"

Jesus smiled at him gently. "My loyal friend," he said, "I would ask something much harder than that. Would you love for me to the end?"

Baffled, Daniel felt the hope slipping away. "I don't understand," he said again. "You tell people about the kingdom. Are we not to fight for it?"

"The kingdom is only bought at a great price," Jesus said. "There was one who came just yesterday and wanted to follow me. He was very rich, and when I asked him to give up his wealth, he went away."

"I will give you everything I have!"

Something almost like a twinkle of humor lighted for an instant the sadness of Jesus' eyes. "Riches are not keeping you from the kingdom," he said. "You must give up your hate."

Daniel felt himself trembling. He was torn in two.

Before the appeal in the man's eyes he felt the whole fabric of his life about to give way, and the very ground beneath his feet like shifting sand. He summoned all his strength to battle for the thing that was most precious to him.

"I made a vow before God!" he defied Jesus. "Is not a vow sacred?"

Jesus looked at him steadily, with a look he knew he would never forget, full of sadness, and regret, and a deep loneliness beyond any reach.

"Yes," he said. "It is sacred. What did you vow, Daniel?"

"To fight!" Daniel stopped, remembering the night in the passage, seeing Joel's face, trying to remember the exact words they had spoken. Thacia's voice came back to him. "To live and to die for God's Victory!"

A smile suddenly transformed Jesus' face, the old smile, radiant, full of youth and strength. He put his hand on Daniel's shoulder.

"That is not a vow of hate," he said. "Go in peace, my son. You are not far from the kingdom."

ON THE FIFTEENTH DAY of Tishri, the Day of Atonement, Daniel stood in the door of his shop. Even so early the holiday spirit stirred the narrow street like a fresh breeze. No one in the village appeared to be working. Pious Jews moved with dignity toward the synagogue, looking with disdain on the frivolous folk who took the occasion for an idle holiday. Voices and laughter sounded across the housetops.

Joktan squatted on the doorstep gnawing at the flat wheaten loaf that Daniel had brought out to him. "The apprentices have the day off," he remarked, eying Daniel hopefully.

"Go ahead then," said Daniel. "There'll be little business today." When Joktan had scampered off, he turned back to his forge. Through the morning hours he stuck dourly at his work, trying to ignore the tug of restlessness in the air. Once temptation had come from the distant mountain. This time it came from the city in the plain below.

At noontime the sound of singing drifted into the shop. Daniel laid down his hammer and went into his house.

"Would you go with me to see Thacia?" he asked Leah. "She will be dancing with the girls in the vineyard." He spoke idly, but half seriously too, thinking that her longing to see Thacia might tempt her.

"Are you going?" she cried now. "Then you can tell me about it!"

"Will you go with me?" he asked again.

A cloud shadowed her eyes. "Don't tease me, Daniel. But you will go, won't you?"

"I don't know," he answered, still trying to hide his real intentions from himself. "If I have time. I have to go to the city to take a lock and key to old Omar."

"Not in your old work clothes," Leah protested. "I've seen people going by. They're all dressed up. Wait—" She ran to the chest and pulled out his clean woolen cloak, and laughed at his halfhearted grumbling as she straightened it across his shoulders.

He walked along the road to the city, holding himself aloof from the holiday travelers, his unhappy, forbidding face giving no one any encouragement. In Capernaum, as he might have expected, the house of Omar was deserted, and he left his bundle inside the door.

He still told himself that he did not really intend to go to the festival, but his steps turned, almost against his will, toward the long slope of the vineyards. It was not hard to find his way. Voices and laughter drew him on, and he had only to follow their lead. Around one of the vineyards the young men of the town had gathered in a shifting, animated ring. He saw at once that he did not belong here. Even in his best cloak he stood out plainly for just what he was, a peasant and a smith. He dared not even approach too near to these elegant youths with their gaily striped cloaks, their leather sandals, their carefully oiled and combed forelocks and beards. They knew each other, called out greetings, jostled and jested, while he stood awkward and angry and alone.

Suddenly the merriment halted. The ring of boys tightened, drew inward. Daniel, who stood taller than most, craned his neck to see over their heads. At the other end of the vineyard a line of girls wound slowly from the green booths, a weaving line of white-clad figures, with wreaths of flowers in their hair and chains of flowers linking them one to another. The girls' voices, thin and high and sweet, floated among the trees.

> *"Look not, young men, upon gold or silver,*
> *Nor upon beauty in these maidens.*
> *Look only upon the good families from which they*
>   *spring,*
> *So they may bear thee worthy sons."*

Still keeping well behind the row of listeners, Daniel watched the line weave nearer. Then his breath caught as he saw Thacia. He had never seen her dance, but he knew well that sure flowing grace. He had marked it on that first day on the mountain. How gently she moved. Not like some others, striving to attract all eyes, nor yet fearfully, like those who crept with downcast lashes. She simply danced, as though she loved the motion for its own sake, her head up, her eyes shining, her lips parted in a little smile as she sang. As she came nearer, he saw that from time to time she gazed directly at the line of men, not coyly, not boldly, but with searching. She was looking for someone, and suddenly Daniel could not bear to see her face when she found him. He was shaken with terror. In a moment she would pass by where he stood, and those seeking eyes would find him out, standing there

229

in his homespun garment with his soot-grimed hands and his bare feet. Would she go on, her eyes still seeking as they were now? Would she dare even to show that she knew him before these others? Or would she be ashamed? She came nearer, the line weaving and swaying. All at once Daniel turned away, pushed through the line of watchers, and plunged down the hillside.

He had gone only a short way when her heard her voice. Looking back, he saw her running between the rows of vines, the white veil floating behind her. She came to a stop a little distance from him, out of breath, with color flaming in her cheeks.

"Why did you leave?" she cried.

"You know why," he answered. "I was a fool to come."

"I invited you."

"You did me no kindness."

He saw the quick hurt that leaped, like the mark of a blow, into her face. "I know you meant to be kind," he stammered. "I'm glad I saw you dance. Now I can tell Leah."

"Is that the only reason you came—to tell Leah?"

He stared at her miserably. "You should go back to your friends," he said. "You belong with them."

Thacia moved forward, slowly, until she stood quite close to him. "Do you still think I am just a pretty child, Daniel?"

He flushed wretchedly. So she had remembered. As he stared at her, the lips that spoke the words trembled, and the dark eyes had a bright sheen of tears.

"No!" he blurted, the truth wrenched out of him in a headlong need to make amends. "I did not mean it even then. That day—when I woke in the passage—it was a

woman's face I saw. The one face I will always remember
—as long as I live."

Thacia did not speak. She stood, straight and proud,
with her face lifted to his, and did not try to hide from
him what his words had done. The deep shining happiness
was like a lighted lamp, glowing brighter till it threatened
to blind him.

"Don't, Thacia!" he choked. "I never meant you to
know."

"Why not?"

"Because it's no use. I ask only one thing of life. I have
no right to the things other people have."

"Is this thing worth so much? Are you sure, Daniel?"

"I have taken an oath."

He watched the light waver and die down.

"I took the vow too," she said. "We vowed to live and
die for God's Victory. There is more than one way of
fighting. Joel sees that now."

"I only know one way to fight," he said. "I don't have
words like Joel's. I have only my two hands."

Her voice broke. "Will there never be an end to it—
the hate and the killing?"

"Thacia!" he burst out. "Don't torment me! I have to
see it through alone. There's no room for anyone else."

She did not speak again. She stood still, taking this
truth as she had taken the other, with her head lifted, not
trying to hide the hurt any more than she had hidden the
happiness, wrapped in a sort of pride that made the ordinary pride of women seem silly.

"Let me go now, Thacia."

She nodded. "God go with you," she said. "Whatever
you do."

He looked back once and saw her still standing on the slope, looking after him.

He walked the miles back to the village as he had come, aloof from the others, protected behind his dark scowl. He was weary and sore in spirit, and he did not want to talk about the festival, but the moment he saw Leah he knew he could not escape. She waited like a good child, her hands folded in her lap, her blue eyes eager.

"What was it like? Did Thacia look pretty? What did she wear?"

"Some sort of white thing," Daniel answered indifferently. Then, looking at his sister, he felt through his own hurt a fresh pain at the thought of her waiting here in this dingy room while the other girls danced in the sunlight. The least he could do was tell her.

"They had flowers in their hair," he began with an effort. Then, on an impulse, he stepped outside the door and pulled up a handful of cockle blossoms that had sprung up by the house, looped them into a garland and set them on the golden hair. "Like this," he said. Enchanted, Leah put up her hands to touch the flowers.

"Then they formed in a long line and danced."

"This way?" Leah began to sway from side to side, lifting her feet, her arms raised over her head. Astonished, he watched her. How could she know what it meant to dance? Those untaught motions had an instinctive rhythm.

Surprised out of his own gloom, he actually smiled at her. "You should have danced with them, Leah. You're as pretty as any of them."

She stopped dancing and stood in front of him, her blue eyes grave. "Am I pretty, Daniel?"

That he, of all people, should have been asked such a

232

question twice in one day! The memory of Thacia's glowing beauty made him answer his sister very gently.

"Indeed you are, Leah."

"Truly, Daniel? As pretty as those girls you saw today?"

"Much prettier than most of them."

He had meant to please her, but he was surprised that his answer should seem so important to her.

"Thacia said so too," she said seriously, thinking this over as though it were something she had never before considered. "Do you think perhaps someone else might think so, not just you and Thacia?"

"Joel said so too."

With a little smile she dismissed Joel. "He is kind, like Thacia, isn't he?" she said, her thoughts elsewhere. Then she made one of her surprising turns to the practical.

"Your supper is ready," she said. "I have a surprise for you."

The mat was already laid out for him, and he saw that he would have to eat, however little he wanted to. With the garland still in her hair, Leah unwrapped the bread and set out the bowl of boiled carrots and onions. Even in his own preoccupation he noticed the trembling eagerness with which she watched him eat, like a child brimming with a secret that can scarcely be contained.

When the vegetables were finished, she went behind the curtain in the corner. She brought out a woven basket of fruit. He saw at once that it was very fine fruit, sleek scarlet pomegranates, plump juicy figs, the sort of fruit that no Galilean ever kept for his own table, and only once a year dared to reserve for the sacrifice of First Fruits at the Temple in Jerusalem. What neighbor could have brought such a gift?

"Is this payment for your weaving?" he asked her.

"No," she said, breathless with pleasure. "It was a present for me."

He waited, puzzled.

"Marcus brought it today."

His teeth, already sunk into the first luscious bite, stopped as though he had struck a rottenness. "Who is Marcus?"

"You know. The soldier who comes on the horse."

He sent the pomegranate spinning across the room. He heard the sickish splash as it flattened against the wall, and saw the basket rolling from his vicious kick. He was on his feet, half blind and shaking. With a wail, Leah went down on her knees, scrabbling on the floor for an orange, sobbing, trying to wipe it against her dress. He snatched it from her hand.

"How do you know his name?" he shouted. "How dare a Roman dog bring you anything?"

Leah cowered against the wall.

"Answer me! How do you know him?" He reached out, gripped her shoulders, and held her up. Without a sound Leah drooped.

He heard his own voice, shouting words he had never used before, words he had heard in the cave. Then slowly the whirling blackness slowed down, and his sight began to clear. In the center of the blackness he saw his sister, shrinking under his hands, the garland of flowers slipped sideways on the streaming golden hair, her white face averted, waiting for his blow. His hands unclenched and let her fall. Shamed, he stood back.

"I'm not going to hurt you," he said more quietly. "Answer me. What has this man done?"

Faintly, her voice came from under the screen of hair. "He has been my friend."

"How long?"

"Since last summer. He has come to see me when you were gone away."

He held himself rigid. "You have let a Roman come into my house?"

"No—no! He has never come into the house."

"What then? Tell me."

"He—he sits on his horse outside the garden wall and talks to me."

"Only that? You give me your word?"

She raised her head and looked at him with such a strange dignity that he backed away.

"What does he talk about?"

"He doesn't know many words. He tells me about his family—they live far away in a place called Gallia. He lives in a little village with a forest all around it. His village was conquered by the Romans. He has a brother and two little sisters, and they all have yellow hair like mine. I wanted to tell you, Daniel. So many times I wanted to! But whenever he came to the shop, when you even thought about him—your face was so black. I was afraid."

"You should have been afraid. I would have torn his tongue out! I will yet, when I find him."

Her face went gray. "No! Oh no!" Suddenly she flung herself at his feet. "Don't harm him! Tell me you won't harm him! Oh—if you hurt him I will die!"

He looked down at her, loathing her. But he knew that she had told him the truth. The Roman had not come into his house.

"Stop groveling and listen to me," he said cruelly. "If I do not kill him, you must never speak to him again."

"No. Never!"

"You must give me your solemn word."

"I do. I promise anything you say."

"You will not show yourself where he can see you."

"No. I will never go out into the garden again."

"You have brought shame on my house, and on Simon's house and on our father's name. On the name of Israel, even."

She began to sob again.

"Weep!" he railed at her. "Weep your silly tears! See if you can cry your shame away."

He turned blindly toward the door, wanting only to be out of sight of her. She lay with her head against the earth floor, her face hidden. For an instant he wavered. Then he remembered something. When was it—on a summer day—she had said, "He is homesick." Even then! All this time she had deceived him. He plunged through the door and out into the street.

For hours he walked, rushing through the village streets, trampling the pastures on the slopes, striding along the road, drenched by intermittent rain. At first he had some wild thought of finding the Roman. For most of the night he did not really know where he went. As the first pink streaks of light streamed up in the sky he turned back toward the village. He was exhausted and empty, and his shoulder throbbed with pain. He had walked out the fierce anger that had driven him. Now, in its place, shame flowed in.

It was a good thing he had not met a leigonary in the night. He might have brought down a reprisal on the whole village. Now that his head was clearer he saw that in spite of his bitter loathing, no one else would recognize his claim to vengeance. The Roman legion had its own laws, as strict as those of the Jews. But it was unlikely there was any law, either Roman or Jewish, that said a Roman legionary could not speak to a Jewish woman over a garden wall.

What did Rome mean to Leah? She had seen a boy, scarcely older than herself, with yellow hair like her own. But why hadn't she been afraid?

"I shouldn't have shouted at her," he thought with shame. "I will try to make it up to her. I will show her that she does not need to be afraid of me."

But let that Roman never set foot in his shop again!

The house was very quiet. On the floor of the room the spilled fruit lay in the dust. Leah sat in a corner, a wilted blossom still clinging to her hair. When Daniel came in, she did not raise her head.

IN A FEW MOMENTS he had undone the work of months. Overnight Leah had become again the wan ghost who had cowered beside her dying grandmother. She did not comb her golden hair, or sweep the floor, or speak. She did not seem to recognize her loom. All day she sat with her head bowed and her hands idle. It was as though everything that had happened since the day of Daniel's homecoming had never been, except that one thing had changed. Now, above all else, she feared him.

In a torment of remorse, Daniel did all the work about the house, the sweeping and washing and baking. He steeled himself against her constant trembling, and the cringing whenever he came through the door. When she refused to notice her food so long as he was in the room, he left the bowl on the mat beside her. Sometimes when he returned it was half empty; more often it was untouched. He pleaded with her very gently. He was more patient than he had ever imagined he was capable of being. But her eyes, when he glimpsed them rarely, were like empty windows. He dreaded to look lest he should see the demons staring out of them. He was sure now that they possessed her completely.

Just when the hope of Jesus began to work in him he did not know. It began as a small flicker in the darkness of his mind. All day at the forge the hope grew slowly, till it filled his every thought. They said that Jesus could cast out demons, demons so terrible that they made a man tear his own flesh. Could he cast out the silent demons, too, those that hid themselves deep in the shadows?

Could he ask anything of Jesus, when he had refused to follow him? And did he dare to ask Jesus to help Leah, when he knew in his heart that he himself was to blame that the demons had come back? Yet he remembered how Jesus, in a way he had never understood, had somehow lifted from him the terrible weight of Samson's death. If only he could take to Jesus this heavier burden of guilt. In the sleepless hours he forgot the doubts that had confused him that night on the rooftop. He remembered only the infinite kindness of the teacher's eyes. He did not think that Jesus would turn him away.

There came an afternoon when his mind was suddenly made up. He laid down his hammer and took the road to Capernaum. He reached the city toward evening, and made his way at once to the shore.

The fishing boats were deserted. A single aged man, his crutches beside him, stared out over the water.

"They have all gone," he whined. "Not a thought for us who couldn't walk."

"Gone where?"

"Who knows?" the man sighed. "They have been gone all day. They followed the master; a great crowd of them. He went out in the boat, and Andrew rowed him across the lake. The people ran after him along the shore. Hundreds of them. I couldn't keep up."

"Which way?"

"To the west. Toward the plain."

Daniel hurried away. He was in no mood to wait, especially in this dismal company. He would go out to meet the returning crowd. For the first time he understood why they had refused to be left behind. This time he wanted something himself, and he knew their impatience.

It was not hard to follow the route they had taken along the rocky shore path. He began to realize, as one excited person after another pointed the way, that a very large crowd had passed by, and that many along the shore must have dropped their work and followed after. He saw before him a barren rise of hills. The light was failing fast, but he could just distinguish a great mass of people, more than he had ever seen before in one place, clotted like a vast herd of sheep on the slope. What were they doing there so late?

Presently the sound of their voices reached him like the roar of the sea in a storm, louder and louder, swelling wave on wave. The master must be through speaking, for no one could possibly make himself heard over such a tumult. Above the roar he caught an occasional scream, hysterical, high-pitched. He had never heard a sound quite like this. His heart began to pound.

He caught up finally with the rear of the crowd. They were all on their feet, pushing, shoving, craning their necks with a frenzy he had never seen before. Up ahead their voices rose in a sort of chant.

"What is it?" He caught the arm of the man nearest him. "Why are they shouting?"

"Why? Where are your wits, boy?"

"I've just come. Tell me."

"It's the Messiah! Listen!"

As he grasped the words his heart gave a great leap. "Hosanna! Blessed be He that cometh!" Over and over, over and over.

"It is the day of the Lord!" screamed a voice above all the rest.

He has declared himself! Daniel thought with rapture, forgetting Leah, forgetting his exhaustion and doubt, forgetting everything but the fierce joy that shook him from head to foot.

"Did he tell you?" he demanded, still clutching the man's arm. "Tell me—what did he say?"

"Say? He did better than say. He fed us. Don't you see the bread? Pick some up for yourself. There's plenty." The man shook himself loose. "Praise be!" he shouted, pushing forward. "Salvation is come!"

Daniel looked down. He saw a glimmer of white on the ground and stooped to it. Bread. He held it in his hand. Farther on he saw another crust, and another. Bread? For all these people? People all over the hillside? There must be thousands.

"Wait a minute!" He ran after the man. "Where did the bread come from?"

"How do I know? All I know is they sent back word for us to sit down. Then someone passed me bread."

The shouting was growing more frenzied. "Let him be king!" they screamed. "He is our Deliverer! Down with Rome!"

Still Daniel could not see Jesus. He began to push his way through the jostling bodies. If only Joel were here, he thought with sharp regret. The end of all their waiting, and Joel was not there to see it!

"Daniel!" Out of the darkness came a familiar voice.

"Simon!" The two friends grasped each other's arms. "Where is he, Simon?"

"He has gone."

"Gone! They're going to crown him king!"

241

"I know. But he has gone. We pleaded with him. But he told us to hold back the crowd, and then he went, with Simon and James and John."

"Where?"

"Back into the hills somewhere."

"We must go after him! Hurry!"

"We will not find him. He said that no one was to follow him."

Daniel rocked back from the words as from a wall. Baffled, he stood quivering, his eyes straining ahead. Where could he look in the darkness? Numb with disappointment, he stared at his friend. Then he realized that all around him, like a bonfire that had leaped too high, the exaltation was dying down. Shouts of joy were giving way to cries of anger. Like Daniel, the people could not believe that Jesus had gone. He must be hiding, waiting to be coaxed. Here and there fierce sudden arguments broke out. If the man wanted to be king, why didn't he stand up and act like a king? Women threaded through the crowd, searching out their men and urging them to go home. Slowly the tide turned back down the hill.

"Come," said Simon quietly. "You can spend the night with me."

"Simon—why?" Daniel burst out. "They would have given him a crown!"

"I don't know. Perhaps it is not time."

"When will there ever be a better time?"

"That is for him to choose."

"But will he? What does he want? What sort of man is he, anyway?"

Simon looked back at him. In the darkness his eyes suddenly blazed. "I believe he is the Messiah, sent from God," he said.

Daniel felt a chill along his spine. "Has he said so?"

"Not to me. Perhaps to those three. I think Simon knows."

"Then why would he not be king?"

"I have told you, I don't know."

"If he is the Messiah, how soon will he lead us against the enemy?"

Simon walked on for a time without answering. Finally he spoke. "He will never lead us against Rome, Daniel. I have given up all hope of that."

The quiet words had the force of a blow. Daniel had his answer at last. Joel had tried to tell him, and Thacia. Even Jesus himself. Now Simon had confirmed the doubt that all these months had blocked the way between him and the man from Nazareth.

"Then why do you stay with him?" All the boy's bitterness broke through the reproach.

"Where else could I go?" Simon answered.

"What has he offered you that is worth more than Israel's freedom?"

"He has offered me the kingdom."

Daniel's anger was rising. "When do you think you'll have this kingdom?"

"You will not understand this," said Simon. "In a way, I have it already."

"That's fine!" the boy's scorn was close to tears. "You have the kingdom! You can shut your eyes while all around you—"

"I have not shut my eyes," said Simon. "I know well enough that nothing in Israel is changed. But I know that it will be, even if I never live to see it with my own eyes."

"Listen to me, Daniel," he went on. "You've seen him caring for those people—the ones so low that no one, not

243

I or anyone else, cared what happened to them. When I see that, I know that the God of Israel has not forgotten us. Or why would He have sent Jesus to them, instead of to the rich and the learned? Like a shepherd, he says, who will not let any of his sheep be lost. I'm a poor man, and ignorant, but I know now that with a God like that I am safe."

Daniel stood staring at his friend. Simon had lost his senses altogether. "Safe? Jesus has put you all in danger!"

Simon's voice was steady. "Jesus has taught us that we must not be afraid of the things that men can do to us."

"Suppose they put chains on all of you and drag you off to prison?"

"He says that the only chains that matter are fear and hate, because they chain our souls. If we do not hate anyone and do not fear anyone, then we are free."

"Free? In chains? Simon—you know what they could do to you! How could you possibly not be afraid?"

"I don't say I am not afraid," said Simon. "But Jesus is not. And he is the hope of Israel."

"What has he done to prove it? How do you know you're not risking your life for nothing?"

"We can never know," Simon answered slowly. "God hides the future from man's eyes. We are forced to choose, not knowing. I have chosen Jesus."

"This was his chance tonight. Do you think he will ever do anything now?"

"I don't know what he will do. It is enough for me that he has promised."

"It is not enough for me!" Daniel cried. "Promises are easy. They are nothing but words. I want a leader who will make his promises good!"

He flung himself away from Simon and stumbled ahead

into the darkness. He could not see his way, but he knew that from now on he was alone. There was no friend to fight beside him. There was no leader to follow. There was nothing left to him but his hatred and his vow.

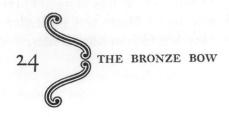

SPRING BURST over Galilee. The curtain of rain drew back from a clear, brilliant blue sky. The rich green slopes dropped down to a gentle sea. Flowers flowed along the roadways, trickling through every crevice in the rocky banks, splashing the gray mud walls, spraying from thatched roofs, washing in a wave of color up to the door of the house.

But the door was shut against them. Inside the shop Daniel worked steadily with a grim averted face. In the gloom of the house Leah sat, her hands idle in her lap. Dust gathered on the threads of the loom. They were both alike, Daniel thought, turning his back on the blossoming roadway. They could not learn to hope again.

Yet he was still stronger than Leah. While she had lost everything, purpose remained to him. His hatred was as strong as ever, so strong that unless he found some outlet for it soon it would destroy him. He was like a man imprisoned in a pit, raging and helpless.

If he were free, he could find a band of Zealots. They existed, everywhere in Galilee. Men spoke of them furtively. In some village, in some cave in the wilderness, men gathered and made ready, and they would welcome him. But he was chained to his forge in an endless round of work to keep alive a girl who was indifferent that she lived. And even if he found a band, how could he recognize a man whom he could trust? How could he be sure that he would not be duped again?

He trains my hands for war,
  so that my arms can bend a bow of bronze . . .

What use were his strong hands? God did not mean the bow of bronze for him.

In the first month of spring, Leah was betrayed by the one remaining thing to which she still reached out. The little goat failed her. The kid which was born in Adar was puny, and brought only the lowest price, and when it was taken from her the goat drooped. The milk she gave scarcely provided Leah with a cupful once a day. There came a morning when the little creature could not stand on its feet. Daniel looked at it with dismay, remembering that goats were subject to a peculiar fever. He brought it into the house and tried to coax it to eat. The little goat huddled beside Leah, as unresponsive as its mistress. Two mornings later it was dead.

He thought at first that Leah refused to eat from grief, but he soon recognized that she too was feverish. She lay on the rush mat, her eyes glazed and unaware, her cheeks flushed, her lips parched. From time to time she cried out in terror. She seemed to be wandering in a distant country, peopled with dreadful shapes he could not even imagine.

By the next morning he saw that she was very ill. The physician, loath at first to come, looked down at her and shook his head. There was too little blood in that thin body already, he said, laying aside the bottle of leeches. He left a concoction of rue and departed, with a resigned shrug of his shoulders and a gentle pity in the wise eyes behind their wrinkled lids.

"I cannot work today. My sister has the fever," Daniel told a customer, and bolted the shop door as the man backed away. Word must have gone quickly through the village, because no other customer came to trouble him.

He sat beside Leah's mat, bewildered. One by one they had all left him, everyone who had touched his life. Rosh. Samson. Joel. Thacia. Simon. Jesus. Now Leah was slipping away. With Leah's death he would be altogether free. But freedom seemed suddenly a terror of emptiness, and he had nothing to fill it but hatred. Leah too, he thought dully, must be avenged.

In the stillness the words came back to him. *Can you repay love with vengeance?* Leah had loved him, with a simple trustful heart, as Samson had loved him. But vengeance was all he had to give. It was better than nothing.

Leah, like Samson, had perished by the sword he had meant for Rome. And like Samson she would not leave a single person on earth save himself who would know or care. Then he remembered that this was not true. Thacia would care. Sometime during the day he became convinced that Thacia should know. There was nothing that she could do for Leah now, but he knew that she would care.

How could he let her know? He remembered the message that Simon had sent him almost a year ago. Rummaging in his shop, he found a bit of broken pottery and scratched with a nail the same message Simon had sent: Leah is dying.

Joktan sat outside the shop, halfheartedly filing down a set of nails. He had no more than glimpsed the girl who lay dying, but the heaviness inside the house seeped through the door and made him uneasy. He was glad enough for an errand to do. Daniel gave him the directions to the house of Hezron in Capernaum and told him to leave the message with the porter at the door.

Joktan did not return. Three times a day Daniel went to the village well to get water, using it recklessly to bathe Leah's hands and face. He came and went with his head bent, looking at no one, speaking to no one. On the second day, as he came slowly back along the street, he saw the Roman soldier Marcus standing before his house. He stood still, his legs suddenly weak. A red mist blurred his vision. His arms trembled till he could scarcely hold the water jug. Here, in this one hated figure, was concentrated all the misery of his life. With all the strength of his being he wanted to hurl himself at the Roman boy, to feel the throat between his hands, to hear the life gasping out. But something held him back. He could not kill the Roman while Leah lay dying inside the house. It would have to wait.

Marcus stepped forward, to stand between him and the door, and Daniel was forced to stop. He could not prevent the soldier from speaking to him, but he turned his face away. When, against his will, he had to see why no words came, he saw the boy's face was contorted in an effort to speak.

"I have heard that your sister is ill," he stammered. "How does she today?"

Daniel spat on the ground. He charged forward so fiercely that Marcus involuntarily stepped out of the way and let him enter his house. On the doorstep Daniel turned. "What is it to you if another Jew is dying?" he snarled.

On the third day of Joktan's absence, Daniel came back

249

from the well slowly, his limbs dragging with weariness, heavy with dread that Leah's anguished breathing might have stopped while he was gone. He took no notice of the soldier who stood across the road as he had stood for the past two days. Every hour that the boy had off duty he spent simply standing there in the blazing sunshine, with his eyes on the house. This time, however, Daniel saw that the Roman was crossing the road and waiting for him, as he had before, between the road and the door.

"I must speak to you," Marcus said, as Daniel halted.

Daniel did not look up.

"You hate me," the boy said. "I understand your hate. I am German. My people were conquered by Rome."

"You serve them," said Daniel with scorn.

The soldier shrugged. "All of my tribe are fighters. At the end of my term I will be a Roman citizen."

"You should have died first!"

The boy flushed under his smooth tanned skin. "I tell you I understand your hate," he snapped. "But I command you to listen to me."

Daniel said nothing, waiting.

"My cohort is transferred. Tomorrow I leave for Corinth. I pray the gods I never set eyes on your country again."

Daniel's quick burst of fury died back in helplessness. Even vengeance was snatched from him! Now he would never feel this man's life between his hands.

"Your sister was the only good thing in this rotting land. I will never see her again. Even if she were not a Jew, a legionary is forbidden to marry. I want to see her before I go. One moment. That is all."

Thunderstruck, Daniel looked directly at the boy before

him. That a Roman should bend his pride to speak so to a Jew! Then the very humbleness of the request maddened him the more. His contempt overflowed.

"If you could save my sister's life, I would not profane our house," he said. "I would rather let her die. Understand this. If you try to walk through that door, I will kill you."

Marcus was still a soldier. His face went white, his eyes glinted with steel, and his hand moved of its own accord to his side. The two young men stood eye to eye, neither one giving way. Then the Roman heeled about and strode away, his shoulders rigid.

If she is dead, Daniel thought. I will go after him now. I will have that at least.

Leah still lived, but barely. She did not know that he had returned. She lay silent, with no strength to cry out against the demons. She had surrendered to them utterly.

In the afternoon heat Daniel must have slept a little. Sleeping and waking were all one endless sameness. But a sound brought his head up, and he saw the door of his house opening. Framed in it, against the sunlight, stood Jesus in his white robe. Dazed, Daniel struggled to his feet. Jesus moved through the door, touching with his fingers the mezuzah as he passed. Behind him came Thacia. Jesus did not speak. He moved quietly to Leah's mat and stood looking down at her.

Thacia came swiftly to Daniel's side. "We were away," she whispered, "with Joel in Jerusalem. Joktan just found me this morning."

Daniel scarcely heard her. He saw only that luminous figure. Jesus had come! He struggled to believe. Jesus had come to his house! He wanted to cry out to him, to go down on his knees, but he was afraid. Something about the quietness of Jesus held him silent. Jesus sat down beside Leah, and motioned for Daniel and Thacia to sit also, at the other side of the room. Then he bent his head and covered his face with his hand and seemed to rest.

If I could speak to him! Daniel thought with longing. If I could tell him it is my fault, that I have done this to Leah!

Although he held his breath and made no sound, Jesus raised his head, and his eyes met Daniel's. There was no need to speak. Jesus knew. He understood about Leah. He knew that Daniel had rejected him. His eyes, searching and full of pity, looked deep into the boy's and saw the bitterness and the hatred and the betrayed hopes and the loneliness. And then he smiled.

Unable to endure that smile, Daniel bent his head. Suddenly, with a longing that was more than he could bear, he wanted to stop fighting against this man. He knew that he would give everything he possessed in life to follow Jesus.

Even his vow?

He tried to cling again to the words of David that had always strengthened him. *He trains my hands for war—*

But Jesus said that the Victory was God's promise. He called men to make ready their hearts and minds instead.

Was it possible that only love could bend the bow of bronze?

He sat trembling, glimpsing a new way that he would never see clearly or understand. We can never know, Simon had said. We have to choose, not knowing.

To know Jesus would be enough.

Almost with the thought the terrible weight was gone.

In its place a strength and sureness, and a peace he had never imagined, flowed around him and into his mind and heart.

After a long time he felt Thacia's hand close over his own. He raised his head and saw tears on her face.

"Look," she whispered.

He had forgotten Leah! Now, seeing how still she lay, he thought that she must have died. Jesus had risen and stood looking down at her. Then, as Daniel watched, he saw her eyelids move and lift falteringly. The blue eyes were blank, as though she came from a deep sleep. She looked up into the master's face, and slowly her eyes filled with wonder.

"Jesus?" she breathed.

Into Jesus' face came the old smile with which he had so often looked at the children who crowded around him.

"It is—all right?" she whispered.

"It is all right," Jesus answered. "Do not be afraid."

With a sob, Daniel stumbled forward to his knees, hiding his face, feeling the tears he had never known since his childhood, not on the night of his father's death or in all the years between, hot and liberating against his hands. He thought he felt a touch on his shoulder. When he lifted his head, Jesus was gone. He saw Thacia, her own tears shining on her cheeks, her eyes like stars.

"Daniel—" Leah said, very faintly.

Not daring to speak, he reached out and touched his sister's hand.

"I know how she felt," she whispered, "the girl—Jairus' daughter—you told me about."

"I know too," he said humbly.

He heard Thacia catch her breath, and turned and

looked into her eyes. He knew he was not worthy of the gift he saw there, but he knew that at last he was free to offer her all that he had in return. In that one brief look they made a new vow together.

"How light it is," Leah murmured, "even with Jesus gone."

Gone! In sudden realization, Daniel sprang to the door. He could see Jesus far down the street, already half hidden by the people who always gathered wherever he went.

"I must go after him!" he cried. "Before anything else, I must thank him."

He flung himself out the doorway—and stopped.

Across the street the Roman soldier stood alone under the broiling sun.

Haltingly, Daniel walked, not after Jesus, but across the road, till he stood before the boy. He had to try twice before the words would come. "My sister will get well," he said, his voice harsh. "The fever has left her."

A quick gutteral sound burst from the soldier. Daniel looked away. Who could believe that a Roman—?

"I think she would want to say good-bye to you," he said.

The soldier waited, not understanding. Daniel looked down the road and caught the white flash of Jesus' robe. Then he straightened his shoulders.

"Will you come in to our house?" he asked.

ELIZABETH GEORGE SPEARE

Elizabeth George Speare was born in November, 1908, and brought up in Melrose, Massachusetts. She attended Smith College for a year, but received her A.B. (1930) and M.A. (1932) from Boston University. She always wanted to write books but with several years of teaching, then marriage and a family to raise, she contented herself with magazine articles and two one-act plays until 1957 when CALICO CAPTIVE, her first book, was written.

For many years Mrs. Speare, her husband and two children lived in Wethersfield, Connecticut. It was this Connecticut River town that was the setting for her Newbery-Award-winning THE WITCH OF BLACKBIRD POND. THE BRONZE BOW was also written there, but shortly after the manuscript was finished, the Speares moved to Easton, Connecticut where they now live.